To Amy —
the first voice at
Foghorn ... long
may you wave,

C. Pett.

4/11/95

The Search For Goodbye-To-Rains

The Search For Goodbye-To-Rains

a novel by
Paul McHugh

ISLAND PRESS   COVELO   CALIFORNIA

Inquiries and requests for permission to make copies of any part of this
work should be mailed to:
Island Press, Star Route 1, Box 38, Covelo, CA 95428

Library of Congress Cataloging in Publication Data

McHugh, Paul   1950–
    The Search for Goodbye-To-Rains.

    I. Title
PZ4.M14955Se   [PS3563.A31163]   813'.54   79–28565
ISBN 0–933280–07–6

Special gratitude to
William Stoneham, whose original art
graces the cover.

to Irena my muse,
and Mac Aetch,
Who-knows-who-he-is.

You road I enter upon and look around, I believe you are not all that is here, I believe that much unseen is also here . . . . The goal that was named cannot be countermanded.

—Walt Whitman

Open Letter to the Author

June 27, 1979

Dawn takes forever to plumb this canyon. Eastern slopes of mountains receive light first. They swell out of the empty night like long green waves, forever about to break, shrouded with the blue gauze of distance.

But the deep womb of the canyon rock covets shadow, will not surrender the dark possibilities clenched between its eroded lips. Let your eyes soar over the dark rough-and-tumble, the boulder jammed chasm of the Rio Grande! The River called Great.

Remember this place? You were here not many years ago, Steve Getane. Come on back and look over the edge!

Here. It's me, Art Saruthaz. I'm sitting in the cab of that derelict pickup—I'm sure you remember it—that old truck on the west slope of da Gama Mountain in northern New Mexico. The truck that looks like it spent its first twenty years delivering coal to Hell, and the last seven parked where it is right now. Through the glittering web of fractures in the windshield, there is a sweeping view of the plains and the Rio Grande Gorge.

Through its selfless service, this truck has earned the right to dissolve peacefully back into the earth. Already the wheels are canting inward as entropy coaxes the front end into a half-lotus. Soon it will return as a bodhisattva for rust-fearing Chevrolets everywhere. But before it vanishes, it can still be used as a relative constant in our realities. Yours and mine. Then and now.

I don't know where you are, Steve Getane, but I've got something for you. Your journal. It's been slightly retouched, but you'll still know it as the story you wrote down and mailed to me, of your search across

America in those years of the early seventies, when the minds of the mass were taking the Greening of America *off their coffee tables and redecorating with* Future Schlock. *A time when alternate realities divided, forming a door for those who would choose neither that nor this, but instead plunged away to surface* elsewhere . . . *like new creatures that needed to breathe at least once of the frosty emptiness of the Void in order to become themselves.*

You said that I should get this journal back to you if it ever seemed you needed reminding of what it contained. I've been watching the times carefully; the time is now. I don't know if, when you sent me your journal, you were also bestowing upon me the legal right to someday get it published. But I can manage to produce that implication from the vague wording of your note. Especially since I have no other way to carry out the responsibility of getting it to you. The power-of-attorney moves in mysterious ways, its wonders to perform.

And this way, others can read this too. Which is all to the good; they may need to. You were never as alone as you thought.

A. S.

I.
The Six of Pentacles, Reversed

"Sorry I'm late," I said as I got in.

Ursula surveyed me.

"No you're not," she said. "But I *am* getting used to it." There was humor in her smile, but also a twist of disdain.

We pulled away and drove in silence.

"Well, anyway, this one should be easy,"Ursula said, after a while. "She's classic. An Old South Belle who likes to get her philanthropic spasms in the sheets to remind herself and her cronies that she hasn't hit the obits yet.

"I checked the file. Articles on her start with a rundown on her past gifts, size and significance of the present one, hit a dash of human interest, then a complimentary close. We'll expand the human angle, but mostly keep it like the others. It seems to please her, and that's what Max wants."

Ursula tapped out her Sherman's in the ashtray, adjusted her aviator's glasses on the bridge of her nose, and shifted into first. I nodded, acknowledging her efficiency.

Max decided what to write, Ursula decided how to write it, I nodded and took the pictures. Jump into the word and world whirl, make its money, use my Nikon light-trap to help others play the fame-game, forget the *beeeg* changes I was gonna someday help bring about. Easy.

But I couldn't do it. Dissatisfaction burned deep inside, a bitter, acrid dissatisfaction that sent fumes twisting upward through everything I touched and did. Everything had a weird failure in it, even my tools.

Like the camera. If I snapped Ursula right now, what would I get?

Her trim, jogger's body outfitted to the Nth of current chic: perfect image of the upwardly mobile career woman. Right down to the polished nails drumming with rhythmic impatience on the steering wheel, the cleft between brows that gave a hyphen of seriousness to her round, girl's face.

But the camera would not find a hint of the Ursula in patched and beaded jeans who had run laughing into my arms a few years back at an outdoor rock concert by the lake . . . . I remembered long black hair floating out behind her as she ran, breasts signaling frantically under her T-shirt, the impact of her wet, squirming body. The wreath she wore, woven from twigs, straw, wildflowers, pot stems, curls of hair. The ambiance of the old wooden apartment on Bronough Street, full of fringe, incense, and light rays refracted through crystal. The camera couldn't recall the sweet and wild Ursula I had bouts of genuine lonesomeness for, tell how she had changed, or why.

It didn't go deeply enough. For this reason, I began to distrust it.

My real sense when I looked at Ursula now was of a marionette, designed, dressed, and painted for a part. Some of the strings on her used to run through the image of the hippie chick, as portrayed and promulgated by the mass media, music, underground circulations, and all. Fashion turned the other chic. Now stronger, motivated by desperation, strings ran through images of with-it womanhood propagated by *Ms.* and *Cosmopolitan.* Ursula managed a hybrid response.

What frightened, what added fear to the comprehensive dissatisfaction, was that a lot of *my* strings ran to her. She was the one who had gotten us out of the psychically fogged-in farm for lapsed radicals, gotten us both into photojournalism and landed us a job with the same paper. She even did me the favor of defining our relationship, insisting on separate "living-spaces" so we'd both have "room to grow."

Now both of us had strings running to Max, who had them running to the editor and publisher. Which wasn't the end of it, as they had strings running out through the paper to the advertisers and readers, who wanted their reality reinforced. My head spun when I thought about it: everyone was a marionette tied to everyone else, jerking and dancing together. No masters, no free individuals, no leaders, just the foci of greater and lesser strings, that played men as much or more than men played them. A tangled net, a knot of intersecting lines.

The light changed. Ursula let out the clutch and drove us off toward our interview.

I'd always been driven somewhere by something: by the force and form of the society into which I had grown up, by the fads and fashions of the counter-society into which I had been swept up—a puppet, dancing on the strings of current events. Even when I'd felt most deeply that I was thinking for myself, most of the time it was not so. Always, a role to play for someone, an image to measure against, a pop notion to entertain. A sense of claustrophobia added itself to my ache of dissatisfaction. Where could I turn for alternatives?

Certainly not the Flagler Hotel, where Ursula pulled her Toyota to the curb, and stopped.

The Flagler was a venerable brick pile built by Henry Flagler (Florida's boomtime Mr. Wonderful), as a waystation for tourists en route to the fleshpots of Miami. Once a sumptuous landmark, the years had taken their toll with more vengeance than usual; now it was not much more than a glorified flophouse, the city's hotel of last resort.

"*Here?*" I asked, astonished.

"So I'm told," Ursula said. She yanked out her emergency, twisted in her seat to get tapedeck and notebooks from the back. She sat up and gazed at the building reflectively. "It's a good place to be eccentric. I told you she was classic. Let's go."

I followed her up the front steps, past two crouching lions with planters on their backs. Luxuriant weeds sprouted from a mulch of cigarette butts and gum wrappers.

Inside, afternoon light seeped through Venetian blinds over high windows, the slats so yellowed they looked like aged ivory. The light fell in furry bars across the dark tile floors, threadbare oriental rugs. Two of the lobby walls sported long murals, one a flight of roseate spoonbills over a tropical sunset, the other depicting the ecstatic homelife of your average Seminole Indian.

Bamboo couches with lime-green cushions, standing metal ashtrays, a few anemic potted palms were scattered across the lobby. An old man in brown, baggy trousers, newspaper draped over his face, snored blissfully at one end of a couch. On a nearby ashtray, a cigar butt spiraled a thin plume of smoke toward the ceiling.

"Look," I said to Ursula. "He's lost in your article on Ray Hamlin."

She gave me a dirty look and continued toward the desk. She swatted the "Ring For Service" bell, then surreptitiously wiped her hand on her skirt. A black man in a bellhop's uniform and an old white cracker with red eyes came out of the same office by separate doors. The old man adjusted his glasses, straightened his bowtie, and held his fist in front of his mouth in an unsuccessful attempt to filter out his bourbon breath.

"Ma'am?" he coughed gently.

"We're here to see Miss Tallulah Crystall," Ursula said briskly. "She's expecting us."

"Ah, yes," he wheezed. "I'll call, and tell her you're here." He picked up a black phone, dialed, mumbled something into it, breathed heavily, then replaced it on the hook. "Go on up," he gasped. "Fifth floor. Number 504. Elevator don't work. Stairs are to your right." He wheeled and staggered back into his office.

The guard grillwork on the elevator sagged into an empty shaft. It looked as if it had been abandoned shortly after Dante used it to visit Ugolino.

As we opened the door to the stairwell, we were assailed by the stench of stale mouse droppings and rotting wood.

"Let's go back and try the elevator," I suggested.

Ursula took a deep breath and plunged up the stairs. I followed. On the hallway of the fifth floor where we emerged, the smell was even stronger. It almost seemed to form a haze around the two bare bulbs that lit the hall.

"God!" Ursula said, looking around with thorough distaste. She went to number 504 and knocked.

"Who is it?" a voice quavered.

"Weingart and Getane," Ursula said. "Reporters from the *Voice*."

A lock snicked back. Another. Then another. Finally, a crack widened in the doorway. A beady black eye behind a thick lens stared me in the chest.

"Miss Crystall?" I ventured. The eye raised to my face and blinked. I felt faintly ridiculous.

"May we come in?" Ursula prompted. The eyes wavered, then disappeared behind the door. It slowly opened wider.

Walking into the room was like entering a bric-a-brac fairyland. Rainbows frozen in tinted glass wreathed the room. There were shelves of tiny, baluster-stem wineglasses in aquamarine, little candlesticks with knobbed stems, miniature blown-glass creamers colored a deep cobalt blue. Other shelves bore tiny decanters, cruets, and cordial glasses . . . a crowded and endless array of fragile forms.

The door closed behind us and the locks slid home. We turned to see Miss Tallulah Crystall, a short, stout woman, easily in her early eighties. Her black dress hung to a point just touching the floor. Her midriff bulged out against the fabric, stretching the seams at her sides. A faded plastic orchid hung at an awkward angle from her breast. Iron grey hair was drawn and knotted about an ebony pin. On her face, a flesh-toned powder had been applied so thickly that it formed deep cracks around her mouth and eyes. Over this she had brushed lipstick and rouge of a cheerful, unnatural red. The oddest thing was that a triangular

4

plastic shield, attached to her thick glasses, hung down over her nose.

She seemed hesitant, unsure of what to do next. Quick and rolling, like beads in the eyes of a doll, her eyes flicked back an forth between Ursula and me.

"Pleasure to meet you, Miss Crystall," Ursula said smoothly. "Please sit with us, and let us ask you a few questions. Afterwards, I think Steven would like to take some photographs."

Tallulah looked at the camera in alarm. Moving with a peculiar, bowlegged gait, she scuttled over to a sofa and sank down onto the cushions.

"Ah was not told about a camera," she said accusingly. She raised one hand to touch her hair. The other hand started up towards her nose, then sank back into her lap.

"Don't worry," Ursula soothed. "Mr. Getane is a fine photographer. And we won't get around to that until later." She sent me a significant glance. "But Miss Crystall, what I'd really like to know, is how did you arrive at the, ah, inspiration of giving a fountain to the Tallahassee Prison?" Ursula switched on her tape recorder.

Miss Crystall's eyes bulged for a second. She realized she was on the air. Then she looked down at her hands and began to speak. "Well, Ah remember it as bein' a ratha *grim* lookin' place. Ah like fountains, because they are to me like . . . like the nevah endin' joy of Life. Ah gave a big one to the Hospital a while back. Ah give lots of things away. You kin read about it in all the papers . . . ."

As she held forth on her own philanthropy, the voice I had expected to remain frightened and soft became strong and voluble. But it held no warmth. It was only a strident and scrambled retelling of facts. Ursula let her develop her theme for a few minutes, then expertly steered the conversation into the old woman's personal past. Miss Crystall laid down the subject of her largesse with a great and obvious reluctance, like an opium smoker putting down her pipe.

Ursula was hard to resist.

"Yes, Ah graduated from Live Oak College," she said. "How did you know that? Ah believe . . . Ah even have mah graduation yearbook still." She twisted awkwardly to survey a bookcase over the sofa.

"Heah it is!" She took out a tall white volume with a worn binder. "Live Oak used to be an all-woman's college," she reflected, opening the book and turning the pages. "It went co-ed just befoah Ah enrolled, which was quite excitin'. See heah?" She pointed out a picture of an open wagon, laden with consumptive-looking young men, girls in long dresses and large hats. "That was a field trip foah a Biology class." She turned the pages with shivering, clumsy fingers. A loose photograph

5

slid out and fell to the floor. Miss Crystall bent stiffly to retrieve it. The plastic shield over her nose swung away for a second.

Her nose wasn't there. My stomach tightened in shock and revulsion. I had only a glimpse, but it looked as if most of it had been cut off, or eaten away by disease. What remained was composed of ugly-looking sores, dusted with a white powder.

Ursula appeared not to have noticed anything. "What's that picture?" Ursula asked.

"Mah . . . a boy Ah knew," Miss Crystall said. Her voice, so pleased with itself a moment before, seemed to be crumbling from the center outwards.

"Let me see it," Ursula said, with a tone more of command than request. Automatically, Miss Crystall gave it to her.

"Hmmmm." Ursula examined it. "Looks handsome in his uniform, doesn't he?"

Miss Crystall received the photograph back in both hands, cradling it. "His name was Malcolm Scott," she said, in a trancelike voice. She stared fixedly at the old photo. "He went to Europe to serve under General Pershing. Ah moved into this hotel to wait foah him. He said he'd marry me when he came back . . . ."

"You mean you've lived in this same apartment for the last *sixty years*?" I blurted, incredulous. Ursula glared at the interruption.

"Y- yes, Ah have," Miss Crystall replied uncertainly. The wealthy and genteel matron was rapidly vanishing, revealing something like a mad old spinster cowering behind the facade.

"But he didn't come back, did he?" asked Ursula, with extreme unction.

"Oh. Oh yes. He came back. In 1919 . . . ." The doll-like mask of her face stretched and was still. Moisture glinted in the network of cracks around her eyes. She was quiet a long time. Then a weird groan passed through her lips. She blinked and shook her head, suddenly grasping how far she'd wandered from the image she craved to protect. She floundered desperately to get back.

"A present he brought me started this collection," she croaked. Running her tongue over her lips, she got to her feet and walked in that awkward, rolling gait to one of the glass shelves. She picked up a delicate glass bottle, not more than two inches high. It was swirled with opaque stripes, and on one side a heart, initials, and a date were stippled with mauve dots.

"This is a very valuable antique," she said. "A scent bottle in Nailsea glass. Birmingham . . . uh, 1819. A token lovers used to send each other . . . ."

She put a hand over her stomach and went on. Strength returned to her voice as she gave us a tour of her miniature antiques. As she neared the end of them, Ursula maneuvered her near a window, and gave me a signal.

I snapped off a couple of shots. Miss Crystall stared at me in dawning comprehension. Her worst fear had come and gone.

"Cain you fix it so this won't show?" she asked plaintively, gesturing at the plastic shield that dangled from her glasses. "Ah must use it to protect my face from sunlight," she explained. "Ah have very sensitive skin."

Her face looked as if it hadn't been hit by a ray of direct sunlight in thirty years.

"Don't worry," I told her. "I'll have the shadow fall across your face there. Hardly anyone will know you have it on." Bracketing the exposure, moving around her, I came to the end of the roll.

"Well," she said, gathering confidence, "Ah want to see the picture you'ah gonna use befoah you print it. And you, young lady," she turned to Ursula. "Please let me read yoah article befoah you turn it in. Ah want to make sure the information is . . . accurate. Sometimes theah's a detail or two it's best to correct befoah it's printed."

"I understand," Ursula said, with a tight smile. She did, too.

Clean air and sunshine, into which we practically ran, was a dizzy miracle. Outside, memory of the dank hotel seemed even more surreal than it had while we were inside. We got in the car and just sat there for a minute, staring at each other.

"That really happen?" I asked, after a length.

I think so," Ursula said. "I'd have to say, that woman is on the more bizarre side of eccentric."

As we drove off toward the offices of the *Tallahassee Voice*, I brooded, still stunned by the old woman. A wreck of human potential. Wealth, a few newspaper articles and her collection of fragile glass were the only buffers between her mind and the astounding emptiness of her life.

An emptiness infected with fear, despair and terminal syphilis. I didn't know much about medicine, but that last seemed likely, given her rotting complexion, bowlegged stance, and tenuous grip on reality. I imagined those 5 billion corkscrews, awakened from sleep by some inner alarm, burrowing hungrily into the tissue of flesh and bone and brain. Evidently, a delicate scent bottle was not the only remembrance Malcolm Scott had brought his true love from Over There.

I wondered what had happened to him.

"I don't envy you," I told Ursula. "I haven't the faintest idea how you're going to get what's in that hotel room down on paper, but I wish you luck. A whole bunch of it."

"What d'you mean?" She shook her head, smiling ruefully. "I told you this one would be easy. It will. I had most of it done before we went up. All I needed was some human interest and a halftone. Maybe I'll use her glass collection for that . . ." she said thoughtfully. "No one's mentioned it yet."

"*What?*" Anger surprised me with the speed and strength of its eruption. "You're just going to do another kiss-ass article? People should get some of the truth about her so they can help her! The last thing she needs is another paper brick in the wall around her!"

Ursula was exasperated. Her jaw thrust forward as her voice went cold. "Listen!" she said. "That old girl is past help. The only thing left is to humor her until she kicks it! These blurbs are all that give her pleasure, so why deprive her of it? Besides, she said she wants to proof the piece. You think she wants the truth about her to get out? No way! My article will be just like the others, with an extra bit on her unique and valuable antiques. That's what Max wants, and it's the only thing he'll print. So butt out! You've done your job, now let me do mine."

"No!!" I saw it now. It was that dissatisfaction that had persisted beneath the fabric of my reality like a nasty mental itch coming out, bursting into the air between myself and Ursula. "You're restoring the Lie if you do that! Shielding her the same way she tries to shield herself. But if there's anything left in her that wants to *know*, that wants to touch real life after so many years, you're denying it! You're putting yourself on the side of her disease!"

A red flush was creeping under Ursula's skin. The subtle tension that had been growing between us had never erupted like this before. A vein, jumping madly, stood out on her neck. I was on her again before she could speak.

"You know what I mean about the *lie*, don't you? We talked about it just last week! How the media programs bullshit into the population. How the news forms a feedback loop that pumps the excrement of society back into its bloodstream. Remember? I think that last phrase was even yours! Well, here's another one of the twenty chances a day you run into to do something about it! Are you? Or are you just going to take another step in your career and push the real questions to the back of your mind? If that's what you're going to do, you can damn well do it without my photographs!"

"Who the hell do you think *you* are?!" Ursula's voice was strong and strident, but there was deep hurt in her eyes. "You think you don't have your own fond illusions protecting you? Just because . . ."

"I'll tell you something!" I broke in. "Old Miss Crystall. That's what you get to look like after you've lived inside of a lie long enough. That's outside. On the inside, you probably look a little worse."

"God! Listen to little Mr. Self-Righteous!"

We were still having at it when we got out in the newspaper parking lot. It was her turn, and she was laying it on hot and heavy. Pent-up grievances, logically unconnected, added fuel to the flames.

Standing there with my hands on my hips, bent under her withering fire, I looked out across the lot. My eyes were drawn to a window. Through the tinted glass that formed one wall of his office, I saw the editor, Max, whom I detested, watching us. Without another word or a backward glance, I walked rapidly out to the sidewalk and down the street.

Propelled by my anger, fists in my pockets, I walked a long way. Blooming wisteria and azaleas did not distract me, blue sky with white clouds did not attract me, and when I ran out of sidewalk, that didn't bother me at all. I just kept walking on the banks of red clay that lined Route 90 on its way out of town.

Disjointed thoughts tumbled and whirled inside of me, but the essence of them seemed to be this: by not willing anything else to happen, I was stumbling on into a kind of fate. The source of that nagging dissatisfaction was the steady erosion of my will to think and feel and choose for myself, and a growing conviction that reality lay elsewhere.

And yeah, I was getting dissatisfied with my tools and learning not to trust them. Including my own mind. My thoughts and values had been programmed by the games in which I had been steeped. I'd gone with it, played good boy, then good boy gone hip when that was all the rage. Now the Revolution was turning out to be a self-congratulatory half-time between sets of business-as-usual. So even the counter-culture stuff was fodder for the iconochasm. Throw it all in. What was I left with, I wondered, as I walked through the spread legs of the drive-in theatre marquee.

LIVE AND LET DIE
PLUS
2ND BIG HIT!!!
DAY OF THE JACKAL

What did it mean when nothing satisfied? When each day was

getting to be like a pulp book? I'd pick it up, read a page, skip to the middle, skip to the end, throw it down. Food, tempting at first, became dust in my mouth, lead in my stomach. It fed my body, but something within continued to ache. Efforts of others at comedy or significance or satire were getting so shallow and irrelevant, I could no longer even fake a response.

My brains and intestines knotted in on themselves in search of a secret that would nourish. But because it could not answer itself, my body began to burn with the desperate fire of self-loathing. No, loathing for the tangled unreal in which I was enmeshed, rat's nest of puppet strings that wove through me, . . . but from deeper inside than I could reach came a howling for freedom, breaking into the center of my consciousness, to reverberate there, and drown out everything else!

My thoughts had more clarity and calm that evening, as I made my way back into town. Past the glass wall of Electrolux TV Repair, where several stacks of recently healed sets formed a blinking matrix. Wrapped in a spiral of visions from "That Girl," "Gilligan's Island," and "Green Acres," an early news show held forth, "—involving ten cars today at the Indianapolis Speedway, injuring both spectators and drivers. Spectators sitting in expensive box seats only twenty feet from the racing surface were sprayed with searing flames and hot metal . . . ."

Ad for Ford Pinto, soaring along some western scenic highway. Report on scrombotoxins in decomposed tuna packed at Starkist's plant in Samoa. Sorry, Charlie.

Moving on down the sidewalk, towards the newspaper offices, I went by the Latin Quarter Cinema. Another double feature: "DEEP WAYS—Three young girls in search of the true way" and "SEXUAL FREEDOM IN BROOKLYN," with a poster of fake hippies in a pile, from which projected a sign advocating "Passion Power!"

I let myself into the newspaper building with my passkey and went to the darkroom. Quickly, but unsure why I was bothering, I took the roll out of my camera, developed it and hung the negatives up to dry. I made prints that were needed for old assignments.

Then an inspiration struck. Slowly at first, but faster and faster, I began to tear through my files, snatching out negatives from many different times and subjects, making print after print with abandon.

WALE, Tallahassee's contribution to inanity on the airwaves, blathered and crooned from a radio on the wall. The off/on was broken, but the volume was down. It didn't bother me; I concentrated on emerging patterns. Light and shadow fell from the enlarger onto blank paper, then into a pan of chemical with it, and captured time took form. The process made everything seem very accessible.

Made some prints of Ursula. What was her emerging pattern? Would I someday see her on TV, her face devoid of any true emotion as she read the news in those tones of cool hysteria that commentators cultivate? There was something obscene in the daily practice of scraping up the dregs of human events and presenting that as the essence of life in those smug, Chicken Little voices. I loved Ursula! I didn't want to see her disappear into that! But it seemed that was where she was bent on going. What was love? Something less than my desire to accompany her.

I worked on. The understanding grew in me of what I was doing and why. A faint sound echoed down the hall. It vibrated under the darkroom door, crept up my shoulder, crawled in my ear. The membrane moved, hammer hit anvil, stirrup bone jangled, microscopic wheat waved, electricity flashed through memory cells, and recognition lit up behind my eyes. The sound (of heraldic garbage cans being bashed together): KERBASH!

"It's good old Rafe," I said to myself. I made sure all the prints were in the wash, then opened the door and went down the hall. There was Rafe's pushcart, bristling with brooms, laden with cansful of inter-office memos and other debris. There was Rafe.

"Hallo, buddy," I said.

"Well," he said, turning ponderously up from his work. "Hello my fren. What you doin, hangin roun this late?"

"Prints."

I took the cigarette he offered me, lit it and puffed toward the ceiling. Smoke spread out in a soft cloud against the acoustical tile. I took Rafe in as he stood there, beefy and broad-shouldered, but the whole sweating bulk of him poised, balanced on the balls of his feet. For his age, over sixty, the man was in good shape.

"Ah Rafe," I said, leaning back against a wall. "You're a mystery. You look younger and craftier every time I see you."

"Yah," he grunted. "Ah feel that way sometime. Not tonight, though. I aged ten years sense I saw you las."

"What happened? Someone overwind your wristwatch?"

"Nope. Nothin to do with that. Ah'm jus awful tired of this shit here. . . ." He indicated the offices of the *Voice* with a disrespectful mophandle. "These people throw their shit aroun like they didn't have to be nobody to cope with it. They don understan half the stuff they doin, an they don pay real attention to any of it. An then, after they *think* they finished, I got to come along and put ten thousand things right!"

I looked at him carefully. It was obvious he wasn't into a heavy funk, just a little good-natured grousing.

He picked a wad of folded paper out of the trashbarrel. "And what are we helping them do? You seen this afternoon's addition?" Wordlessly, Rafe displayed a montage of rape, murder, and the tawdry presidential striptease over Watergate. Then he flipped inside to the ads, the scenes of airbrushed androids in states of elaborately contrived happiness. He looked at me to see if I got the point.

"Yeah," I said. "The whip and the carrot. That whole rag ain't much more than using sensational information to push you into advertising. Then into the store for the salvation you can buy."

"Who?" Rafe said. "Not me, mah man. Not me. That's why I used the money from this to git me a little place out of town, where nothin comes in that Ah don *invite*. Ah don like the way people in this world are always puttin their minds on you. I want to be free, like a horse."

He underlined this unusual metaphor with a wave of his mophandle, invoking a vision of sagebrush freedom. I stared at him. I'd pursued a friendship with Rafe from the time I first met him, but he always seemed to slip away on the edge of my knowing, escaping into a dimension where he was comfortable, but where I'd never seen him before.

"Ah," I said. "So you're a hippie."

Smiling a crooked smile, Rafe dipped into the trashbarrel again and emerged with a copy of *Rolling Stone*. It was a back issue from someone's desk cleaning, one with a portrait of Dylan on the cover. Wordlessly, he flipped inside to the ads for books, slogan T-shirts, albums, paraphernalia, stereo components.

"Nope," he said.

I sucked the cigarette down to the butt, stubbed it against the side of the trashcan, and tossed it.

"Rafe, you're echoing my own thoughts," I said. "I sure as hell wouldn't mind being free, like a horse, myself. I just don't have a farm to run off to."

Rafe chuckled. "You got feets don't you? That's all you need to run."

I groaned and leaned back against the wall, running my fingers through my hair. "Rafe, I've already *done* that number. I've spent the past year getting a career and a social scene together. You telling me to chuck it all, all over again?"

"What *you* tellin *me* man? Dint Ah tell you bout all the rail-ridin I done in the Depression? Ah know what I'm talkin about. When you loose and on the road, thinkin new thoughts, seein things a different kind of way comes easier. Sounds like what you need. Shee-it, you only twenny-two! You got lots of good miles in you yet!''

"All right!" I said, coming off the wall and catching fire. "All right! Just cut the strings and snatch my body away. But do it different! I get you . . . . But listen. I've got to get my prints out. What if I go, split as fast as I can get it together? Don't know when I'd see you again, or even if! But no matter what happens, I'd like to think of myself as your friend.''

"Well," he said. "I'll let you do that. I'll let you do that.''

We gripped hands. I was amazed at the strength in his huge, warm paw. I turned and walked down the hall. His voice came after me. "Haw!''

I looked back. Rafe held out one fist and unclenched it, palm up. A small, crumpled object on his hand slowly expanded, changing colors as it moved. I took it for a piece of carbon paper, crushed into haphazard resemblance of a flower. It could have been a trick in the reflection of the light, but as I watched, it changed from a black rose, to a red, to a white.

"*Lookit* all this shit," he said. Then he chucked it into a trashcan, laughing to himself.

The blower had dried the negatives from the afternoon enough so I could print them, add them to my collection. Before long, they were in the wash.

In the darkroom, I leaned back on a tall stool, my elbows on the counter behind me. Even though all the prints were fixed, and therefore light-safe, I left the dim red lights on and the door closed. I liked it that way. It was like being inside your own cranium, developing and reworking the images of experience.

Tarot. Photographs. Sometimes I saw photographs as tarot cards . . . energy, life-forces, transformed and held in the images of two dimensions. Sometimes, to me, the photographs were even more accurate representations of those forces than the cards, because they were drawn directly from life, rather than through the symbol factory of the mind. This was one of those times. In the turmoil of my own emotions and the red darkness of the room, I cultivated this understanding.

I stopped the drum and reached into the swirling water. I took the prints out, one by one, and scrutinized each as I assembled them in a stack.

Ursula. I gently laid a portrait of her coming out of Cherokee Sink (nude, one hand wringing her hair dry while the other reached for the sky in exultation), laid it on top of a flash shot of her glaring at me over her typewriter as she pushed to make a deadline.

Radical Jack and assorted pals and gals in the regalia of the hip Saturnalia, the night the ROTC building got torched. Years ago, now. Put that under the shot of the harsh angles of the plaster and plastic student apartment building where I currently crashed, until Mrs. McPeak could find me a new hovel with atmosphere. The pool at the apartment, I remembered, had a set of rules beside it calculated to induce psychosomatic leprosy in all the tenants. You were supposed to do everything short of dipping yourself in Lysol before a swim.

It seemed that most of the students had dipped themselves in Lysol anyway, I reflected, as I added photographs of them to the pile. They'd done *something* to rid themselves of the dangerous Dionysian bacteria that had spread like infectious laughter a few years back. A colorless, unenthusiastic bunch. Safe and serious. Styled hair, fad clothes off the racks, clenched foreheads, armloads of books, beer, and tennis rackets. Remember Kent who? Clark Kent? Kent, like with the micronite filter?

Work assignments. The governor shaking hands with the judge soon to be convicted in a pandering scandal. The lovers: two dolls in rented clothes embracing by wedding cake. Assorted piles of smoking wreckage. And so on, back through frozen slices of my times. And on top, the latest hit, Tallulah Crystall, archetype of the *arriviste* after a lifetime in the Lie.

I hefted the stack of photographs. Here it was, the best my camera could do: a vision of my reality in a double handful of soggy tissue. As I held it, the violent dissatisfaction and piercing anger of the afternoon came flooding back. And something deeper, a spasm of feeling so strong that it frightened me, made my hands start to shake as I gripped the wad of damp paper. Go through it!

I tore it in half. AAAAaaggGHH!!

It is hard to describe. But the very air around me, the quality of material objects around me, seemed to change. I felt as if I had done something apocalyptic.

But I was still in the same darkroom, in the same body, same life, same world, with the same people waiting for me to continue doing the same things. However, I was not going to do them.

Rafe had given me the faint push I'd needed. I had hit the road before, but not the way I sensed I was going to hit it now.

II.
The Six
of Cups

Next morning, I pawned all my camera equipment. I was screwed down to about half what it was worth, but it still gave me a tidy sum. I used it to buy packs, water bottles, a Coleman one-burner, a tune-up kit and freeway pegs for my putt.

Ah yes, my bike. Haven't introduced you. He was one of my tools that hadn't lost favor, a pre-K1 Honda 750 with an 812 kit, Yoshimura cam, Hooker header and modified suspension. I'd just gotten the seat reupholstered, and some exotic artwork done on the tank and sidecovers. The bike now seemed to have a personality, so I named him Franklin Delano Motorcycle. "Frank" for short. That afternoon, as I worked on him, I realized how well the name applied. I wanted him to be my ride to a New Deal.

But which way would I go to get it? That stumped me. Here I was, making ready to charge off, with no direction. Frank had his points. I could tell, I was putting them in. But mine? It didn't seem that this journey would benefit from being aimed at any particular spot. Still, I'd have to pick by *some* method which road to hit . . . .

I tried to keep the quiver of urgency out of my hands as I puzzled over this, squatting in the broiling sun, adjusting clearance on the points.

Done. I banged the seat shut over my bag of tools, just as a long shadow began to slide across the asphalt. I looked up. A long line of thunderheads was drifting with slow majesty across the sky, like a fleet of gaff-rigged schooners under full sail. It was that season in the deep South, when thunderstorms weighed anchor, sailed in, and blockaded a

15

sunny day without warning.

I pushed Frank under the stairwell of the apartment building and tucked him into his tarp. Then I walked to Tennessee Street and hung out my thumb. I made it to the *Voice* building just about the time the first fat, cold drops began to splat against the pavement. I found Ursula's car in the lot. Unlocked. I got in, twiddled my thumbs, watched the rain fall, and waited for five o'clock. I didn't have long to wait.

Preceded by a few others, Ursula burst outside, ran through the rain, and dived breathlessly into the car.

"Hi," I said.

"Hi!" She was startled.

There was a gentle awkwardness in the air between us, as we each tried to figure out where the other stood, after yesterday's conflagration.

"Why weren't you at work today?" Ursula demanded, then immediately amended her tone with some of the warmth I could see in her brown eyes. "I missed you," she added quietly.

"I'm not making it in tomorrow either," I told her, resisting the mute plea of her warmth. I didn't know why it seemed that if I gave in to it, the edge would be taken from my decision of last night.

Ursula removed her glasses and stared at me. There were two spots of red where the frames had rested on the bridge of her nose. They were joined by two blotches that rose in her cheeks.

"Are you *aware* how long it took me to pull together a place for us both to work? You're going to throw it away just like *that*?"

"I'm splitting town," I told her resolutely. I broke eye contact with her and looked out through the windshield. "Gimme the keys."

She put them in the ignition for me. I started the car.

"Just like that, huh? The least you could have done is tell Max," she said.

I looked at her sharply.

"He'll find out soon enough."

A mockingbird hopping in a puddle took flight. The tires splashed into it as I turned out of the driveway. I felt Ursula's attention on me and glanced at her. Her eyes were filmed with an extra moisture, round and dark as a child's. She was looking at me as though I had somehow become a stranger, a point of view I could understand.

"You know where you're going?"

"No."

She slouched back in her seat and stared out the window. I was struck by the fact that I could sense what she felt, almost see it in the air between us. Ever since I'd torn that wad of photographs in half, something had been happening to my perception. It had been cast free, and was finding its own sphere at a deeper level than I'd ever known before. But I still didn't know what to tell Ursula, what words would have the power to clear the air between us, so she could see how vitally necessary my change was to me.

"Want me to drive you home?" I asked lamely.

"I'm trying to not care what you do . . . ."

"All right."

A corner of her mouth jerked and twisted downward. She rolled down the window, and turned her face to the wind and the rain.

I drove out the Lake Bradford Road, and turned down a long, sandy driveway. Grey Spanish moss that plumed the trees was already turning faintly green in the rain. I stopped in front of the cabin she rented, where both of us had lived at one time, and kept the engine running. Ursula looked askance.

"Need to borrow the car," I said. "Got to drop off the stuff I'm not taking at Goodwill."

"DAMMIT Steve! Look, I don't know why this thing with Miss Crystall is so imp— . . . ."

"It's not just her. Not just her. I need to not go any further into . . . what you're getting into." I cursed my inability to articulate it. "At least, not until something changes inside of me."

She shook her head. "We spend four years together. Then you just up and say, 'That's it, I'm leaving.' " Suddenly, Ursula's face tightened. "And you're so cold! And matter-of-fact about it!" She got up out of the car and slammed the door behind her. "OK, *take* the god-dam car! And when you come back, just throw the keys under the seat and leave it. I don't want to see you!" She half-ran toward the cabin.

"It hasn't been *our* relationship these past few years," I said to her retreating form, even though I knew it wasn't true. "It's been *your* relationship."

I threw the car into reverse and spun back out of the driveway.

It didn't take long to stuff my extra clothes, bedding, books, and whatnot into boxes. I didn't have that much to begin with. Cutting free the excess was like dropping ballast from a balloon—it made me feel light, free, able to climb faster. Not unmixed with guilt, I had the same feelings about cutting free from Ursula.

Goodwill was grateful.

Back on the street, I noticed the sky was clearing. The armada of thunderheads was crowding on canvas for Pensacola. The air was clean, sparkling, charged with a thousand fresh smells. I felt a moment of regret that I would be leaving behind the lush and lovely Tallahassee summer.

I knew I had to perform some ritual gesture of farewell.

Several miles northwest of town, off the Old Bainbridge Road, was a small meadow centered within a stonehenge of live oaks and their fallen logs. Year round, this meadow was thick with fragrant grasses, loud with crickets, and bright with butterflies in the spring and summer. I used to go there often when despondent, for rest, or when parched for inspiration. I'd found it one day while out looking for *psilocybe cubensis earle*, a fungus with unusual properties. I found no 'shrooms, but I did find this spot, imbued with a powerful and subtle charm.

Today, driving out on Old Bainbridge was like moving down a long tunnel under the interlaced trees, filled with a soft green light. I made the turn onto an abandoned logging road. The car rocked and the clutch whined as I navigated some impressive ruts. Ah.

I switched off the internal combustion, got out of the car, and walked through the trees. A few last drops spun lazily out of the sky. Overhead, to the west, the departing clouds churned in a broad, ragged mandala of grey and purple shadow. In the middle of the meadow, in the wet grass, I sat crosslegged. I closed my eyes. Aha. The restful power I'd found here so many times before seemed even more concentrated now.

Now. An image of Ursula's uncomprehending and reproachful gaze floated before me. I brushed it aside. Then I saw myself as I had stood last night, a tight, crazy smile on my face, a wad of torn, dripping paper in each hand. Why? Why was I bent on tearing apart a reality Ursula and so many others had made and shared with me? There was a tearing pain in my heart as I thought about it, and a fear of going deeper into the subject. But what *was* it that repelled me from joining or allying myself with anyone or anything? I'd gone through the motions while shrinking back inside even further.

It was a momentum begun a few years back when young folks—who had the least to lose, who had high spirits and as-yet uncompromised ideals, pot for a sacrament, a rock'n'roll banner, and Vietnam as a cause célèbre—had taken the risky shift of pressing for change and renewal. Now that wave was spreading out on the beach, sinking into the sand. But the last of its thrust was still carrying me.

The "wornout and soldout!" visions we had attacked. Our institutional inheritance. State, church, world economic machine, trend, counter-trend, psuedo-trend, expressing themselves in a thousand thousand interlocking structures, recreating the earth in their image. And the cancer riddling it was fear. It was not that the dreams originating these structures were not positive, necessarily, it was that too many people, for too long, had chosen them out of fear rather than love. Fear, blindness, and a lack of alternatives.

It wasn't only that the structures had gotten their hooks into the people; the people had *their* hooks into the structures. That neurotic clinging was what made the whole mess cohere. All institutions were nebulous and vulnerable, because they were man-made. But everyone, including the critics, preferred to treat them as a product of some Divine Beyond. That way they could cling to them or curse them without taking any responsibility for them.

Thus the dreams, calcifying for a lack of real life energy flowing within, became enclaves with neurotic adherents manning the battlements. The brief, hairy rebellion had been a reaction against that. But did a return to business-as-usual mean a return to the same vices? A return to dealing with the Lie thrust in from every side, scared that there might not be an alternative and lacking the courage to create one? Like Hamlet, I thought. We'd rather cling to the evils that we have, that we understand and have worked out compromises with, than fly to others we know not of.

There *had* to be something else! More essential! Apart from the ebb, flow, and sticking places of pop belief!

I could visualize the cognitive coordinates where the answer *should* be. I almost saw it—a single brightness like a navigator's star, half-glimpsed through the fog. I pursued the trace of it through my mind and memory. It was like following a silver thread through a dark tapestry unrolling before my inner eyes. Scenes appeared, scenes that were never a part of my life as I knew it, though they were imbued with a haunting familiarity.

In a tent made of skins, an old man squatted before a fire and tossed colored powders into the flames. The half-glimpsed star flared briefly as one bright spark.

That spark was also in a brass brazier, where a priest sprinkled incense in homage to a jackal-headed god.

The shadows in the temple, light from the torches, smoke from the incense, all swirled together to form the skyscape of a departing storm.

There was a child, gazing up at it. I remembered that; I was the child. I could feel the firm roundness of my limbs, sweet pulse of my breath, the clear light in my eyes. The time was the early 1950s. I was standing on a log thickly shrouded in gold and green moss, near my home. In the storm I felt a powerful presence, blowing energy through me like the wind, and asking for . . . recognition. Acknowledgment. I was infused with a ripe golden happiness and yet a curious longing to go deeper. I felt as if I were being taught the dreams of the rain.

The image that summarized all I felt was the light of that elusive star, hovering in the clouds. Two curving walls of purple formed a ragged oval. Through it, a fan of light poured, to lose itself in a purple mist.

Only then did I realize that my eyes were open. It wasn't *then*, it was *now*!! The exact pattern of light glowing in a memory of childhood, was also before me in Tallahassee of '73! I couldn't tell whether I was in the past or the present. Hair stood up on the back of my neck, droplets of sweat broke out on my face. I had a dizzying sense of vertigo. My mind felt stretched, like a compass, between two points of being. It seemed that a small motion of my will would catapult me headlong into the past. Then the clouds shifted, the light was eclipsed, and I plummeted like a stone into the continuity of Tallahassee.

The door had closed, the starlight was gone. I yearned after it, the way I'd always imagined Ulysses straining against the cord that bound him, hearing the sirens sing. But it was no good. Strings of time and space, momentarily stretched, snapped back and held.

I reached down and touched the wet earth beneath me. It occurred to me that I was going mad. The prospect frightened me, but somehow . . . I liked it.

Even as I rose woodenly and walked back, the intensity of that moment of vision stayed with me. It seemed to form an actual distortion in the air, hovering at one corner of my physical sight. Several times on the way back into town it sent lines of force out through everything else I could see, as if the entire world were about to rise, shift, and go swirling down into it. It made me dizzy; it gave me an unnerving sense of the bizarre, but I was fascinated by the *quality* of the being whose presence had dominated the experience. It felt as if *that* were the touchstone of a change, connected with the deepening in what I could see and feel that had begun last night in the darkroom of the *Voice*.

I tried to explain it all to Ursula when I returned. I did *not* just park the car and throw the keys under the seat, but strode into the cabin burning with exhilaration! As if I had just run many miles in the rain.

Ursula turned in her chair, by the desk in the bedroom, when I entered. There was surprise in her eyes, but also a certain calm and distant knowing, as if she had been receiving thoughts and drawing conclusions of her own while I was gone.

I knelt. I don't know exactly what I said. I do recall that I tried to get it all said at once, my hands sculpting in the air the forces of my story whenever words failed.

"You know," she said, when I had finished and we were just there, staring at each other in silence. "You know, with you like this, I'm going to have to look out for myself."

I nodded. That was what I wanted. The look that passed between us was pure understanding. At that point, in my mind, she began to recede from me. But she came forward once before she moved back. Her eyes on mine, smiling with a sweet sadness, she rose slowly from the chair. I switched off the light. She lit a lamp. Then, by the side of the bed, her fragrant dark hair falling over my arms, I felt for the buttons at the back of her dress. Soon, it was her soft nakedness that I pulled against me. Her warmth, the familiar smells, familiar shape of her body. I think that, at that moment, I loved her more than I ever had before, more than I ever would again.

The next day, after she left, I spent excited hours bringing my gear over to Ursula's cabin, packing and repacking it, and doing a final check. Then I stacked everything by the front door and waited for Ursula to come back.

She didn't.

Shadows of the lakeside cypress stretched across the sand in the driveway. Out of things to do, I sat on the porch and watched these shadows lengthen. It became glaringly apparent that she wasn't coming home. I got angry. What was she doing, striking out at the mood of my journey, trying to ruin the thing that was freeing me from her? Well, I thought, that probably being the case, I can damn well celebrate a good-bye party on my own.

I hopped on Frank and torqued out of the driveway, clawing a roostertail of sand into the air. I went to the Pastime.

Now the Pastime Tavern was a den of sweet iniquity. A squat building on Route 90, it combined low lights with get-down sounds. An electric bass always seemed to be throbbing slowly and wickedly in the basement. More drug deals, character assassinations, assignations, and good old time-wasting had been perpetrated around its ring-stained, butt-scorched tables than anywhere else in Tallahassee, . . . with the possible exception of the State Capitol Building.

As soon as I walked in, I entered a haze of perfume and perspiration, of smoke that had been collecting against the ceiling for twenty years, of a warm buzz of conversation punctuated by scattered laughter. As my eyes grew accustomed to the light, I looked around to see if I knew any of the night's revelers. I did.

Ursula sat on a bench near the front, with half a dozen empty glasses stacked on the table in front of her. I should've expected it. That was her favorite solution for troubles: one part vermouth to six parts gin, and a twist of sorrow.

But the juice had had at least one good effect. Despite the fact that she was in her work duds, the alcohol had relaxed the nervous stiffness that usually went with them. Her body seemed to thrust itself against the fabric in a hundred different beguiling ways. She didn't lack for appreciation.

The man sitting next to her had his hair in a Shag, a sculpted affair combining sterile diabolism and conservative chic. A way of showing his cool, without bringing down the ire of the *Voice* publishers, who were still alarmed at the decadent implications of hippiedom. He also had an acrylic pullover with a silk-screened sunset, a silver bracelet, a pair of tight flared jeans, and Frye boots with brass buckles on the sides. He looked like a man in a filter cigarette ad, or the answer to "What Kind of Man Reads Playboy?" This was Max.

I walked up to their table.

"Meeting fancy you here," I said.

Ursula looked up. "Oh yeah, really," she replied. "What are you up to?"

I paused. "Looking for you," I lied.

"Here I am," she said, raising her glass in a mock salute.

"So I see." I began to feel somewhat nauseous.

Max leaned back, unlit cigarette dangling from his lips. Slowly, he brought a lit match to the tip, inhaled, and blew a puff in my direction. I thought about how suave he'd look with that cigarette sticking out of his ear, coal end in.

"I've got a check for you," he said.

"Why don't you use it to buy yourself some aftershave?" I suggested. My voice was higher than I wanted it to be. Feelings I still had for Ursula burned inside. But I sensed barriers between us now like invisible concertina wire, landmines of things I could say wrong, bombed bridges that had been our points of contact. I wanted to smash through the whole intricate mess.

"Ursula," I leveled. "What are you doing?"

She stared at me laconically through half-closed eyes. "Isn't it obvious?" she said.

"Yeah. You coming back to the cabin tonight?"

She shrugged. Max smiled in thinly disguised triumph. An icy calm descended on me.

"Hey," I said to Max. "Lemme bum a hack."

"Sure." He reached into his pack with two fingers, extracting a cigarette.

I tapped the end on a thumbnail, then let it dangle from my lips in a burlesque of his style. I put my hands in my pockets and hunched my head down into my jacket collar.

"I see your Jagger," I told him, "and raise you a Bogart. See ya later, schweetha'ts. Beast of luck." Then I turned and shouldered off through the crowd.

As I brushed past the bar, I nearly knocked Dr. Eugene Gaunt, an Ichabod Crane double from FSU's Theology Department, off his barstool. A half-empty liter of the house red sat at his elbow. In front of him was a yellow legal pad on which he had scribbled extensively. He caught my arm as I bumped against him.

"Don't be so rude, dude!" he said. "What's up?"

"Hi Gene," I muttered, trying to pull away.

"Hygiene is up?" he said. "What's that, a drug company? I'll check my *Wall Street Journal*. Thanks for the tip!"

"Uh . . ." I began, intending to say that the last thing in the world I wanted right now was to get sucked into one of his lunatic conversations.

"Hey," he interrupted gravely. "The Wasp of Doom is coming, sometime this summer. So watch out. It'll scare the bejabbers out of the Treacle Drinkers, and nothing's more lachrymorose than a Treacle Drinker who can't find his bejabbers. The world will drown in tears . . . ."

"What?" I said. That seemed to be the only possible response.

"Sit down," Gene said generously, "and I'll explain."

"No, Gene. I was just on my way to . . . ."

"Then suffice it to say that the Wasp packs the poison of cynicism and apathy in his poignant little stinger. His day approacheth like unto a garbage truck. The wholesale iconoclasm, the rabid-rapid rape of social dreams, the creed of disbelief, the phenomenon of trendy metaphysics, are all psychological correlatives of the end of the Piscean Age, which I can prove by algebra, interpolation, and a little guesswork . . . ."

"Gene! Stop! I've gotta go to the bathroom! Let me go or I'll whizz on your Adidas!"

He glared at me over the rim of his wineglass. "Should I tell him?" he asked the glass. "Or let this enthusiastic—if un-disciplined—former student stride off into his prolonged adolescence unwarned? Make me belch twice for yes, once for no!" He tossed the wine down. He belched long, loudly, and once.

"The entrails have augured!" he shouted. "Get lost!"

"Gene," I told him, "you're hard to like. And as for the Wasp, don't worry, I'm already stung. It ain't so bad. *Ciao.*"

I pushed my way back through the billiards room. I discovered, to my amazement, that I really did have to pee. The light in the men's bathroom was, as usual, not working. I left the door open a notch and went to the approximate location of the toilet.

The thin slab of light that came through the door illuminated a graffitum: "Just because you're paranoid doesn't mean they're not out to get you." As I read it, I proceeded to piss all over my boots. That destroyed the last of the icy calm that had descended while I talked to Ursula and Max. I was now certifiably miserable.

Walking back through the billiards, the snick! click! that rose from the tables was like the random ticking of an erratic clock. A timepiece for my new schedule, I thought ruefully. As I passed the bar, I saw Ursula and Max disappear through the front door.

Probably headed for his apartment. Wise of Max to make his move so soon; if I knew Ursula, after that number of drinks, she'd be snoring in half an hour. Well, at least now I'd be able to stay. Possibly I could stir up a loving farewell from *someone*.

I headed downstairs into The Pit, the Pastime's basement nightclub. The poster over the spiral stair announced tonight's band: Loose Change, featuring! Jo Guiness and her Big Bend Bluegrass Boys.

Jo was an oldtime Tallahassee mamma, a ravishing poetic lady with heartbeats in her dark eyes and an incredibly edible body. Despite her smooth skin and sweet good looks, she had done a whirlwind bout of addiction with almost every drug available, had gone through scores of old men with the abandon of a bumblebee in a buttercup field, and had been arrested once in a spectacular scandal involving a married state senator from Miami. She had a quick mind, a sweet sad smile, and one helluva voice for the blues. I loved her to death, because she kept alive a wild energy that Ursula had exorcised long ago. Jo and I had never gotten around to consummating our friendship, but we enjoyed pretending that at any moment we were about to.

In the basement. Spotlights blew light through red gels toward a low stage. Jo, nursing a beer in an hourglass-shaped stein, was sitting at one of the small, round tables. Behind her, the Big Bend Bluegrass Boys were tuning their equipment. They were all backwoods longhairs who liked to spike their bluegrass with rock'n'roll.

"Hi, honeybum," I said to Jo, as I pulled out a chair.

"How you?" she said.

"Dunt esk."

"That bad? Poor baby." She puckered her rosebud in a pout of commiseration.

"I'm blowing town, Jo. Don't ask me why, I'm not too sure myself. Got to get loose of things and take another look. But does Ursula help? No, she rags on me and hops in the sack with that geek Max. I guess she wants to twist the knife just so I'll have something to remember her by."

Jo looked at me shrewdly. "Awwww . . ." she said.

I laughed, despite myself, and shook my head. "I dunno why that should strike me as funny. Minute ago, I was eating my heart out."

"I am the muse of irresponsible laughter," Jo said. "All who taste of my graces become swine."

"But I haven't really tasted of 'em, Jo . . . ."

" 'S okay. In our capricious omnipotence, we've given you a special dispensation."

"Oink."

She turned in her chair to see how the band was getting on. I saw a silver pendant in the form of a naked woman hanging from her neck. The lines of face and bosom were definitely familiar. I didn't have to look far for a parallel.

"Jo, did you model for that pendant?"

"Well-l-l, yeah," she admitted. "Stan did it for me."

"Isn't that a taste solipsistic?"

She didn't look abashed for more than a second. "Isn't everything?" she countered.

"Who the hell wants to live in a house of mirrors?"

"Who the hell can get out?"

"If I make it, I'll send you a card."

"Do that," she said. "You do that."

One member of the band, with long blonde hair and moustache, walked up and mumbled to her. "Aha!" she said. And to me, "It's time."

Soon, between a lead guitarist with gyrating Chuck Berry hips and the blonde bassist with his flashing silver rings, Jo sang with all her vibrant sadness about the "White Line Fever." Gradually the floor became crowded with dancers from the tables, and others who rushed downstairs when they heard the band start up.

I sat wallowing in a sense of loss for what I was leaving, and apprehension for what I would be traveling towards. I wandered through memories of university madness, bluegrass festies, sinkhole swims, and young love. I thought, I've seen the era of my ways. When will I again see the like?

In front of me, a horde of dancers whirled, a kaleidoscope of blending, blinding flesh. I kicked myself in the ass and joined them! One last time . . . ! Everyone cut loose and let themselves get shook by the music real good. I caught Jo's eye and she winked. Her green blouse was hugged to her breasts by sweat. Denim bells, also wringing wet, stretched across her trim ass. She let go of the mike and danced with abandon.

Between sets, we went out to the parking lot behind the Pit, and sprawled on the hood of somebody's Lincoln. Jo sang softly to the crescent moon, "Will the Circle Be Unbroken?" I pulled open the front of her blouse, and blew air down between her sweating tits.

"That feels good," she said. "Wish I could take the goddam thing off."

"Go ahead."

"Nooooo!" She blushed. It was strange and delightful to see her so child-modest, after a night of earthy song and earthier dancing.

The sound of guitars being tuned drifted out into the night. "C'mon!" We ran inside.

Dance! Chairs were folded up, pushed against the walls. No one who sat could stay that way long; the magnetic vitality of the music sluiced them back out onto the floor. It seemed to me that this joyful, sweating, panting crowd—all high on the music and each other—represented the best of the moments my generation could create, moments that, just this year were becoming few and far between. I was glad to have caught this one, but I could see that it was no longer enough.

The last number, "Do Right Woman," brought the crowd down gradually and ended in a shower of fading notes. I wrestled my way through the bodies, and helped Jo down from the stage.

"Wanna help me finish off my goodbye in style?" I breathed in her ear.

"The party's over," she breathed back. "For me, anyway." She nodded toward the blonde bassplayer. His moustache had lost its zap about halfway through the evening. Now it made an exaggerated downcurve on his face like the mouth of Tragoedeia. I saw him glance at us as he knelt to put his guitar in the case. "Obligations . . ." she said.

I studied her, looking into her green eyes. I could feel her stout loyalty, the nature of her love for this man. That shocked and impressed me: I could feel and appreciate her love for someone else. In that moment, I sensed a trace of that thing I would be traveling in search of. The room became too small. My dissatisfaction, temporarily suppressed, ignited again inside me. Already, in my mind, I was out thrusting down the cool, empty roads of night . . . .

"Hey," Jo said. "C'mon. Aren't we friends?"

I returned to the space behind my eyes, and looked at her. "Uh, yeah."

"Well, friends kiss each other goodbye, don't they?"

"They do," I agreed. "Ya ready?"

"Shoot."

Crotch-squeezing, thigh-rubbing, juice-dripping, tonsil-swabbing, lip-crushing, breath-sucking SMACK!! Then away! Away! Into the dream-haunted night!

I stood outside the Pastime, jangling my motorcycle keys, looking up at streetlamps and the silver slice of moon. And thinking.

I could feel it inside, some kind of psychic pregnancy—a clamoring force that could not see enough, feel enough, be enough, demanding release! Already it had forced itself far enough to tear through the patterns of my life, to change the very nature of my perceptions. My old reality was a suit that could no longer fit, my old concepts like a set of inch-scale tools confronting a metric problem. I had nowhere to go but out. OUT!

But I still didn't know what direction to take . . . . Then, I did. It was obvious. The impulse, the starlight by which I would navigate further into the unknown would be the trace of that strange yet kindred energy, that powerful source of understanding I had seen shining yesterday in the stormclouds, a presence I realized I had always sensed springing from some deep ultrareality, behind and beneath my experience.

But what in me could track or trace this thing? The same inner sense that had motivated me in the darkroom, led me out to that field on the Old Bainbridge Road, shown me a way to appreciate Jo's love for someone else—that piece of navigational equipment which for lack of any other name I began to call the astrolabe of the heart.

As I saw that, thought that, felt that, I knew it was time to go. GO!!

The sand lot before Ursula's cabin glowed with faint brushwork of shadow and moon. Otherwise, it was empty. She hadn't come back. Of course, I shouldn't really have expected her to. Ursula was wise. She knew what she had to do in order to remain herself. I felt another pang at the impending separation from her, but it was soon replaced by a curious detachment. I had my astrolabe, and I had my star. Somehow, tonight, that seemed to be enough.

I got the knapsacks of gear from the cabin, carried them out, and strapped them to Frank. His kickstand sank in the sand, so I stuck an old hunk of board under it. Then I made my last trip in, to put on my riding leathers. I had oiled them; they were glistening and warm to the touch. Then I was sitting on Frank, revving the engine. I shifted into first and slowly released the clutch.

In the cool dark of the early morning, I came to the truck route encircling Tallahassee, a road called the Capitol Circle. North? East? South? West? I had postponed my choice of directions until this instant. West, suggested the internal astrolabe. That was the direction the storm-cloud had taken, bearing in its mist the vox voci. West it was.

III.
The
Star

Blipping through small towns at steady speeds, little panhandle burgs with names like Two Egg and Chattahoochee. Through the smell of dew-wet Georgia pines, through the new light of rising sun coming through the clouds behind me. Steady hum of Frank's exhaust was a sweet lengthened note, a chant, a song to the wind. Unphotographable moment! There was regret for what I was leaving behind, but, by and large, I cut through ribbons and ties like a drunken mayor opening a freeway. Light rock with a driving rhythm was making up songs about me, and I began to grin into the wind . . . .

Hours of giddy delight lasted until I came upon my first rainstorm, a dark coagulation of clouds straddling the road. It almost seemed that my magical storm of two days ago had moseyed down the road a piece and just stopped to wait for me. In any case, I had no intention of getting my enthusiasm dampened. I started to look for cover.

After the next few curves, I came upon another rinkydink town, of six or seven doddering old buildings with front porches that looked like dropped and stepped-on false teeth. I pulled in under the sagging awning of an abandoned gas station, through patches of weed and fragments of beer bottle.

I parked Frank by the battered gas pumps. Panels had been torn off, exposing their rusty innards. The pumps no longer cared; they just wanted to decay back into the earth and get their incarnations as gas pumps over with. Small flowers sprouted through a concrete slab cobwebbed with cracks. The building itself was white stucco, with red dust lying in the curls of plaster. A large plate glass window, surprisingly, was intact. It too was covered with a patina of red dust; letters could easily be traced on it with a finger. In this way, it had become a gypsy bulletin board, one that gradually erased every time a truck barrelled through town. Current listings:

KAREN EATS MEADOW MUFFINS

announced a scrawl in the lower left corner. Someone, probably Karen, had tried to rub it out. In the center of the window was a homily on dualism:

LIFE IS LIKE A DICK
WHEN IT'S HARD, YOU GET SCREWED
WHEN IT'S SOFT, YOU CAN'T BEAT IT

And on the right:

GOD LOVES EVERYBODY. EVEN GODDAM REDNECKS
THAT WON'T PICK UP HITCHHIKERS!

Under that was a single word of advice or warning:

PUSH

I took off my helmet and sat down to wait out the rain. Down the street was a Rebel Mini-Mart, the one tacky new structure between all the old houses. As I watched, a pickup full of crewcut farmers splashed through the puddles and stopped in front of it. I could just make out the sticker on the front bumper:

THE KNIGHTS OF THE KU KLUX KLAN IS WATCHING *YOU!*

I felt a twinge of paranoia. I knew that the Pigs vs. Freaks game was passé, but I didn't know if *they* knew. If any place ever looked like a pocket of lingering resistance to change, this town did.

No! I thought. Don't react the usual way to this. Break out of that! Keep following the magic. But I could find no catalyst within me to change my reaction. And there was no one around to help me with it, either. I began to feel the edge of a tremendous loneliness. So. Where was the light of my halcyon star now . . . ? Try to choose it. *Try* to have it manifest here.

I rummaged in my food pack for something to pour into the void. As I reached for my canteen, something touched me, made me glance up. No one and nothing there but my own reflection gazing back from the dusty plate glass, with the word *PUSH* lettered across my forehead. The reflection winked at me.

I unscrewed the canteen cap and suddenly froze. Now wait a minute! *I* hadn't winked, but the face had! Somebody else had to be standing behind that glass, watching me, winking when he suddenly caught my eye! Startled, scared, I looked quickly back up.

He was still there, someone standing on the inside of the abandoned station. Hard to make out his features through the dusty glass, but he looked enough like me so that it was easy to see how I'd mistaken him for my reflection. He was talking.

I motioned that I couldn't hear. He gestured, and I felt an inner pop in my ears, as if I had swallowed while changing altitudes.

"Skeered the shit outta you, dint Ah?" he said. His voice was thin and whistling, like a wind in dry grass.

"You still are," I said. "Who the hell are you?"

His grin was lopsided, crazy. "Whattsa matter freako? Cantcha read?"

"*PUSH?*" I hazarded.

The face sardonically raised one eyebrow, and nodded. Then it vanished.

I stood still, stunned, uncomprehending. Then I ran for the shattered door that led to the room behind the glass. I stood on the threshold and looked in. Shadows, cobwebs, and dust. Nothing else. The broken door was the only way in or out; it had been in my view the whole time.

I slowly retraced my steps, while my mind groped frantically for an explanation. I examined the place on the glass where the face had appeared. A faint pattern in the dust suggested the outlines of it . . . . That pattern, my reflection, and a bit of overactive imagining might have combined in a temporary hallucination.

But now that I thought about it, the face had looked unlike me too. The hair was curlier, the bone structure more refined . . . elfin even. And how to explain the words, the eerie accent? I winced. How far, how fast, was I moving into madness if I not only imagined faces and voices but actually conversed with them?!

The place gave me the creeps. In a matter of minutes I was aboard Frank and riding away from it, through the drizzly remnants of the storm. What was I driving myself further into?

C'mon, c'mon, my sanity reasserted itself. If it happens again, worry about it then. If it doesn't happen, you've got nothing to worry about.

My train of thought was derailed by a sudden thump from the tires. I had just crossed from the smooth pavement of Florida on to Alabama's brand X variety.

I crossed a small river called the Styx, turgid, sticky, and black—probably where the road department dumped the asphalt that should've gone on the streets. To my right, a huge billboard proclaimed

WELCOME TO ALABAMA, without a trace of sarcasm. There was a portrait of George Wallace on the sign, with his black eyebrows knitted together in a look of dawning comprehension, his mouth frozen in its dour little pout. A line of script beneath the portrait urged the jaded traveler to "take a fun break!" while in Alabama.

I passed a mule, hitched to a wagon, tethered by the roadside.

I spent some time dwelling on my attitude of psuedo-hip chauvinism, making up thoughts like, "This entire state should be bronzed and made an adjunct to the Smithsonian, before it moves into the 20th Century!" But I was unable to spend much time doing it. Reality was about to intrude in the form of another storm. An ugly looking mass of purple, vortexing inward ominously, this storm was considerably larger than the one I had just ridden through. And darker. It was the stuff of which twisters are made.

Heavy rain, for a motorcycle, is deadly. It transforms pavement into a carpet of ball bearings. Brake too hard on one wheel, overestimate a curve or ability to stop, underestimate speed or distance, and you *will* wind up on your ass. Hopefully, not under the wheels of the semi-truck with the sleepy driver coming up behind you. I knew I could improve my chances by staying ultra-alert, maximizing distance between myself and other drivers. But what could I do about twisters? Lash myself to the handlebars? Pull out my sleeping bag, zip it over my head, and set an alarm clock for next week? Get under something solid, like a building?

That last seemed to make sense, except I was now in heartland Alabama, and an aura of imminent danger was drifting up in my mind from the recent story of a hitchhiker I'd met, who told me of having his head shaved with a rusty razor by sheriff's deputies in Alabama, then being beaten near Baton Rouge. . . . Things are changing, I told myself. You can't afford the luxury of paranoia. You have to find shelter, and quick. Of my two available choices, I picked an International Harvester dealership. The least evil I could expect was to be cursed back out into the rain. Since the worst was too horrible to contemplate, I didn't think about it . . . just stopped, got off, and stomped on into the office like a delivery boy taking orders for Mason jars of cardiovascular antifreeze. Several crewcuts in coveralls stared at me.

"Howdy!" I gave them my best grin. "You got a spot where I can park me and my scooter 'til the sky clears between here and Mobile?"

"Ask Roy," growled a short, stocky man. He aimed a screwdriver at another man walking up between the parts shelves. Roy had heard me ask my question. His tanned face was expressionless as he scrutinized me from head to toe. Our eyes locked for a fraction of a second.

"Gowannahead," Roy said, pointing towards a work bay. "Park it raht inside theah.''

I drove Frank into an empty bay, surrounded by disassembled pickup trucks and tractors, the clatter of wrenches, a general aura of grease, metal, and work. There was also a gingery feeling in the air as the men looked me over. A mechanic near me was having trouble with a bolt, so I went over and held one of the wrenches for him. After that, the vibes seemed to ease up a bit.

Outside, the rain came down like Babe the Blue Ox pissing on a flat plateau. A giant puddle crept under the door, began expanding relentlessly across the concrete.

''Migod!'' I said to myself. ''It found out where I am, and it's coming in after me!''

''Maybe we'd better throw you back outside,'' Roy said. He was suddenly standing behind me, wiping his hands with a coarse rag. Up close, I could see that face was as wrinkled as a leather door hinge, with lines worked into the flesh as if it had been used endlessly for every conceivable expression. Why, I wondered, did he have his poker face on for me?

''Does it do this often here?'' I asked, pointing at the deluge.

''Hit'll start doing it pretty regular now,'' Roy said. He walked over and poked his head outside. When he turned back towards me, I saw some suppressed emotion finally beginning to erupt on his face. ''You don't need to worry about this one, though. It's all over.''

''All over?'' I echoed. This is it, my redneck paranoia informed me. Any minute, a spanner would descend on my nut from behind.

''All over but the rain!'' Roy haw-hawed and slapped me on the back. His face crunched into a broad smile.

A big bean farmer came in to get a part from Roy. He lumbered into the shop, big and hearty as a bonfire, downhome as a boiled spud. He had red cheeks, massive arms, and black hair all over his body. He gave me a suspicious glance, then pointedly ignored me. But I still hung around to pick up on the conversation.

''Whattaya want this part for?'' Roy asked. ''It's rainin, Burt! You can't plow in this!''

''Whattaya *mean*? Mah kid's already out plowin in it with the other tractor. This ain't rain, just extry-damp fog. Now, gimme that hose.''

''Sorry, Burt. I don't want to be responsible for you catching cold, so I'm not gonna sell you this part until tomorrow. It's for your own good.''

''Goddammit, Roy! Gimme that hose, or tomorrow they'll be plowin *you* under!''

Their faces shone with the joke they shared. I basked in it too, proud of these two fellow humans, delighted with the heavy, earth-loving fire of the bean farmer. He wasn't about to let rain dampen his enthusiasm or his purpose. He'd just wade on out into the bright green leaves, the air throbbing with thunder, the smell of freshly turned earth, and *enjoy* it!

Burt finally got his hose, splashed out to his truck, wheelspun in reverse through the slop, and careened off down the road. A small tag on his front bumper informed me that,

ONLY LOVE BEATS MILK

Roy must've had something in him that beat milk, because he kept his shop open, and hung around a half-hour past closing time, just so I wouldn't have to ship out onto Shit Creek. My redneck paranoia, mortified at the failure of its predictive abilities, slunk off into a corner of my psyche to lick its wounds. During that half-hour, Roy and I sat and made conversation. My astrolabe of the heart pointed somewhere into the space behind his eyes, and I think his was pointing back. As the rain began to ease, I got up to go.

"Let me give you my nephew's address in Jackson,"Roy said. "He's young and proud and crazy, like you. Even got a scooter, except his is a lot funnier looking. It's got one of those front wheels that stick out into the middle of next week! Bought it after he quit the Baptist seminary. He took some time off to think things over. I 'spect he'll be goin back there one of these days."

He wrote the address on a torn piece of bag with a grease pencil. As I took it, I had the sensation of receiving a message, an invitation from the *presence*. I folded it into my wallet, and thanked him.

"Here's the lull," I said, looking outside. "I've got that now-or-never feelin'. Thanks, Roy. A lot."

"No sweat," he said. "Take care. God bless you."

"Sure," I said. "Whatever."

Then. Vvvvroom, shift, vvvvvrooom, shift, vrooooom! I had a rain-wet wind in my face; I was on the street; I was lookin' for traveling room! A light grey drizzle eased earthward. I did not think it could get any worse. I was amazed to discover that it could.

The memory of Roy's kindness was a spot of warmth in my mind. I had to smile, though I was getting progressively wetter and colder.

I passed the spooky, moored battleship Alabamm, just able to see her muzzled muzzles thrust up into the mist. Then I slid into a damp knot of downtown traffic. Since I didn't know my way through town, I was caught in it a long time. No one in cars or trucks was smiling.

The sun plooped down on the horizon like a grey, wet blob of tissue. The darkening glut of inner city concrete at last gave way to the trimmed lawns and hedges of greater suburbia. Where in hell was I gonna camp on this highly damp first day of traveling? In this darkening hour, did I begin to lose heart? I soddenly did. It's hard to be an effective dreamchaser when you're cold, miserable and far from friends; when it's late and giddy tiredness circulates in your veins instead of blood.

The suburbs became thickets, became second-growth forests. I glanced down several overgrown sideroads until I found one that looked interesting. Ducking branches, I pushed through on it until I came to a tiny clearing. Frank shut down with a sigh.

In the stately patter of downdrop plops from the tips of leaves, under pearl pale last ray light, laced with grey rain, I pitched my little tent, threw a plastic tarp over Frank and gear, and stripped down to my shorts.

"If I'm gonna get wet, I might's well get *wet*."

I lit my Coleman and hunkered down beside it to boil some noodles. After they were done I mixed in some miso, and ate while I heated some water for coffee. The rain on my back was cold, but not unbearable. In other words, I wandered back and forth between cursing my fate and accepting it.

Rinsed the gear and stowed it. All the light in the sky had fallen to earth. I crawled into my miniscule tent, prepared for mystic dreams and dry slumber. *Thrip*. Throp. Whazzat? Cold rain dripping on my naked spine. The goddam brand new go-everwhar, guaranteed-in-a-Himalayan-blizzard tent LEAKED. With the gut resilience of the utterly exhausted, I accepted this as simply another disaster. I balled up my sleeping bag and plunked my head down on it. Then I plopped my feet in a puddle of water that had been quietly collecting at the foot of the tent. Far out. I had a tent that leaked water in but wouldn't leak it out. At this rate, I'd drown by morning. Which was OK; probably a more merciful death than the pneumonia I would have contracted with just my feet wet all night. So I embraced this evil too. Anything to get a little sleep.

I had just about got the puddle around my feet warmed up to skin temperature when a sinister hum sounded an inch or two from my ear. At the same moment, a hypo filled with formic acid was slammed into a minor nerve on my back. The damn camel-humpen, shit-sucking sieve that some noxious manufacturer had disguised as a tent leaked mosquitoes, too. I think, at that point, I fainted.

The next thing to leak into the tent was morning. When I opened my eyes, I could see! My arms moved! And most of my blood was still in my body, instead of flying around Alabama in the bellies of a billion mosquitoes. I unzipped the tent, wormed out, and rose on my hind legs in a world filled with the scent of wet woods. Everything glittered with preternatural stillness. I did a stiff little dance under the grey-gold morning clouds, and promised myself I would hit the road as soon as I saw a patch of blue.

A sound, like a chuckle, behind me! I spun. Nothing. Only a twig, nodding up and down as if a bird had just flown from it.

I looked around. This tangled backwoods road was like thousands of others across America, where Carol the cheerleader popped her cherry after the Thanksgiving game, in a car with steamed-up windows and a fifth of Jack Daniels on the front seat. Where boys and their dogs scrambled on May afternoons, pursuing the summer to come. These things were suspended in the air here, either because they had happened, or because they were waiting to happen.

Hot coffee, handful of bread, sack of dates. Lo, the poor traveler, munching, meditates. That *presence*. That storm star. Could I truly sense the trace of it, or only imagine that I did? I took out the address of Roy's nephew in Jackson and pointed the inner astrolabe dead at it. Nothing. Maybe I'd be better suited to just wandering in any direction that seemed mysterious enough, until I stumbled across something. What was it I'd done the last time I doubted the presence and desired it manifest? *Focus* on bringing it here, making it appear. Maybe I should perform a spell, like a magician drawing his circle for summoning, his octagram or pentagram, then stepping within. I put my finger to the dust. Somehow, none of those signs seemed appropriate. So I drew a question mark. I stared at it. It seemed to glow. Obviously, just an effect of staring at it too long. I looked away, but when I looked back it was glowing even brighter. I blinked and began to get scared. Just exactly what was it I was screwing around with? I threw a handful of leaves at it, but that didn't stop it from changing.

The question mark became an ear. The point at the base of the question mark became a gold, circular earring. Then a face began to take form, filling in the rest of its lines, taking on color. It rose up from the ground, turned toward me from profile, adding a third dimension almost as an afterthought.

The eyes were the worst.

I avoided their gaze.

"Go back," I said.

"No," it replied. "Stop fear."

"Change?" I asked, hoping for a reprieve of some sort.

The form began to dissolve and shift. As it did, I bit my tongue. Here I was, talking to it again. I had already recognized it by the tone of its voice, or its energy, which amounted to the same thing. It was Push. The disembodied storm star was hard enough to conceive of. I didn't *want* to be dealing with this apparition again, much less the questions it raised about my sanity when it talked back.

The apparition resolidified. Instead of that strange, floating face, he had become a small man about three feet high, with a trim, nut-brown body, complete with furry legs that ended in delicate hooves instead of feet.

"This homey enough for you?" he asked.

It wasn't. It was tempting to forget about the level of free and willful power I had seen in those eyes, but I couldn't. No matter how cute he made himself.

"Who or what are you?" I demanded, admiring the steadiness in my voice. Fearing his answer.

Push stared at me without answering. He stuck a finger up his nose and rooted around. When he pulled it out, a bit of green moss adhered to the tip. He regarded the moss solemnly for a second, then licked it off. Having effectively lampooned my fears of the demonic, he looked at me and smiled. Still, I was only partially reassured.

"Who or what are *you*?" he demanded.

I was surprised by the shift in tables. I didn't have a ready answer. "I asked you first," I protested.

"So what?" Push leered. "Your grasping mind wants to label me so I'll be easier to categorize. Humans. All alike." He looked down at his own body as if contemplating its possibilities. Then he walked over to a pine tree, turned, and began scratching his back on it. In between little gasps of pleasure, he continued his harangue.

"Soon as you've got something labeled, you cease to regard it as magical or alive in the truest sense. Once it's under your cognitive thumb, you concentrate on making it merely useful. You crazy buggers. Through the ages, you've tried to do that to the entire earth, and now you dream of doing it to the stars. Drop your pants and grab your ankles, Universe! Here comes Man!"

Push leaned away from the tree and came over to look into my eyes. "But you wanna know something?" he said softly. "You haven't touched the earth at all, just laid a crust of your half-baked reality on top, according to a recipe handed down and complicated by each succeeding generation. You don't want to experience life, just control it. Which means, all you really want to experience is your own mind. You'll get your wish. You always do. One day your race will wake up in a hall of mirrors that is a quaint hell of its own devising. When that happens, don't blame me.''

Push sat down crosslegged a few feet from me. Golden cobras of light danced in his brown eyes.

I swallowed and cleared my throat. "That was misaimed," I croaked, then cleared my throat again. "I'm on a flight from the way I was taught to see. Seeing you is proof of it!''

"Do I terrify you?'' The deep voice that boomed out of the tiny body, did, in fact, terrify me for a second. I was unsure whether or not to take it as self-mockery. But suddenly, just to realize that I had that option was reassuring.

"You wouldn't,'' I said, "if you would just give me some indication of the forces you work with, and where your influence might lead. See, I'm after something . . . .''

"So what do you want? My Diner's card? Do you want to know whether I'm good or bad? Mainly, I'm indifferent.'' Push shrugged. "What is it you're after?''

"I don't know,'' I said, irritated now more than frightened. "I haven't got it *labeled* yet!''

Push laughed. "Good! Good. In that case, you stand a chance of letting it get creative with you. How do you see it?''

"What do you mean?''

"How do you sense, single out, search for this?''

I was silent. He peered at me, then pointed at my heart as if in recognition. "Ahh! That way. Hmmm. Astrolabe? That what you call it? Ha! Vasco on the horns, eh? Does it work?''

"Well,'' I said. "No matter what it's worth to you or anyone else, it's all I've got, so it's worth a lot to me. Everything else I've ever heard of or used required a little bullshit to grease the works.''

Push's eyes sparkled. "So? Did you dig up the X on the map yet?''

"I've got a line on it,'' I said. I wasn't sure how much more I wanted to share with this entity, even if its malignance was primarily manifesting as sarcasm.

Push clapped his hands and pointed directly at me. "Bean Farmer Rain Bliss, right?''

"*What*?'' My forehead wrinkled.

"Elemental harmonies. Rain is cold and wet, can refresh or sicken you; meanwhile, it goes about its real business, watering the beans. What the farmer showed you—water and electricity; a thunderstorm is your kith and kin. Let it fall and flow like a cycle spinning through you, and you say goodbye to rains as some alien force and greet it. Sensual. Direct. Hello, free.

"Shut yo' mouf," he added pleasantly. "You'll catch flies. And before I go, I'd like to point out that I've answered your original question. You'll know me by the effect I have on you. Only way you ever know anything, really. Buy their fruits, remember?"

From his sitting position, Push leaned forward and banged me on the forehead before I could block him or duck. My eyes shut from reflex; when I opened them, he was gone.

Disoriented, disbelieving, I stared at the spot where he had been. A patch of earth in every way normal, except . . . it seethed with unmitigated being. Ants scampered madly in all directions at once. Beetles, with limbs and appendages jointed and socketed improbably, moved ponderously over the same ground. Grass thrust itself up with a green vibrancy and sheer will to exist that was alarming. Each translucent, fragile blade was insistent on its right to be precisely so, thrusting, like my blood, up toward the sun!

Blue explosions were ripping through the clouds everywhere. My promise was fulfilled; I could go on.

Then I noticed what all those ants were scampering towards: my food knapsack. "Hey!" I shouted, forgetting all about Push. "Distract me with beauty while ya rob me blind, eh? Larcenous little buggers!" They grinned, ran in a circle, bumped into each other, and staggered off under the pine needles. *Los idiotas*.

IV.
The
Tower

Miss., Hattiesburg, was a snarl of poorly timed lights, traffic jams, overheating cars and drivers. I was fairly steamed myself by the time I made it through, so I putted into a Muckie's for a shake. I went in warily. This was a middle-crass American watering-hole, and full of danger.

Managed to keep my eyes averted from the racks and shelves of souvenirs on my way to the counter. But the lady was busy. Reluctantly, I turned around to see what there was to see: brown plastic anchors with MISSISSIPPI in scarlet script; kiddie underwear with GRANDPA LOVES ME stitched over the bottom (Ho ho! You *bet*!); bumper stickers urging folks to honk for the deity's firstborn; shrunken heads with rayon hair, glass eyes, and teeth that glowed in the dark (perfect nitelite for overfed young ghouls, so they could fumble their way into the head, instead of going tinkle on the linoleum); an array of plaster-plastic-glass-tin kitsch so extensive and varied that it boggled the mind even as it turned the stomach. How any mind could pervert itself to the task of turning resources into fodder for the cheapest and shallowest of tastes and sentiments, I could not imagine.

An old woman was picking through all of this. For all the world, she looked like a tramp I'd once seen rummaging through garbage cans in Miami's bayfront park. The main difference was that the old lady had rouge to hide her grey hunger, and the tramp had a greater chance of finding something worthwhile.

As I raised my eyes to check out what visions might be passing

40

outside, a Teen Angel strolled in through the front door. She had wavy red hair and a softball team of freckles strewn across her upturned nose. She had pert leedle teats, an innocent wiggle in her slim, young hips, and—bless her—a frilly white blouse covered all over with red valentine hearts.

I immediately lost my desire for the milkshake. I wanted *her*. Right now! Right here! Right before that granny tourist with the rhinestones (so help me!) on her sunglasses! Whew! Surely the walls would crack, doves descend, and the ungrand mother be cured of her craving for kitsch, if the skintones of me and this sweet suthun belle should ring together. Her curves, and my clapper. Her slim fingers laced against the back of my brain while my licker lapped like a flame . . . . Whoo! We'd melt every plastic knickknack in the place wif the whitehot purity of our flamen passhun!

The angel noticed me noticing her. Demurely lowered lashes informed me that my stare had done its work. To my surprise, she continued her airy walk around the counter until she faced me from the other side.

"Sorry I'm late, Sue," she said to the other girl. Then, to me, "Have you been served, sir? Do you know what you want?"

I hesitated so long, the reason for my hesitation became clear. Her cheeks lit up under her freckles.

As soon as I saw that, I backed away from causing her any further embarrassment. She was a virgin clear through and her magnolia-blossom charms, just in bud, needed something other than a heavy hand like mine. She needed . . . probably, someone like Roy's nephew Carl, the Baptist ex-seminarian I was on my way to see in Jackson.

So I ordered a chocolate shake. "Shake one and burn it, Sue!" she said over her shoulder in jerk jargon.

It was horrible. Ah, I thought, should a truck driver happen in and foully assault my teen angel, I would simply skewer him on the milkshake straw. The poison on the tip would finish him off in minutes. Aside from that, I couldn't think of any uses for it. I put it down and bid the Angel farewell. Then I went into the bathroom to wash the taste out of my mouth.

There was no graffiti in the men's room. In Muckie's, once every hour on the hour, a man comes into the bathrooms and hoses down the walls with a mixture of Lysol, whitewash, and Woolworth perfume.

As I exited, my eyes seemed to astigmatize. One caught the Teen Angel bending over the syrup vats, the other randomly wandered until it caught that grim old matron gloaming over the garbage. Their images briefly superimposed and blended in my brain. I shook my head and it all straightened out.

41

Then! Buckle on the helmet. Start. Go. Disappearing on Frank's ascending note. . . . Soon I was dialing down on the expressway offramp into Jackson, to check out the scene.

The Scene: The given address was an old apartment building. An aura of WW II efficiency housing hung around it, inseparable—and in fact no different—from an aura of mildew and dry rot.

I tapped on the door with the appropriate number. No response. Evidently, Roy's nephew was not in. My dream of mooching a steaming bath and hot supper, even at the price of an hour of Fundamentalist dialectic, evaporated with a sigh.

I spent a few minutes flinging myself aimlessly around the parking lot, trying to decide what to do. I could cruise for hotspots, see if I could pick up on a temporary roommate. Or go find a state park. Or, hell, just camp right here! String my hammock between two posts of the building, cook up some veggies and crash for the night.

As I walked back toward Frank, through the warm nuzzles of summer dusk, I saw a young girl walking up the stairs on the outside of the huge, barracks-style building. I felt her eyes on me also, as if at any moment she were going to say . . .

"Hello."

"Hiya," I said, looking up at her. "Carl Wiggins live here?"

She leaned forward, both arms on the bannister, regarding me coolly. "Yeah, but he's out. He's off to some biker orgy in the hills or something."

"Oh really?"

Unusual place for a Baptist seminarian. Maybe he was going for converts. I wished him luck.

"You friend of his?" she asked.

"Just passing through," I told her, with a gesture. "Carl's uncle gave me his address."

She gazed at me thoughtfully, then smiled. "Well, why doncha come up and have supper with me? Maybe Carl'll make it back a little later on."

"Awreet! Sugah, you've won my undying gratitude. I'll be up in a flash. By the way, name's Steve."

She waved a languid hand. "Joyce."

A flash passed, and I was sitting in her kitchen chomping on a reheated tomato, cheese, and hamburger casserole. Joyce seemed amused by the abandon of my appetite. In between gulps of food and air, I studied her.

She was thin, just saved from being gaunt by the firm roundness of her limbs. I was able to explore this extensively since she was only wearing a halter-top and cut-off jeans. Her face was long, but cheekbones, nose and chin were jutting and emphatic, an effect pronounced by the way her light brown hair was tied back.

Something about her reminded me of a plainswoman in a movie of the 1850s—wiry, determined, resourceful, but at the same time imbued with an essentially daunted quality. The plainswoman virtues seemed to wrap around a core belief that somehow, anyhow, nothing would ever amount to much. I imagined this fatalism, deadlocked with just enough strength to survive it, was laminated into the virtues of her soul, giving her that harsh and desolate beauty I thought I saw in her eyes. Was I really seeing that?

I felt guilty and ungrateful for jumping on first impressions and visualizing her that way. I glanced around for clues that would disprove my presumptions. Unlike any other young woman's space I had ever seen, it was spartan and unadorned. No posters, potted plants, tiffany lampshades, tapestries with tassels. No mandalas, stuffed toys, knick-knacks or even magazines lying around. Just bare walls and the stark essentials of living.

"You from here?" I asked.

"Nope," she said. "Hitched in from Nebraska, last year."

"Ah. Just roadin'?"

"No. Runnin'. I was still wearing band-aids on my face from this big fucking bowl my mother threw at me. She didn't especially get off on having me around."

"Howcum?"

She fixed me with a speculating stare. "What the hell," she said slowly, "Why shouldn't I tell you? It wasn't because I was Miss Teenage Nebraska, you can be sure of that. I was one of those girls all the other mothers talk about when they break for coffee at PTA meetings. I was pretty heavy into soapers and sex . . . kinda lost it for a while. Some pretty nutsy things went down. Like one night, my father and me . . . well, it wouldn't have happened 'cept I was high and he was drunk, . . . and it prob'ly wouldn't have gone all the way anyway . . . ."

Her face was smooth and untroubled, but I could see something flickering behind her eyes.

"Then my mother walked into the room, and the shit really hit it."

"Oh," I said. "I can see where she might have found you hard to like, after that."

"That ain't the punchline," Joyce said. Her smile was as tight as a scar. "Since then, he ain't been able to get it up; with her, or anyone else as far as I know."

"Yark." I was getting a bit more of a story than I had bargained for.

She glanced once directly into my eyes, gauging my reaction. Then she got up and began to clear the table. "So I hitched out. My first ride ended right here in Jackson. It was far enough away and looked like as good a place as any; so I found a job as a cocktail waitress and started pulling down the bucks."

"Cocktail waitress? How old are you?"

"With makeup on, twenty-one."

"Oh." I looked around the barren apartment. "Watcha doing with all the bucks?"

"Buying presents."

"No kidding?"

"Last Mother's Day, I sent my mom an Accutron watch with diamonds on the casing."

"You trying to patch it up with her?"

"Not really. It's more like a joke. The way she feels about me, she'll never be able to wear it; and the way that watch looks, she'll never be able to *not* wear it. See?"

I nodded, thinking to myself, watch out for this one. To cover my uneasiness, I got up from the table and stretched. Peered out the uncurtained window to the parking lot below.

"Doesn't look like Carl's back yet."

"You kin crash up here if you like."

"Huh? Oh. Well . . .sure. Thanks."

I made three trips between Frank's rack and Joyce's living room, carrying in my gear. Every step of the way, I puzzled over what kind of a scene I had stumbled into; or been sent into, I thought, remembering the way I'd felt when I acquired Carl's address. How did thin, strange Joyce fit into the picture? What lessons could I learn or unlearn from her, what information would I glean to help me in my search for the *presence?* Ah well. Only one way to find out.

I collapsed on Joyce's couch and let the delicious warmth of tiredness flood through me. Tinkling sounds of silverware and plates came from the kitchen. I began to fall into sleep with a headlong impetus known only to the dying and those of us who tour the countryside on motorcycles. Suddenly I found myself literally chewed out of my drowsiness. Fleas! A whole circus of them had jumped from the couch onto my body, where they cavorted merrily, taking frequent breaks to chomp at my flesh. Anger competed with curiosity; I'd never been bitten by a flea before. Anger won, hands down. Pants down, too. With a killer instinct, most of them seemed to be headed for my crotch.

"Balls afire, Joyce! Your goddam couch is alive with fleas!"

Delighted laughter floated out of the kitchen. Joyce came to the door, her hands dripping soap.

"Oops. Guess I should've told you about that."

"You're dam' tootin' you should've told me! This another of your black jokes?"

"No. C'mon. Listen. Just go take a bath and shampoo. That'll get rid of 'em. They're nowhere near as sturdy as crabs. Anyway, you could use a bath."

I bowed sarcastically and stomped off to the bathroom. Copious amounts of hot water and soap eventually reduced the division of fleas to a few hardy, isolated snipers. I sent my fingernails on a search-and-destroy through my pubes while I speculated about where I was going to sleep. Could still string up the hammock. . . .

With a towel wrapped around my can, I padded back through the apartment. Joyce was sitting in her bedroom, toking on a nightcap reefer. Blue smoke from the joint mingled with swirling plumes from a joss stick in a sweet, spicy haze. I walked in. She held up the joint. I nodded, and sat beside her on the bed.

As I puffed, I looked at her. In the soft light of a solitary candle on the dresser, her hard plainswoman's face seemed to relax and soften. I looked at her long, smooth legs, the young breasts poking impudently against her halter. Her eyes were on mine, fixed with a penetrating expression. I was suddenly shocked, aware she was sending out waves of desire, patiently waiting for me to be washed in. . . . Both my faint repulsion to her and the desire she excited in me shot up, but remained equal in strength. My instincts were to back out.

"Well," I said. "Think I'll hang out my hammock and go swing for a while."

"You don't need to do that."

"I've already given half my ass to the fleas on your couch, Joyce. I need the other half to sit on." I got to my feet.

"You could sleep in here." Suddenly she was no longer inviting, but challenging me. "How about it? Can you get it up for me, or not?"

I wavered. Then, by way of answer, I shucked the towel and threw it in the corner. I stretched out on the bed. It was set in motion. She quickly shed her clothes then, and her round limbs gleamed like old ivory in the light of the candle. Her nipples were roseate and small, on high cupped breasts. I saw the soft brown hair, unusually thin and fine, on her

cunt, before she slipped into bed. I wanted to erase the impression of in-
decision I'd given her, so I began to touch her with firm grips and
movements of my hands. Her eyes closed. Slowly, gently, her breath
began to quicken. As I touched, touched, stroked her clit with the tip of
one finger, her breathing changed to rhythmical sighs. She reached down
and began to pull on my cock, strongly, demanding it. I mounted and
entered her. She was as tight as a virgin. With her warm fist of a vulva
clamped down on me, I began to undulate into her slowly. I could've
come right away, but held off for a long time while I felt for her mind,
gradually losing all sense of distinction between my body and hers. Then
I found her, deep inside, stretching out a hand like a child, for me to take
and hold. And as I reached, it seemed I was reaching toward that valentine heart teen angel; the energy was the same. But as I touched, the
child abruptly changed into the old ghoulish grandmother, demanding I
caress her withered heart. I looked for Joyce and she was far away,
laughing mirthlessly in a place no one could reach, asking for love and
refusing it at the same time . . . . I couldn't do it! I freaked, backed
away. And I spurted into her then. It was like a shout in an empty room.

I was a long time coming back to myself, lying there panting, feeling angry and—somehow—duped. Whether by myself or her, I didn't
know. Not a spark of the star. I abruptly disengaged. She snuggled up
against me. The room had become stifling hot. I pushed her away and
got up.

"I have to piss," I said.

I went into the bathroom. While I was pissing, I stared morosely
at my cock. "You got me into this," I accused. It shrugged and went on
pissing.

Back in the room, Joyce had fallen into real or feigned sleep. She
looked calm but not innocent. Stale air! I walked over and yanked open
the window. When I laid down again, cool air came flowing over us like
water. A thought came to me as I fell asleep.

At least, now, we know something of each other.

I awoke at the first hint of dawnlight. Arose, looked down, and
saw how Joyce slept on in fragile aloneness. I dressed, went to my pack,
and found the roadmap. I took it out on the balcony, to study by the pale
light.

Some of the same dissatisfaction and desperation I had felt in Tallahassee was whirling inside of me now. I didn't know whether to leave or
stay. I fervently hoped that last evening with Joyce was not the sum of
what was going to be given me during my search in Jackson. The inner

astrolabe, when I had quieted my mental turmoil enough to consult it, was mute. It was not even sure it was there any longer.

I sighed and focused on the map. The only thing that drew my attention in the least was the blue splotch of a lake, not far from town.

To my surprise, I found myself half-hoping that the hallucination, or cognitive poltergeist (a corner of my mouth quirked at the label) that called itself Push, would put in an appearance; if not to stimulate my sense of direction, at least to provide a feeling of *depth*.

A few minutes later I heard the bang of a pot, phut of a match. The screen door on the apartment creaked tragically as Joyce came outside. Her hair was brushed and tied back with a piece of yarn. She had on yesterday's clothes. There was something disturbed and questioning in her eyes. "Good mornin', " she said.

"Mornin'."

"You been up long?"

"Few minutes."

Her eyes searched mine for the answer to an unasked question. I went cold as those grey-green orbs looked into me. A look of disappointment flickered across her features. I felt a moment of hesitation; perhaps I'd misjudged her, perhaps not really seen her at all, but only my pictures of her. Guilt.

Joyce turned away to go back inside.

"Joyce. Wait a sec. Look at this map. See that big blue blob? What is that?"

"Ross Barnett Reservoir. Why?"

"Is it a nice blue blob?"

She shrugged her thin shoulders. "It's OK."

"Want to help me explore it?"

She brightened, suddenly returning to the curious and friendly personality I had first seen in her. "Yeah!" she said. "Good deal. I'll throw together some breakfast, and roll a doobie to take with us."

And so, in more time than it takes to tell it, we were zooming on Frank down the sunny, empty streets of Sunday Jackson. We went out of town to the north, then headed east on a winding country road. Soon we were riding on top of a dam, with a roaring spillway to our right and a shimmering expanse of water to our left. But the surface of the lake was crowded with boats of every description. The shoreline was jammed with cars and knots of people flowing between picnic grounds, campgrounds and marinas. I was able to fight down my nausea until we passed a crackerbox assortment of shoreline condominiums.

"Jeez," I said over my shoulder, as I pulled over and idled by the side of the road.

"Let's go over by the spillway," Joyce suggested. "That's a little better."

"Mmph."

We retraced our route until we came to the dam spillway. The water cascaded down blackened concrete to empty into a river that had a rugged-looking road along its north bank. I looked askance at Joyce and she nodded, so I headed down. Rough and tumble all the way, but Frank rode it out with poise and aplomb. No mean feet for *that* motorcycle. We slid, roared and bounced to the end of the road.

As we dismounted, I looked back up the road at an old man we had passed. He was sitting in a carved, high-backed chair, perched on the river's edge. The ornate chair would've been much more at home at the head of some magnificent mansion's mahogany table, except that it had evidently been used in this peculiar function so long that its finish was cracked and flaking. Apparently oblivious to anything else, the old man sat there, completely still, hunched over his pole. He wore a kind of brimless cap, crowded with broken lures that had been attached by their hooks. I wondered how he kept their points from digging into his scalp.

I turned to Joyce. "I think it's about time to fire up that doob you brought," I said.

"Matches you got?" she asked.

"Nein."

"All I need is one."

"Nein. Nyet. Non. No."

"Oh."

"Maybe we can get a light from somebody around here."

As we headed for the path that led down by the river, we came to a battered blue Chevy pickup parked behind a bush, its bed laden with traffic cones, rope, and a litter of miscellaneous.

"Hmmm," Joyce said. "Now that looks familiar."

I looked at her inquiringly.

"It's Carl's truck," she explained. "Carl Wiggins, the dude you came to visit."

We looked in the cab. On the front seat, a young man was stretched out, arms entangled in the steering wheel. He had blonde, curly hair and fair skin, now flushed and perspiring. His face nuzzled one sticky armpit as he snored resonantly on.

"Carl?"

Joyce shook her head. "But I'm sure he's close to hand." She gave me a meaningful look the significance of which I failed to grasp. Then, nearby, we found him . . . a short, stocky man passed out in a hollow on top of a mound of dead leaves. His face resembled Roy's—

square, country-pleasant, and peasant-honest—but the flesh around his eyes and mouth looked puffy, and seemed shaded a faint and unhealthy brown. The aromas of sweat and rancid beer hovered about him.

"An outstanding candidate for the ministry," I observed.

Joyce giggled. Something about Carl's condition satisfied and amused her. She leaned over him and rummaged through his pockets with all the gentleness of a camp-follower looting the dead. She yanked out a book of matches.

"Hey, thanks for the light, Carl."

"Maybe we ought to cover his face, so he won't get sunburned," I suggested.

"Maybe not," Joyce said. "If he ever found out you tried to do anything for him, he wouldn't like it. Best thing to do with Carl is to stay out of his way." The look of the plainswoman returned to her face, like a fierce bird coming home to its roost. "C'mon," she said. "Let's get out of here. You'll have your chance to meet him, if that's what you really want."

As we went further up the bank, the path gave us frequent glimpses of the river. It was pretty gruesome with its brown water, streaks of floating garbage and filthy foam, flies, crumpled paper flowers, oily rainbows coiling around dead fish floating belly-up.

"Amazing," I said. "What did that sign at the top say the dimensions on the reservoir were? A 30,000 acre septic tank. What a tribute to the human presence."

"Guess what the name of the river is," Joyce said.

"I can't imagine."

"The Pearl."

"Fits." Sold all we had for it, I thought.

Finally we found a patch of clean sand, shaded by the roots of a fallen tree. We kicked back and lit up, toking in silence. And in that curious interchange of cannabis-mind metamorphose, we did a trip on the mobius strip of things as they are, and emerged on the other side of the same place. I became unable to disregard the thrust and flow of crazy energy that was the communication between myself and Joyce. Before I knew it, my head whipped up and I caught her for a second, pinned her real *presence* right there in her startled eyes, and immediately began to feel as if I was understanding her again. I saw that strange attraction/repulsion I felt with her was based, as I probably should've suspected, not on any way we were different, but on the ways in which we were alike. She punished herself, desiring and demanding love and communication; but when it became available she would abruptly define herself as being unable to have it, then scorn the individual stupid enough to offer her something she couldn't have. I sensed I had a mechanism operating in a similar fashion on a larger scale.

Joyce knew how I was looking at her. For an instant her pupils widened in desire or fear, then her energy flipped back, and reappeared as the valence of an inquisitive, if shy, young girl. I realized that her seduction of me was over. She would not risk being caught again. That suited me. There was something between us that I was also unwilling to look at.

It was hot! The temperature was rapidly climbing to the point where leaves droop and people wilt. The day was turning into one of those Deep South scorchers, where everything seems to float a few inches above itself, fixed in a hard light.

My eyes were drawn across the water.

Near the other bank were three madmen in a boat, making their way upstream with one paddle and some difficulty. I felt an immediate rush of recognition. Howcum?

Was it because one wild dude in the bow, long hair crowned with a green metalflake hardhat, paddled like mad, while the others, laughing like mad, grabbed branches on the shore to keep the boat from moving? Or because the huge man in the center of the skiff was playing king-of-the-icebox, shouting, punching, nearly throwing the other two overboard when they tried to get a beer? Or because the guy in the stern saw me and Joyce passing a cigarette, made the connection, and waved a lid from the boat by way of greeting? All of the above. And more.

Our mimed inanity was infectious, self-reinforcing, and progressed with geometric disregard for the constraints of civilized, or even recognizable behavior. Finally, things reached such a pitch that these vulgar river boatmen decided to cross over to our side, to lessen the gap in the current arcing between us. They shoved off from the south bank, nearly capsized, rallied in a massive slapstick recovery, and struggled on. The bow man flailed at the water with his paddle like a GI digging a slit trench 'neath an incoming rain.

"Sh-i-I-T!" he yowled. "I'm fixin' to wear this dude out or break it, one!"

The others sat back and offered taunts of encouragement.

I pretended to be a newsman, scooping the landing, taking imaginary photographs with a nonexistent camera. As soon as they saw it, they all stood and struck dignified poses: Benedict Arnold crossing the St. Lawrence; Charon crossing the Styx; Tennyson crossing the Bar. The boat lurched alarmingly. The first two broke their poses and grabbed at the gunwales with comic haste. The last one snatched, missed, lost his inebriated balance, and did a creditable back flip off the stern thwart.

Then the one in the metalflake hardhat began to paddle in earnest, while the large man shouted encouragement to the one in the water. "Swim, flybrain! How do you expect to catch up treading water?"

The swimmer gargled back half-audible but palpably obscene curses as he went into a stroke that combined your basic Australian crawl with a good deal of random, if inspired, thrashing.

The ship of stooges beached. The man in the hardhat leaped to safety. But just as the big one scrambled out, the man in the water reached the boat. He gave it a tremendous shove to one side. The big man teetered on the edge for a second, then swung over and sat in the shallows with a resounding splash. He looked angry for a second, then got up and threw an arm around the shoulders of his friend. "You are a turd," he told him affectionately.

Streaming brown, smelly water, they came and stood before me. The longhair in the metalflake hardhat introduced himself.

"Greetins bro!" he said. "I'm Cheney."

Cheney's small, compact body reminded me of Push, but his handsome features were somewhere on a continuum between Errol Flynn and Burt Reynolds, smack in the middle of a *Cosmopolitan* cover-girl fantasy. But something about his face was stiff, as though he was reluctant to alter the lines of his classic looks by using them for expression.

"Pleased," I said.

"This here's Big Daddy, in case you couldn't guess."

Big Daddy rubbed his hands on his belly and thrust out one paw, like a lumberjack passing someone an axe. Some of his 360-odd pounds sagged off his six-foot frame and hung over his belt, but most of it was concentrated in massive chest, shoulders, and arms that nearly exploded the seams of his polo shirt. The alligator on his pocket looked uncomfortable.

His black, brilliantined hair, sculpted early Elvis style, had been inserted carefully into a Caterpillar tractor cap. Along with an outstanding body odor, he exuded an aura of impregnable confidence. His round, dark face was gathered in an expression of mildly amused drunkenness.

Just a big ol' good ol' boy, I thought. Then I glanced into his eyes. They were electric with intelligence.

"Charmed," I said.

Cheney said, "Now the only reason I'm introducing you to Ding at all, is so you'll be able to yell at the guy who drank up all the beer."

"BULL!" Ding protested. Ding was obviously over thirty, with a golden beach-boy act that looked as if it was getting a little hard for him to sustain. Dressed only in a pair of ragged shorts and sneakers, it was easy to see that his cultivated musculature was going to flab, his years of

51

bronzed skin were culminating in an expanse of chocolate scale, and that his sunbleached goldilocks were simply falling out. Even the way his hair was brushed, it was getting hard for him to hide the long purple scar that ran down to his right eye socket from a dent in the side of his head.

Ding went to the skiff, plunged his hand into the cooler, and returned with three cold ones—Miller's High Life. He gave one to me, kept one, and (pointedly ignoring Cheney) waved the other one in the direction of Joyce, who had been gradually edging closer to the conversation, evidently trying to convey the impression that she had stumbled onto our little gathering by accident.

She shook her head and Ding gave it to Big Daddy. Tops popped in unison, we raised the cans and tilted some of those cold suds down. Oooh.

Cheney was looking at Joyce in curiosity. Joyce was looking at Cheney with fascination. "Hey," he said. "I've seen you before. You're the chick that lives upstairs from Carl. Joyce, right?" She nodded. "Well, I'm Cheney." He stuck out his hand and touched her on the arm, while his matinee features worked up an offhanded, boyish grin.

Joyce's sorrow-laden heart fell like a boulder into the sand between her and Cheney. It lay there, beating and crying, for the rest of the afternoon.

"Can you roll?" Big Daddy asked me.

"Blindfolded, dead drunk, in a cave at midnight!"

"Well here," he handed me the lid. "Mizzippy homegrown."

"Papers?"

"Don't have any," Cheney said. "Been using these bank receipts."

"*Bank receipts*? Why not newspaper?"

"Don't have any," Big Daddy said. "But hell, the very first joint rolled by the first caveman was prob'ly done with a bank receipt. They didn't have Zig-Zags back then."

"If I can't do it with proper materials, I ain't gonna roll. I got my pride." I passed the bag to Cheney. He expertly swaddled a pinch in a receipt, licked it, and passed it back.

"I will, however, smoke." I skritched a match, lit up, and inhaled deeply. Then I coughed until tears came to my eyes. It was like smoking a length of rubber wrapped in cardboard.

"Takes a strong will and a weak mind to smoke one of these," I choked.

"That's me," Ding said. "Pass it over." He toked and held, much to my amazement.

"Guess I qualify too . . . ." Cheney did the same.

"What were you dudes doing on the river?" I asked.

"Fishin," Big Daddy replied happily.

"Naw-w-w. I can't believe anything edible lives in that crap."

"Well, you're right. We're just using fishin as an excuse to get high and take the day off. See, we all work together paintin lines on the highways."

"You stoney ding-dongs? I can just see some poor devil following one of your damn lines right off a cliff."

"Nossuh!" Cheney said. "We paint the straightest lines in the country. We got this good ole boy drivin." He clapped Ding on the shoulder. "He gets so tanked we have to prop him against the steering wheel. Don't hear him say anything but 'Sho is' and '10-4' for the rest of the day. Just point him in the right direction, he'll say '10-4' and start off. A bit later we climb in the cab, give him a beer, and ask if everything's OK. Sho is, he sez. He never gets off the ropes more'n half an inch. People come all the way down from New York just to see our lines. Go away shakin their heads. Can't believe how good we do 'em."

Embarrassed by this high praise, Ding turned to amble down for another beer. Except, he preambled by tripping over a log and rolling most of the way down the bank. Inebriated amusement spread over his scarred face.

"Ding!" Big Daddy shook his massive head. "How drunk can a man get?"

"Now that there's a question we'll just have to answer," Cheney said. "Get me one too!"

"One two?" B. D. repeated incredulously. "You mean twelve? Greedy, greedy!"

I was served, too. Ding plonked a cool, dew-beaded can into my waiting hand. It felt fine to be guzzling golden brew on a gold and blue sun-crazed June day, such as this. The whole concept of being dissatisfied with anything, or going off in search of anything else, moved steadily further away from me. And Joyce? She was having a fantastic time falling silently and hopelessly in love with Cheney. The only thing that made this possible was that Cheney was ignoring her. If he had responded, the whole deal would've been off.

"Hey! Looky there!" Cheney said, pointing upriver. "Here comes Bunnytoes."

Bunnytoes? I looked. It was the fair-haired boy from the cab of the blue truck. He was struggling along the bank of the river with the aid of a walking stick about twelve sizes too big. Carrying it impeded his progress a good deal more than it helped. As I watched, he fell to his knees by the side of the river, and splashed some of the brown, tepid water on his face.

"Eccchh," I said.

"You ain't kidding," B. D. said. A heavy scowl knit his eyebrows together.

"Lighten up, Daddy," Cheney said. "It's the coming thing."

"Wal, mebbe so, but it ain't comin with me!"

Cheney cackled.

"Is what I think, what it is?" I asked.

"Prob'ly," Big Daddy said. "What you see comin downriver is on the receivin end of Carl's latest plunge into decadence."

"So you guys know Carl pretty good."

"Oh yah, we know Carl," Cheney said. "He works with us. Matter of fact, he owns two of the trucks we use. Where do you know him from?"

"Traveling through Mobile. His uncle Roy gave me Carl's address, said I oughta stop by. So I did, but he wasn't home and I wound up with Joyce instead."

"You got a better deal," Cheney said. Joyce smiled at him.

"The thing I don't quite get," I said, "is that Roy had Carl connected up with a Baptist preacher school . . . ."

Big Daddy laughed. "Carl hasn't been near a Bible in three years. Ever since he got away from it, he's been goin for the devil 'bout as hard as he can. Which Roy had a hand in. He fronted Carl the trucks for the business. And without income from the business, Carl couldn't afford half the shit he's into."

"You are all in business together?"

"Keerect. We put it together two years ago. Until then, we were just a bunch of chopper nuts that liked to ride together. Now we are Snortuppe Line Corporation."

"Who came up with *that?*"

"Me," B. D. said modestly. "I'm the brains of the outfit. I knew the ropes and the contacts for the state contracts. Carl had the bucks and some new trucks. Ding knew how to drive. Cheney didn't know his ass from a hole in the ground, but we had to let him in or risk hurtin his tender feelins. Which normally we wouldn't giva hoot about, but when he's feelin bad, Cheney don't tune our bikes worth shit."

"OK for you baby," Cheney said in a menacing voice. "You best make sure I'm in a *real* good mood when I put in your new clutch."

"Most of the time, though, he's fantastic," Big Daddy said.

The fair-haired boy staggered up to the group.

"Hi everybody!" he said breathlessly. Everyone said "Hi" back except for B. D., who grunted. The boy glanced at him nervously, then fixed on Joyce with something like desperation.

"Hi," he said. "I'm Freddie."

"Joyce." She smiled superficially, but something in him arrested her. Perhaps, a level of hopelessness she could relate to. Anyway, she rescued him from the caustic comments of B. D. by maneuvering him toward the log Ding had tripped over, where they began to talk. I saw her glance at Cheney to see if he was getting jealous yet. He wasn't. He was talking to me about motorcycles.

"From Florida on a 750 Honda, huh? That's what we all got, but they're a long way from stock. Sounds like yours is too. How's it run?"

"Tops. Got trouble keeping the carbs tuned, but that's just because they're cable type, instead of the rack linkage."

"Maybe not," Cheney said. "Those pre-K-1's have another little problem that's easy to fix sometimes. Nothing to do with the cables. Why don't you bring it by my shop tomorrow? It'll only take a second to check out."

"Dyno. Where?"

He wrote the address for me on the back of a Snortuppe Line Corp. card, then turned to Ding.

"Well Ding ole buddy, how drunk *can* a man get? You want to find out?"

Ding nodded enthusiastically. Arms over each other's shoulders, they went down to the coolers and pulled a dozen cold ones from the ice. Then, with the beer at their feet, they sat on the bank, clinked two cans together and yanked the ripcords. They drank them straight down, crushing them as they did, as if to squeeze out the last drop. It seemed a ritual perfected through considerable practice.

"What a pair," B. D. sighed and rolled his eyes to heaven. "We were *supposed* to work today. But those two crazies came to my door at three this morning, screaming and yelling. They had a six-pack down me before I even had my pants on. Ah well. Maybe we'll get to it tomorrow."

"Maybe not," I suggested.

B. D. gave me a calculating stare. "You think we're all a bunch of alky losers, don't you?"

"B. D.," I said earnestly, "I've never met anyone quite like you guys. I haven't the vaguest how to label you, even if I wanted to. Looks like you enjoy yourselves, though."

He grunted. "Take a look at Ding. More there than meets the eye. He was a big surf champ, until he stacked his board against a cliff in Peru. He came home to Jackson to get away from the ocean for a while, but he'll be getting back to it.

55

"Cheney's a racer. He's just getting started on dirt track, but he's got what it takes. I'm coachin him. Top national material, potentially. He's got a little race tomorrow that he's just gonna whoop up on."

"How about you?"

Big Daddy sucked in his paunch and drew himself up to his full height. "I, sir, am a proud product of our state university system. I have a Masters in EngLit."

I adopted a similar pose. "Yeah, I can put on a college cranium too. Worldviews! Rebuttals! Somebody else's carefully stacked ice! Lot of damn good it does me. At least we can say we went to separate schools together. That's a bond."

"Oh, come on," B. D. said. "When conversations lag, you can always use that stuff. It passes time. Occasionally, you can even find out something new and useful."

OK I thought, looking into his eyes, pursuing the energy of consciousness I saw imprismed there, and its kinship, if any I could find, to the *presence* of the storm star. So. This time the astrolabe would point through a matrix of literary associations, cats-eyes and maggies in the glass bead game. What questions would bear on what I was doing?

"I'm game," I said casually. "Who was the most significant American writer of the fifties?"

"Faulkner," he answered promptly.

"Not the best, the most significant."

"Faulkner?"

"Nope. Kerouac."

"That strung-out beatnik?" Big Daddy snorted.

"Sure. Faulkner's characters grappled with a world that was long gone, conflicts that had crystallized and were just hanging there in the air. He was a hot craftsman and so-so existentialist, but he mainly portrayed consciousness running naked and terrified through walls of reality that cannot be altered or moved. Kerouac cracked those walls, as much by the way he wrote as by the things he wrote about. Then he climbed through the breach, taking notes for us: a hyper-mobile, post-iconoclast generation that would search out new roots and new freedoms. . . ."

Big Daddy watched me without blinking as I orated. His comprehension did not waver. When *he* spoke, he dropped most of the country drawl I'd thought was his natural tone of voice.

"Well and good for you, a young head roaming from city to city for visions and kicks. Of course you're partial to Kerouac; right now you're following one of his benzedream scripts! Look. You're from Florida, which isn't the South, really, not like it is here. The head is different. Here, we recognize the past as imbuing our present, reaching through it to shape our future. Faulkner understood that, and his concerns were not with the elements of time, new *or* old, strictly speaking. He just used temporal elements as a frame in which to make statements about the human soul.

"Now, I grant you that Kerouac had that raw talent and the kind of beserker watts you need to go busting through walls. But once on the other side, he was lost. He didn't have the skills to settle the new terrain, which are the kind of spiritual resilience and creativity you find in Faulkner, . . . not just the writing but the man himself. Kerouac was obsessed with one phase in time; Faulkner was essentially timeless. So which one is more significant?"

"I don't know," I confessed. "I lost the thread of what I was driving at."

You'll find it again," B. D. encouraged. "We can always pick up this conversation again at some other point. That's the beauty of this shit. It's like correspondence chess."

"Agreed."

We bowed deeply to each other and clinked our Miller's cans together.

We turned toward the river. Cheney and Ding had fallen into the same rhythm, gazing spellbound at the flowing water (sip, watch, sip, watch), two friends who had gotten drunk together so many times there wasn't anything left to say.

"It's a great life," Big Daddy soliloquized, "that we have together. But we ain't accomplishing anything. Not a goddam thing. But how many people who *are* accomplishing a goddam thing are having as good a time as we are?"

His laughter rang out and floated in the golden afternoon, to dissipate and become lost in the vast air like torn and drifting smoke.

The setting sun had just impaled itself on the spires of Jackson's skyline when Frank putted into the parking lot behind Joyce's apartment.

"I want to be alone for a while," I told Joyce. "Got to run some things through my head."

She nodded. "You've got to run some things through your head," she repeated. A sunburnt spot on the tip of her nose glowed faintly in the gathering dusk.

"I'm gonna walk around. I'll pick up supper somewhere."

"Enjoy," she said, without inflection. Then she went up the stairs. "By the way!" I heard her call out after me. "It ain't Faulkner or Kerouac either one, wise guy. It's Sylvia Plath!"

57

When I turned to look up at her, she was already gone.

I walked down the sidewalk—old concrete, humped and cracked where blind, struggling roots had forced themselves beneath.

Joyce was strange. But what was the difference between her schizoid despair and my relentless dissatisfaction? Well, she seemed stalled out while I was still furiously looking. But suppose I was only fooling myself? Suppose the innate hunger had no object? What if visions of star *presence* and daemonic guides were thin delusions that one tore through, to arrive facing a blank wall at the end of a blind alley? In that case, the solution of Big Daddy and his band of lotus-eaters was not only logical, it was preferable. They had a comraderie, a reckless human warmth that drew me! *Why* couldn't I just let myself have it?

I ate at a boardinghouse several miles from Joyce's apartment. Guy at a newsstand told me it had a good smorgasboard. It did. It also had a large population of grey drifters, disenfranchised family men, and huge old women who bulged out their tent dresses in unlikely places. I embodied the only youth present, and I dined surrounded by hungry eyes, like those cartoons of African explorers.

I avoided conversation and left as soon as possible. What was the point of these old lives, waiting patiently or impatiently to end? What, even, was the point of my youth, seeing where I'd wind up after exploring the inherent meaninglessness of various games . . . including, probably, the question game I was playing with myself right now? Each human generation suddenly seemed like sparks from a bonfire, rising luridly and briefly towards a vast cold void—the blackness of things as they ultimately came not to be. The only thing *to* do in the face of that was get warm and drunk!

I was in a state of resplendent depression when I reached Joyce's apartment and opened the door. She was in the bedroom. I grabbed my sleeping bag from the pile of gear and went back out on the balcony. I lay down on the planks, in the dark, to stew in my own juice.

Before Joyce was up, I was gone. Had breakfast at a greasy spoon. Over stiff eggs and cold toast, I swilled coffee and scanned the paper. The headlines were full of Nixonania and other malformations of global angst. The comic strips weren't funny, which I found amusing.

I putted around the city until midmorning, eventually making my way to Cheney's shop. After rolling in the back door, I removed my helmet and took a whiff of old grease and new rubber. Eau de motorcycle shop. The same around the world.

I spied Cheney, in stained coveralls, up to his elbows in the chest cavity of an old BMW. I imagined him as a kid a dozen years ago, kicking a can past the open back door of his local Harley shop. There, in the cool dim cave, he saw a mechanic, a middle-aged Vet maybe, squatting by a huge hog and surrounded by a galaxy of glistening parts. Cheney sidled in to watch . . . the mysterious, laconic skill of the mechanics. Learned the inside jive and shop jokes between the employees and steady customers. Even got to hold a wrench sometimes. Then he heard the thunder of a motorcycle he had worked on when it was restored to bellowing health, and he was hooked. Now, he was well on his way to being that mechanic to younger boys, the mysterious figure with tools that could do anything, the same greasy half-moons of mechanic's dharma jammed under his fingernails.

"Hey Cheney! Get your hands offa that glorified Black Forest clock and put 'em on a real bike!"

"You made it!" He turned his too perfect face to me and beamed. "I'd rather work on your hot Honda any day. These Kraut machines are too much hassle for too little result."

His eyes were still puffy from yesterday, but he seemed surprisingly cheerful. Wiping his hands with a rag, he came over and patted Frank on the tank. "Carb probs, huh? Let's see if I'm right. Start 'im up."

He listened to Frank burble a few minutes, then grabbed the throttle and gave it a healthy yank. "Looky," he said. "That adjustment screw. See it vibrate? Lot of 'em get that way. But don't worry. I'll fix it up by messing it up."

"What?"

"Watch." He hit the kill switch and took out all four screws. Ignoring my protest, he crunched their threads with a pair of pliers. He put them back in and hooked up a set of vacuum gauges. He gave the throttle another yank. The screws didn't budge. He switched the bike off.

"Ta-da!" he said. "There you go. Tuned to 'G'. For good."

"Ah-h. Many thanks, 'Melican motocycle maestro!"

A man from the parts desk came over.

"You're lucky," he told me. "Only a select few get a free tune from ole Cheapo Cheney. We don't like to say it to his face, but he's one of the ace grease monkeys in town."

"Why not say it to his face? Does he get a swelled head?"

"Oh no. Cheney's head is mostly steel plate and plastic. It can't swell. Can't crack, dent, or even think for that matter. The reason we don't talk about how good he is, is so he won't ask us for a raise."

"Oh yeah? Well listen buddy, I may have a tin head, but it'll hold a lot more beer than yours will."

"I can vouch for that," I said.

"Yeah," the parts man said. "That's Cheney all right. Old Keg-Head. When he dies we'll just stick a tap in his ear and get it all back."

"Ah, don't listen to him," Cheney said. "Parts men are crass. All they can do is push metal, they don't know how to give it any soul. Piss on ya. I'm glad I'm racing this afternoon! That way I don't have to hang around and get myself insulted by uppity *clerks*. C'mon. Take me to my apartment on your putt, then we'll use my car to go to lunch." I had to laugh when I saw his car—a black shiny, 1956 Cadillac hearse.

"Like it?"

I nodded. "A low-slung, sleek chariot. . . ." I dodged his punch.

"It sucks gas like a fiend, but I can put two bikes in back, and it's solid as a tank. Anytime I drink and drive, this is what I go in."

We pulled out of the parking lot and slinked into the traffic. I watched a cool, green-tinted world slide by.

"What did that guy mean about your tin head?"

Cheney glanced at me. Even when he smiled, his movie-star face seemed stiff.

"Christmas, last year, I stacked my Datsun against a phone pole. The police report said I was doing in excess of eighty per. Sounds about right. The car looked like a stepped-on egg crate and my face looked like a busted jar of raspberry jam. I was five days in a coma while they wired me back up. I've got a steel forehead, a plastic nose, a rebuilt jaw, and not too damn many of my original teeth. They didn't even try to get me back to the way I used to look—just went ahead and fitted me up for this Hollywood Halloween mask."

"I see."

"If I ever get hurt again I'll have to go to a body-and fender shop instead of a hospital. But you know what bummed me out? Lyin in bed over New Year's with cement around me up to *here*." He tapped himself on the chest. "I didn't get to party! Now I got this Cadillac halftrack, and you know it's gonna take one *hell*uva wreck before I miss a good party again!"

We ate at an uptown cafeteria. Cheney's greasy coveralls and my riding leathers were a bit misplaced amid the neat, sweet and petite of the business world. We didn't care, just hunkered down and chomped, swapping stories like kids with handsful of alternate bubble gum cards.

"So. What's this about a race today?"

"Oh, there's a dirt flattrack outside the city limits. Every once in a while a bunch of dudes get together and have a race on it. Sometimes we do it with the AMA, sometimes we just *do* it, you know? No points, just fun." He grinned.

Why do you race with a head that comes apart? Aren't you scared of stacking it again?''

The grin vanished. "I ain't no coward."

"I didn't mean scared *that* way. I mean, since you drive that huge Cadillac for . . .''

"Look," he said testily. "I ain't scared of drivin and I ain't scared of racin. Got it?''

"Got it."

If I didn't get it, it was a safe bet I'd be leaving the cafeteria by myself. And there was still something with Cheney, B. D. and the gang that the astrolabe kept me focused towards.

"OK." The stiff, winsome grin returned. "Sorry if I got hot for a sec, but I wanted you to understand how it was." He glanced up at the cafeteria's pussycat clock. It's tail was a pendulum.

"Hey! Time to move it! They'll all be waitin on us!"

We jumped into the hearse and drove back to Cheney's apartment. It was a line of brick boxes, the monotony broken only by the changing numbers on the doors, except for Cheney's.

His was the only one with a squadron of lean choppers parked outside, chrome sparkling in the afternoon sun. I recognized Carl, Roy's nephew, conscious at last, among those standing around the bikes with cans of beer in their hands.

"Whooooo! There he is! The Man!" They all clustered around Cheney, punching him on the shoulders and pushing beer into his hands. "Let's get him warmed up! Somebody check his oil!"

Carl stood apart, not joining in the general hoo-ha over the arrival of the hotshoe hero. Erect and sober now, he seemed less flabby, more muscular and vital. His features, from his thick wrists to his freckled nose, suggested he had been formed to fill some adman's fantasy of a country boy. Give him a straw hat and a fishing pole, and he could sell a million "Silkies! The Cigarette With The Scent of New-Mown Hay!" But where I expected to find the prescribed solid country nature in his eyes, the content of a man who knows his place and digs into it, there was instead a hard sadness.

Ah, I thought. The farmboys of America are all lured from the corncribs of paradise to the saloons of disaster. I walked up to him.

'Carl? Hi. Steve Getane. Your Uncle Roy gave me your address and told me to visit. He said you could tell me about, oh, current trends in the Baptist church.''

"Hi." His look was direct, but guarded. He didn't extend his hand. "There *are* no current trends in the Baptist church. What else you want to know?''

Our attention was distracted. Cheney had just been hoisted on the shoulders of the assembled, for an honorary splash in the apartment pool.

"What a crazy outfit," I said.

"Yeah," Carl agreed. "And who else but Cheney could be the star?"

"What d'you mean?"

"You comin to the races?"

I nodded.

"You'll see," Carl said. "You'll see."

Dripping wet, Cheney ducked into the apartment to change. The troops gathered by the front door. Big Daddy saw me, and gave me a bear hug calculated to reduce my coat-size by half.

"Hi guy!" he said. "Glad you made it."

"Oof," I said. "Arrgh."

"This gonna be your first outlaw race?" he asked.

"Uh? Outlaw?"

He nodded. "A race without AMA approval, officials, or rules. The whole thing is one big swarm of macho chaos."

"Sounds delightful."

"It is," Carl said. "You should've seen it last month. Some flak came down on Cheney because he rode in the wrong class by mistake. That wouldn't've irked them, except he won. Some dudes got hot and came stomping over. Now, anyone with a plastic face is in no position to hassle anybody, except by phone."

"So, there was the undoing of all that surgery staring him in the face."

"Right! But then came the marines. B. D.'s van came tearing out onto the track, with a bunch of us hanging out the doors. We jumped out and piled into 'em. Big Daddy had one of 'em under each arm and was bangin their heads together, when this other cat jumped him from the back. B. D. just stuck the one under his right arm down between his knees, reached up, grabbed that other fool by the scruff of the neck, hauled him down, and began bangin all *three* of their heads together!"

It was nice to see Carl shrug off his jaded expression and look excited about something.

"Then the county fuzz made the scene, along with all the unofficial officials. They tried to separate the fighters, and the brawl immediately became twice as big. There was people punchin cops, cops punchin promoters, riders, fans, everyone!"

"That's when I saw my chance," B. D. put in. He had been standing by, looking modest, while Carl recounted his exploits. "I bounced the guys I was holding off the hood of a police car, pushed

Cheney into the van, and took off. Last I saw of the rumble was a big cloud of dust on the track, with cusswords shooting out of it.''

"And they're letting you guys race again?" I asked incredulously.

"Sure!" Carl said. "They *want* us to come back. That's the most fun they've had all year!"

When Cheney emerged from his apartment, wearing padded leather pants and a Snortuppe Corp. T-shirt, he held aloft a glistening key, as though it opened a secret back door to the bedroom of Miss Nude America. "Who wants to let Elsie out?" he asked.

"Gimme that!" B. D. snatched the key out of his hand. "She likes me better than the rest of you clods, anyway!" He unlocked Cheney's garage door and went inside. He returned pushing a motorcycle whose entire being was devoted to the impulse of speed. There was a gleaming alloy frame, a Matchless Single engine that looked as if every cubic centimeter had received concerned and constant attention, spool wheels with no brake drums, black-taped handlebars, a gas tank, and a seat. Period. Things a street rider would have considered essential to safe, or even *sane* driving had been eliminated, and whatever remained had holes drilled in it to reduce weight. Elsie was one lean, mean machine.

"Looks like she'll git when you goose 'er, but how do you make her stop?" I asked.

"Well, Cheney usually handles that by falling over," Carl snickered.

"The hell I do!" Cheney said. "This baby has never gone down, and ain't never goin down!"

"That's right!" Big Daddy glowered at Carl. Big Daddy, glowering, was a sight to see. He looked like a muscular volcano a few seconds before eruption. "So knock off the negative vibes, already. You want a hero, you've got to root for him."

Standing beside Elsie in his racing leathers, sun glancing off her chrome and his custom face-job, Cheney was a thumbs-up, safe bet for anyone's hotshoe hero. I felt myself rooting for him, and felt also a bit of sincere envy. He seemed to fit so well into this place and time, into this circle of friends, as if he had been made for the part.

"Awright!" Big Daddy said. "Everybody take a look at the happy young couple. By the authorities interested in me, I pronounce you man and machine. Now let's get cracking!"

Elsie was loaded into the hearse and strapped in place. Cheney grabbed another beer and got in the front seat. I rode shotgun. We formed a long convoy as we pulled out of the parking lot: first the hearse, then the long line of gleaming choppers, with B. D.'s Dodge van bringing up the rear.

As soon as we got on the street, one of the bikes shot out in front—Carl's. I had a glimpse of a black head with protruding velocity stacks, a Sportster tank, a wrought-iron sissy bar, as he flashed by. He dropped a gear, grabbed some revs, and popped the clutch. Wheelie! With his long hair swinging over the pavement, he stayed up in the air for an incredible number of yards, accelerating all the time. At the last second before the on-ramp, Carl dialed it down. The bike wiggled, flexed, fishtailed, then banked into the curve as Carl calmly shifted into third.

Cheney shook his head. "That guy don't like to ride in *no* kind of order." Then, admiringly, "He can drive though, cain't he?"

We arrived at the track: a circle of sleazy-looking bleachers and chicken-wire on the outskirts of town. The air was brash, brass and blue. A layer of hot, dusty light pressed against the earth, pierced by shouts and the whizzing of machines. On our way in, we passed a dirt-bike lying on its side. An angry-looking teenager was tickling its innards with a long screwdriver. As we watched, he threw down the screwdriver and gave the bike a hearty kick in the crankcase.

In the pit area, a lot of people were standing around with cherry pop cans, looking very pleased with themselves. B. D. explained to me that since no drinking in the pits was the only standing rule, booze in rinsed out cherry pop cans had become a standing joke.

Cheney warmed up his bike, then lounged picturesquely beside it, while B. D. and I went to watch the qualifying heats in the smaller classes. Out of the corner of my eye, I saw Carl walk up to Cheney and give him a can of cherry pop.

Dirt flattrack was the wildest form of motorcycle racing I had ever seen. On a short track that looked hardly a quarter-mile long, four to six riders mounted on overpowered, brakeless bikes, accelerated madly towards a curve then threw their bikes into a broadside, fighting for position. They steered and braked with the throttle. The ones who made it around the curve, repeated the whole insane business for five laps. The ones who didn't make it, usually broke traction at some critical point in the broadslide. Then, man and machine would go tumbling and sliding to the outside of the circle. But the race would go on. Surprisingly, no one seemed to get hurt. We watched several heats and races, then it got close to Cheney's class, the Unlimiteds.

Back in the pits, a girl in sunglasses, jeans, and a halter top about the same size as the sunglasses, was giving Cheney hits off a joint. He sat on Elsie looking like he'd already won. The actual race was mere technicality.

His class was called. He fumbled his helmet on, gave everyone the high sign, then rolled out to the starting line. I imagined how he felt, a man with his mechanical ability, aware of the pistons going up and down, the oil circulating, the valves ta-tappeting, the short, furious lightning bolts darting along the wires.

Ding, Big Daddy and the others stood with me at the side of the track. I could feel our combined energy beaming out to the champion. It seemed that, if he won, in some mysterious fashion *we* would be vindicated also . . . that which we believed in would have triumphed. We were spellbound with an almost reverent fascination.

The flag! Elsie leapt forward, ahead by a length! Also, totally out of control. She went down in the first turn. The other bikes scattered around her and roared off.

Elation of a minute before collapsed. A faint nausea took its place. Cheney pulled his bike up—it was still running—mounted, and got back in the race. By the time he got up speed, he had already been lapped by the leaders. The humiliation was devastating. He completed the remainder of his laps clumsily, like a fat kid on a stand-up coaster.

I scrutinized the Cheney cheering section. Disappointment was on every face, but there seemed to be a hint of something else . . .fear? Of what? Was it entire lives and lifestyles that Cheney had been expected to vindicate? I looked back out on the track, and I saw grown men, riding in circles on dangerous toys.

Cheney rode back into the pits. He yanked his helmet off and bashed it on the ground. There were tears in his eyes. "Dammit! That's the last time I drink before a race!"

"That's what you said the last time," Carl said. His voice was dry and sarcastic. "The time you got mixed up and raced Amateur. Remember?"

Big Daddy glared at Carl. He seemed *very* close to eruption this time. "Who gave him booze in the pits, Carl? Don't think I didn't see you! Why, if not to enjoy this right now? I'm gonna take you apart. And when I do, I bet I'll find out that shit is all that holds you together!"

Carl's voice was shaking. "I gave him one beer. Big deal! It wasn't the beer that stopped him, and you all fucken know it!"

"Hey!" I said. "C'mon! It was nothing; it was just one race! The kind you learn from, y'know?"

"Yeah," someone said. "It's cool; he tried."

"You looked good on the straights," Ding put in. "All you have to do is practice up your cornering."

"I'll say," Carl said. "You were thrashing around out there like a madwoman in a shithouse.''

Everyone got real quiet. Big Daddy started for Carl, but Cheney stopped him with an outstretched hand. Cheney's jaw tilted up as he stared at Carl, eye to eye. Then he started chuckling. "You turd," he said. "You're right. It must've looked pretty funny." Everyone began laughing and the tension eased.

"C'mon!" someone said. "It's time for the final. They had the second heat while everybody was jawing!"

We trooped across the track and took up positions inside the oval. All except for Carl. I saw him walking across the parking lot, helmet dangling from one hand, heading for his bike.

It was the final race of the day, pitting everything from a stripped down, overbored Triumph Trophy, to a jacked-up vintage Superhawk.

"Look," Cheney nudged me. "Dude on a Superhawk." Cheney seemed fully recovered from the anguish of his loss. I wondered how much of that was real.

Like all the other bikes, the Superhawk was stripped down to the nitty necessities. The gaunt frame and tiny engine looked even smaller next to the lemon-colored Triumph that blurped and idled beside it on the starting line. But once the Hawk rider blipped his throttle, you could hear the little engine grabbing revs smoothly and effortlessly.

"Hot damn," Cheney said. "He's got a cam in that thing that won't quit!"

I admired my detatchment. I had learned my lesson on the last race. I wasn't going to get sucked into identifying with anyone. If I had any hopes, I could . . . .The flag dropped before I was ready. The Triumph snapped into the lead, a lemon shaft of lightning, with thunder hosing out of the pipes. He was followed by a two-stroke banshee, a Kawasaki, and the Superhawk. The rest of the bikes packed up, and for all intents and purposes left the race, They stayed on the track, but mainly functioned as a mobile obstacle course for the three leaders.

The positions stayed the same through the second lap. Going into the third, the Trumpet had the lead by several lengths, but the 'Saki and the Hawk were closing in, even as they jousted for second place. The Hawk was much quicker than anyone could've expected. The bland-looking powerplant was obviously a furnace full of goodies.

I found myself jumping up and down, punching the air with my fist. Cheney and B. D. were doing the same. Our wills were plugged right into that Superhawk, our energy sloshed in his gas tank. He may have been the underdog, but by some mysterious alchemy, he had become *our* underdog.

The 'Saki knew his life depended on keeping the Hawk jock

squeezed out of the corners, but even on the straights the Hawk was giving him trouble. It was no sweat for the Triumph as long as his two competitors kept each other tied up. He just invoked his power on the straightaways and invested his handling in the turns. He would've come up a winner, but coming out of the last curve of the third lap, he tried for a few foot-pounds too much, too soon. His rear wheel broke free and he slid wildly across the turn. Clawing for traction, the tire bailed out chunks of dirt like a gravedigger on speed. The dirt flew up and battered the 'Saki rider's faceshield, making him hesitate and swing wide to avoid it. That opened up an alley for the Hawk. Dancing easy on his throttle, he popped in. The Trumpet jock got his hotshoe back on, and felt confident enough to risk a glance over his shoulder. He saw the Superhawk staring back, only inches away.

He was in trouble. He couldn't cut corners like that torquey li'l mother, his only hope was keeping the gate closed. This he did, while the Hawk buzzed and strafed his ass. In the dust-dusky air, a small green idiot light taped to the Superhawk's handlebars was glowing like an errant green star.

On the first turn of the last lap, the Hawk wicked it up to slither by on the inside, but the Trumpet, cued to his dirty pool, backed off his throttle and used his slower speed to cut in, closing the gate, forcing the Hawk to stay behind or crawl up his tailpipe. But the Hawk wasn't buying either one. He went for a third option. Veering to the outside of the curve, he wound up his bike so far it started to sound like a turbine. Green means GO! In the last full curve he pulled ahead on the outside, deeding the Trumpet the gate. The Hawk was fixin to show some class! As the trumpet banked for his turn, the Superhawk wailed off the wall like a Jai-Lai superball. By the time the Trumpet came out of the turn, the Hawk was already going twice as fast, had a better angle, and naturally, handed the Triumph its ass.

He zipped in under the flourishing flag and didn't shut it down until the next curve, when he slowed and threw it into a broadslide, then snapped out and popped over the edge . . . a nice jump in the suddenly listening air, in the advent of warm evening, coming down on his rear wheel to land off the track. He cut a circle and came to a stop. He pulled off his helmet and grinned, as a horde of back-slappers and arm-pumpers descended. I walked over to see the hero of the hour. He was *young,* a teenager with thick brown curls plastered to his forehead by sweat, bright untroubled eyes, and now, a glowing aura of flesh fulfillment. He's not human for a moment, coming rather from some astral planet of speed angels that never die, will never age, but are glowbodies of eternal energy who will be always full of the glories of this hour! That's how he feels . . . .

Cheney came and stood beside me. "He can drive, cain't he?" There was respect and envy in his voice, and a few other emotions I didn't particularly feel like deciphering.

The girl in the halter top, who had given Cheney the joint, was working her way through the crowd to the Superhawk jock.

"C'mon," Cheney said. "Help me load Elsie and we'll run on back to my apartment for the party."

"What? You're still going to have the victory party?"

"No, mon. We always have a party. If we win, it's a victory party. If we lose, its a consolation celebration." He gave me the old Cheney grin, stiff but sincere. "Either way, we get to party. That's the important thing!"

We drove away from the track in a welter of motorcycles, cars towing motorcycle trailers, pickups with motorcycles leaning in the beds. Headlight beams scissored across young men with dusty faces, walking with helmets and tools dangling from their hands.

When we made it back to the place, Cheney kept the engine running as I got out.

"What's the word?"

"I'm gonna go out and scare up some action," Cheney said. "Maybe I can't put a tiger in my tank, but right now . . ."

"A little pussy will do," I finished for him. "They say that in Florida, too."

"Yeah. Well, I met a barmaid last week who seemed real friendly. And if she don't work out, I got other possibilities."

"Well, if any of the possibilities has a sister, ask her to come along."

"Do my best."

"No doubt."

Cheney's apartment was a cacophony of popping beercans, loud laughter, farts, grunts, screams. I hadn't been inside before. Aside from the ripe odors of so many bodies in such a small space, the apartment itself had a peculiar redolence all its own.

Big Daddy sat apart, observing the party with the impartial benignity of a buddha. He hitched his pants up to a new fold in his belly and wallowed back on the couch. Under cover of darkness, his hair was liberating itself from the viselike grip of his Elvis hairdo. A halo of black, spiky tendrils spread out around his face.

Just then came a lull in the conversations, coinciding with the end of a loud jazz tape no one had been listening to. Big Daddy found the opportunity favorable to speak. He didn't use the tone and language we had indulged in on the banks of the Pearl. He was craftier than that. For this particular tract, he stuck to his native dialect.

"Thing that was screwin Cheney up today I've seen many times. Got nothin to do with how well you can ride, hell, anybody with an ass and two hands can ride. The secret's in your *attitude* toward ridin. If you cain't cut the shit, it's usually because you ain't payin attention to what needs doin and then goin for it with everythin you got.

"Bein nervous is a waste. Even thinkin can be a luxury when you're supposed to be *goin for it*. You cain't wait aroun 'til you're 200 percent in control. That never happens anywhere, anytime, with anythin! Fact is, if you're not a little bit out of control on a racetrack, you're not goin fast enough. Same might be true of life. You can slab yourself good if you're wastin time thinkin over mistakes, when what you *should* be doin is hauling your ass out of a tight spot. Y'see, Cheney was all there out on the track today. His body was, but his mind was off in his Datsun that time he stacked it. Or mebbe on his bike that time he went off the bridge. . . ."

"You mean he's had two of those?" I broke in.

B. D. snorted. "He's had a hell of a lot more than two. He's got so much tin in his bod he could walk *naked* through one of those airport gates and still set off the beepers. But lemme finish tellin you about the bridge.

"We were out in the boonies on these 250s I got, and I'm jammin it on 'cos I'm tryin to show Cheney how to go for it. It'd just rained, so everythin was slicker'n snot. I zipped around this turn, and dead ahead was this two-log footbridge covered with leaves and mud. Man, I dint worry oh no am I gonna make it, is my life insurance paid up, do I want to be buried or cremated. Y'know? Just banked that baby over and tooled it across. But ole Cheney went into the deep freeze, . . . started to worry about the worst thing that could happen to him. Sure enough, it did. He hit that bridge with the ass end of his bike passin the front, spun off it and slammed down into the ditch. Broke an arm, a leg, and his collarbone. Knocked loose what little sense he had. Which I can prove, because he still wants me to teach him how to race! But he won't learn to just drop everythin and *go* for it! To *ride* when he's ridin, and think when he's sittin in an armchair and cain't hurt nobody. That's what all you suckers need to learn! Speed is a harsh mistress; if you're gonna chase her, you gotta have some concentration!"

After this sermon, Big Daddy leaned back and awaited the amazed agreement of his listeners. It wasn't long in coming.

"What you say, B. D.? You snort speed with your mistress?"

"Nah, he's tellin you how to ride an armchair. Think!"

"Somebody give him one, so he can start!"

"Look! Look! He's startin now. See how his forehead kinda puckers?"

"Cut it *out,* you guys! You get him thinkin, he'll drive off the road into a tree. You want that to happen?"

"Yeah. I wanna see what happens to the tree!"

"Shithead!" Big Daddy heaved his can of beer at the last speaker. He ducked. The can bashed against the wall and spilled out foamily on the carpet. I suddenly realized how Cheny's apartment had acquired its peculiar odor and emphatic lived-in look.

"All you guys do is play games!" Big Daddy glared around him in a rage. "All you do is get doped up, talk about how doped up you were, and how doped up you're gonna be. And when I try to explain something, help you change things a little bit, you all get on my case! God! I've spent the last six years making friends with a pack of morons!"

Everyone laughed. I didn't. I felt a wave of dissociation sweep over me. I felt B. D.'s pain. I knew then that the warm comraderie I had admired was not operating at a level that would satisfy my search, or even distract me from it much longer.

Carl, also, did not laugh. He emerged from the bedroom of the apartment with fair-haired Freddie in tow. Carl's eyes were shining with some unnatural light; his voice was low and amused.

"Hey B. D." he said. "Freddie's not so dumb. He's got something we can all agree on. It's got everything . . . lines, getting doped up, speed, and concentration. Show 'im, Freddie."

Freddie dipped into a pocket of his slacks and pulled out five small plastic envelopes. He moved with a spacy confidence and precision I didn't think he had in him. He spread the packets out on the littered coffee table with one sweep of his hand, like a poker shark laying down his cards. A fine white powder gleamed inside the plastic. Everyone fell silent.

Ding edged up to the table. There was an expression of utter fascination and longing on his face. "Speed, smack, or coke, Carl?"

"A combination of things, my friend. A unique and interesting combination of things. You want to *go* for it?"

As full of strange energy as that moment was, it still felt tightly confined. The way everyone's attention was riveted on the packets of gleaming powder—lying amid the overflowing ashtrays, crumpled paper flowers, empty bottles and crushed cans on the table—it felt like a roomful of people seeking exit, crowded against a door that would not open.

I looked away, at the wall. An oblong patch of paint, a shade darker than the rest, caught my eye. As I gazed at it, I realized that a painting or photograph had once hung there. One of those things a human hangs on a wall to make a facsimile window, opening on a world where his dreams or fears or hopes become more real than they do in the place where he finds himself. Evidently whatever had been hung there hadn't worked, had stayed flat and two-dimensional. And had been taken down.

But now, I thought, that square of unfaded paint could be taken as a subtle piece of found art in its own right. Something that spoke not of escape through the wall, but of the wall itself. Another painting in the Wall Series—at once abstract and representational—unsigned by an unknown artist who is nevertheless much anthologized and frequently imitated. This work, entitled "Wall" has no frame. As soon as the work is perceived, its statement spreads by a series of geometric leaps to the walls behind and around you. To the carpeted floor. To the acoustical ceiling and on down the hall, where soft lights extend an invitation to explore the closed alternatives of a world maze.

The work achieves its statement. You are encircled. You are trapped, in finite time and finite space. Having been born here, you will die here, and nobody really knows what you are supposed to be doing here, in between these walls. Think of freedom! Hurl yourself against the walls, and they become twice as real. They spin around you, and you return to the center of the room. Distract yourself, then. Race in circles, win trophies, Olympic medals, degrees—the approved goals that society has stretched like a membrane of illusions between the human mind and the terror of the walls. The walls spin once around you, and you return to the center of the room. Shoot up! Fall down. Scream, if you like. Dance! Drink! Die . . . who cares?

Was there a way away from the walls? A way through them? Did Carl and Freddie have it in their plastic packets? I thought not. The passing thrill of the drug would be like a painting hung on a mental wall, offering awhile the illusions of a window. Then the drug vision would end, the walls would intrude upon awareness again, perhaps with twice as much force as before. *They spin around you and you return to the center of the room.*

I thought of all the things I'd tried, the things everyone has tried, to fill mortality with the thrill, the rush of limitless being. To put off boredom, claustrophobia, the feeling of the walls. The seekers of the thrill of acquisition, known as greed. Those who mangled the lives of friends and relatives for the thrill of hate and destruction. We who desperately seek the first rush of falling in love, over and over. We who cling blindly to the large structures of politics, science, religion, causes, fashionable trends of thought (especially the ones that offer freedom if you buy in), and whimper with fear at the thought of confronting our own being, stripped of these associations. We who lose ourselves in history, or the future. Who lose ourselves in a hopeless effort to make our bodies more real than the walls, vainly trying to satisfy or nullify the urge for release.

No one, I thought, can condemn junkies, except for being obvious. We have all sought the same thrill for the same reasons; only the methods have seemed different. But none of these ways of passing through the walls succeeds. Fueled by fear, they make the human soul real in the same way that the walls are real. By running from the walls in this fashion, maybe we were actually running toward them.

I admired the way these thoughts fitted together in a glowing geometry, a physics of the consciousness. The understanding was beautiful, almost a neon effect on a black field. I felt my attention recede from them, in order to put them in a familiar perspective.

I became aware that I had spaced out. The room I was sitting in was empty. Big Daddy was gone. From where I sat, I could see Ding, Carl, and two others clustered over a spoon in the bathroom. Ding had the sleeve of his sportshirt rolled up to his armpit. He knotted a length of surgical hose above the bicep, with his teeth and one hand. His upper lip, drawn back in a snarl of effort, his teeth gleaming in the flourescence, gave him a surreal look of hunger. His inner elbow glistened with small flecks of moisture. He was ready to eat.

Carl finished mashing up the paste in the spoon. He put in a piece of cotton.

"Hit me," Ding said.

Carl filled a hypo from the spoon. He selected a spot on Ding's arm, and pushed it in.

Ding's eyes seemed to flicker and dilate. Moisture beaded on his upper lip. "Yeah. Yeah. *Yeah-hh-h,"* he said slowly. After a few minutes, he got up from the john where he'd been sitting, and glanced in the mirror on the medicine cabinet. It was fogged up; he couldn't see himself.

I had a sense of imminent withdrawal, as if my experience in Jackson was complete, and I was already down the road, moving away. It seemed appropriate to go outside. The air was cool, just beginning to recover from the day's heat. It was a sudden relief to be away from the odor of Cheney's apartment. I had gotten used to the smell without noticing it. I felt a bit sad that there hadn't been more for me here, that my search would not let me stay. I spied Big Daddy. He was down at the far end of the apartment building, leaning against the wall. A spot of red light glowed in his hand, glowed brighter as he raised it to his face. I walked towards him.

"Hello, B., D.," I said. "Goodbye."

"You leaving?"

I nodded.

"Why don't you stick around a couple days longer?"

"Can't."

B. D. seemed thoughtful. The place of the hale-Big-Daddy-well-met act had been taken over by the rather cerebral entity I had glimpsed on the banks of the Pearl. "After what you've seen tonight, I don't blame you," he said. "But you don't see it all. No one does. There are other things going on with us. Where you headed?"

"I don't know yet."

B. D. threw his cigarette to the ground and stomped it out. "Well then. Are you hip to the fact that this whole scene you've found in Jackson is like something out of one of Kerouac's books? The emphasis on speed and travel, on cutting away ties and responsibilities, on jacking your head around with hootch and drugs, is the very thing he praised and helped create?"

"Yeah," I admitted. "I kind of noticed the effect."

"Then why don't you go check out Faulkner now, . . . the themes that go beyond physical excitement and time? You could go right on up to Oxford from here. That's where he hung out. See if you can find Yoknapatawpha, . . . just *go* for it. I'll give you the address of a dude I know up there, for a place to stay. Here."

He wrote on the back of a Snortuppe card and handed it to me. I got a tingle of the appropriate energy. The *presence* was further down this road.

"Why don't you come along?" I asked.

"No. This is my home. These guys are my friends here."

"They don't act like it."

"Let me be the judge of that."

"OK."

"Goodbye."

He thrust out his hand. "Swing by and see us if you come back through. Let me know . . . what you find out."

"*Certe.*"

He smiled back. We shook hands. I turned and walked back to Cheney's apartment, where Frank was parked. A long, black shiny car pulled up in front. Cheney got out, followed by a tall, slim girl with her hair tied behind her. She looked damn familiar . . . ah so, the circle had come full round. The significance of who was doing what to whom seemed complete.

"Cheney! Joyce!"

They waited for me by the front door. Joyce was dressed up and tricked out, which surprised me. There were blue crescents of shadow over her eyes. Her lips gleamed in the light from the lamp by the door.

"I want to give you an advance warning," I said. "They're shooting up saniflush in there."

"Yay!" Cheney said. "Carl found some! Hope they saved a couple of hits for us."

"You do that?"

"I do whatever comes around. Like I told you, mate, I'm in it for the party. You comin in or what?"

"No," I said. "I'm allergic to saniflush."

"That's not all you're allergic to," Joyce said archly.

They went in. I still had to pack up my gear, and I needed a place to crash; so I headed for Joyce's apartment. I could probably sleep in her bed. It didn't seem likely that anyone else would be using it.

V.
Eight
of Cups

I woke before my dreams had time to leave. The dream thoughts were strange, formless, gibbering things, made of grey smoke. They spoke in a language my waking mind could almost understand. Then they were gone. Where . . .? My eyes focused on a dresser, where a burnt out candle slumped in the mounded white scales of its melted wax. O yeah. Joyce's. I got up and began to make the bed.

I felt shitty. I had dreamed grey; it was a grey day, and my path looked the same way. Leaving Tallahassee had drawn some distance between my perception and the feelings that had driven me out of town. This morning, they had caught up to haunt me, coloring everything I saw or could foresee. The star was a will-o'-the-wisp.

My leathers were cold and clammy, and I shivered as I pulled them on. I gathered up an armload of packs and staggered out onto the balcony. There, to my astonishment, he was.

Jack Kerouac was sitting on the bannister. He wore a blue sweatshirt with the sleeves pushed up past the elbows, baggy brown trousers, and a pair of tennis shoes. A flat cap, pushed forward on his head, hid his eyes and some of the angles of his tanned face, but it was unmistakably him. He had a cup of coffee in one hand, from which rose curls of steam and a faint whiff of scotch, and two freshly lit cigarettes in the other. He offered me one of the cigarettes.

I stepped mechanically up to take it, dimly aware that I had dropped my packs and was now stepping over them.

He was a young, virile, alert Jack, the one who had slammed a long roll of paper—the final folio of *On The Road*—down on the publisher's desk. Not the pudgy alky who had boozed away his final days in Orlando, fumbling for a way to write the same story for the twentieth time.

"*Ecce homo!*" he said. "The groggy hero resurrects from his night of foggy dream!" As he handed me the cigarette his head tilted, and I could see the eyes under the visor of the cap. They were golden, glowing and amused.

"Push!"

Telling him how surprised or glad I was to see him, at this juncture, would have been a serious tactical error. So I said, "Thanks for the hack. You want to get lost for a while and let me finish waking up?"

He chuckled and leaned back against a post. "That's what I'm doing. When I want to get lost, I come and talk to you a bit."

I rubbed my face with one hand. It felt like my entire body was covered with stubble. His response had left me with the ball. I tried to pass it back.

"If I'm so lost, how do you always know where to find me?"

"You send out strong signals, bub. I know when that strictly-from-hunger Steve Getane call comes beating on my door. Sometimes I answer right away. Sometimes it's more interesting to wait."

I mulled that over. The startling part was that Push seemed to be laying claim to an objective existence, something apart from my apparent talent for hallucinating him. If that were true, then he had to be some sort of magical entity from another sphere of being . . . a proposition I found hard to swallow, not to mention unnerving. As I teetered on the edge of falling back into profound fear of him, her, it, I snatched a handful of my mental business and threw it at him. If he could supply answers I didn't already have . . . well, I'd have some new information. Plus something very interesting to wonder about. "Push. . . ." He fixed his eyes on me. This time, I didn't flinch away from those inflexing golden kaleidoscopes, with their pits of icy knowing.

"Tell me something about this. Everything I learned, right up through adolescence, seemed to be—more than just information—the mental coordinates of a certain state of being, a state all adults agree on as sanity. Now, this state had its roots and channels coming in from way back in history, and reaching on into the future, forming the lake of the present. It was as if what we know as this life—all the pictures of our culture—were a kind of reservoir from which the newborn are forced to drink, becoming more than brainwashed, becoming actually what they drank. The elixir that would make them real and sane, or at least relevant. Now, the matrices filling this reservoir are caught and held by the walls. . . ."

"Hold it! Hold it!" Push had his hands over his ears. He was laughing, but he seemed to be in real pain. "I've heard of mixed metaphors, but yours are scrambled! Howsabout we try one of mine?"

Exactly what I wanted. "Shoot," I said.

"Once upon a time . . ." he began. I winced. He smiled and continued, ". . . there was a little kingdom in which lived a little prince. The kingdom was called Macedonia, the prince's name was Alexander. Young Alex believed that one day he was going to rule the world. In this, he did not differ greatly from other little boys. But he believed in his ability to bring it off a lot more strongly than others did. As he grew, he illustrated that by breaking a horse that no one else in the whole kingdom had been able to ride.

"One day, he heard of a temple far to the South. Supposedly, in this temple hung a great rope with a fabulous knot twisted in it. It was said Apollo had tied this knot, swearing as he did that whoever parted it would become ruler of the world. Unlike most other gods of his time, Apollo was considered fairly reliable, so the fame of this knot spread far and wide. It was called the Gordian.

"When young Al heard about it, he thought it was right up his alley. He packed fresh goats into some olive skins and set off, undeterred that many had tried before him and failed. He probably would have been undeterred by a tidal wave coming in the opposite direction. That's the kind of guy Alexander was.

"He found the temple and the rope with the fabled knot. He stood before it a long time, trying to figure it out. He stood there a much longer time. He stood there for days. It was not just the knot's complexity that baffled him; it was that there was no particular reason for it to be tied the way it was. The more he tried to reason out its labyrinthine coils and bends, the farther away from any solution he seemed to be. It was as if his brain were tying itself into a knot just like the one he saw before him.

"Finally, his concentration was broken by an old priest, who groveled up to ask if he would perhaps like a sliced goat haunch sandwich for nourishment. At that moment, young Alex was smitten by inspiration. He grabbed the old priest's frock and hauled him to his feet. 'Whoever parts the knot will rule the world, right?' The holy old toot gurgled and nodded; his eyes bulged with terror. Young, would-be emperors and magicians had been know to lose their marbles in contemplation of the knot before.

"Al drew his sword. The old man fainted on the spot. But casting the priest from him, Alexander turned and chopped the knot in half with one mighty downward stroke of his blade. They were sharp enough to shave with back then, you know. 'Ta-da!' Alexander said. He strode away from the temple to claim his empire. The rest, as they say, is history.''

Push stubbed his cigarette butt out on the end of his tongue and swallowed it. I ignored it; I was much more interested in the thrust of his parable than in cheap astral theatrics.

''Yeah! The knot! That entangled state of mind, shit, a whole reality! That's what I want . . . to cut through it! I *know* the thing I'm looking for is right on the other side of it.''

''Ah.'' Push regarded me laconically. ''You willing to commit suicide?''

''*What?*''

He shrugged. ''You have been formed in and of the knot. Your rebellion is only another acknowledgment and reinforcement of the knot's reality, unless you're willing to commit suicide.''

''OK,'' I said, figuring I was calling his bluff. ''How?''

''Glad you asked. Otherwise, this conversation might've ended with you jumping off the balcony. What I have in mind is not as easy. In fact, by comparison, it will be excruciating. Consequently, it will be a lot more fun for me to watch.'' He grinned wolfishly. On Kerouac's face, it looked rather handsome.

''Explain!'' I demanded. ''Otherwise, *te morituri non salutamus*!''

He folded his arms and settled back against his post. ''It wouldn't be a knot,'' he said, ''unless there were forces in it that sought to bind, now would it?''

''Individuals, institutions . . . ?'' I hazarded.

He gestured impatiently. ''Whatever reigns here. Who benefits from power that is bound in place? The ones that do the binding, that bend reality and human lives into their own shape. One form and phase after another. You know what I find most amusing about you humans? The great eagerness with which you swap one form of bondage for another, convinced you're gaining in the exchange.''

''But I. . . .''

''You're different, right? You're gonna cut through the reigns of the world by ruling yourself. However, before you rule yourself, you have to cut yourself free. It all ties together with double-binds. That's why it's in the form of a knot.''

''All right. So where do I start? Or do I just give up?''

''Giving up might work. But it would take someone like you a thousand lifetimes to do it. You're better suited to the cutting approach.''

"Well," I said, "I need more knowledge of how and where to strike."

"You're asking me?"

"Well, yes, I'd like your op—. . . ."

"The reigns of the world are maintained through desire and fear. When these emotions occur, if you pay attention, you can feel the patterns of conditioning and control set off within you."

"Yes. Go on."

"Your parents raised you in the desire that you would grow up like them and in the fear that you would not. You speedily learned to desire their pleasure and fear their displeasure in this regard. The patterns from these experiences still hold you. And in the areas where you've rebelled against these, the rebellions still hold you as much as the original patterns did.

"Educators imprinted you with thought-forms, nursing your desire for success, your fear of the disgrace of failure. The trace of these motivations still drives you. Peers made you conform through fear of not-belonging. You still desire to be comforted by the warmth of the crowd. It has so much power, that whatever it thinks is right.

"The business empires want your desire so that you will work, so that you will get paid, so that you can buy and keep buying, and move up in status in their organizations. They want you to feel humiliated in the eyes of men for not having. When you destroy these fears and desires, you break this reign. I don't really need to tell you how priests and preachers, policemen and judges, and all the other hookers and hawkers use fear and desire, do I?"

I shook my head.

"Watch out for me," Push winked. "Even the champions of the Truth That Frees frequently desire that you help reinforce their choice of specialties, to erase nagging doubts over whether or not they really do have an option on the Door."

"And if I'm lucky or smart and I get past you?"

Push grinned. "Then, you must undo the next dimension of the knot, where it ties into your mind and life, and becomes you.

"Deep within your personal psychology, you preserve the *essence* of desire and fear through successive judgments you use as crutches for your own identity. But an identity thus conceived is a child of the knot. Progress past this point depends on whether you can become something other than a bundle of preferences.

"Remember those two at Muckie's? The teen angel and the old granny ghoul? You called them that, feeling lust for one and disgust for the other. But was the old one not once young? And will the young one not grow old? They could have been the same person in different stages of the same life. Truly, there is something there different from age. But all you saw was the non-negotiable terms of your personal satisfaction, writ large.

"Or while you were watching the races yesterday. Or while you were sleeping with that nubile, if confused young girl. Instead of completely making love to her on the level where you *knew* she was at, you got pious on her about halfway through, demanding she get on a level she could no more relate to, than you could tell me the color of the lint in an archangel's navel! Partly because of that, she dropped back into her hopelessness, and shot her body full of icky toxins last night. Who the hell do you think you are? You think the whole world revolves around you?"

Numbly, I shook my head.

"Well it *does*, stupid! As long as you are alive in it, you will be one of the things the world revolves around! So get your damn fingers off you own eyes and see where you are perpetuating the blinding pain of the knot by carrying its patterns around inside you. Quit pretending your game of picking favorites is a search for truth!

"You dare talk liberation when it's precious snobs like you, convinced of the superiority of their own vision, who are most responsible for the knot's existence! You say you want to see things as they are, but you really want to pick and choose among them, deciding what is worthy and inspired enough to be on the planet with you, and what is not!"

Push slammed his hand down on the banister, emphasizing his point. Unfortunately, a fly, roused by the warmth of the sun, had chosen that minute to buzz sleepily over the balcony. It had lighted on the rail, knuckling its eyes with its forelegs. Now, its vital juices spread out around its smashed carcass in a little splotch.

I felt a lot like the hapless fly.

"But there's hope for you, m'boy," Push smiled as he combined Clarence Darrow with W.C. Fields in his tone, "which is why I took your case."

"I'm honored," I said, cautiously following Push's abrupt return to humor. "But couldn't I put in a transfer for someone a little less brutal?"

"Nope. A little blessing of your chosen path is that you'll receive vast amounts of teaching. One of the curses is that there'll be no way to avoid it. Consciousness itself will be your teacher. You're going to have to abandon your limitations and infinitely expand your perceptions, which is a joyously agonizing process. You have my sympathy."

For a moment, I felt the astrolabe point dead center into the middle of what Push was saying. Then patterns of the knot drifted across my vision, conveying the predictions, the *assertions,* that I couldn't have the freedom I needed to search for that presence, the star, because it simply wasn't possible. Relentlessly the patterns drifted, blocking the vision. Possibility denied. I couldn't break through these patterns or change them, any more than a man standing on the ground, shaking his fist at the clouds, could get them to stop raining! I thought with envy of that farmer in Alabama. He didn't need to make it stop raining in order to be as, and who, he wished.

"Yes!!" Push shouted. "That's it! What the Bean Farmer taught you! Expand that attitude of goodbye to rains. Keep the wind in your face and wetness in your hair if you want, and leave the rest of your old comprehension behind!

"Cut through the other reigns the same way, the way Big Daddy went across the footbridge. Don't stop to shuffle, deal, and play solitaire with doubts, desires and fears! *Go* for it with single-mindedness. Nothing clings to you; you cling to nothing. Surprise yourself! Always look for ways to violate conditioning, so it is you that acts, not the conditioning. Do things spontaneously! Or totally unspontaneously. Follow first impulses, or wait and follow your thirtieth! Have the kind of mind that the walls of reigns cannot confine! Don't try to fight them on their own ground. By going for your feeedom in this fashion, you will achieve it. You'll already have it!"

I felt a curious lightness spreading through my body, a tingling warmth. A shiver started at the base of my spine and shot to the top of my skull, jerking my head around.

The presence! The star! I could sense it again. Aloud I heard myself say, "Now I'll get it!"

"What?" Push was amused.

"I can't tell you," I told him.

"Aw-w-w, a secret!" he mocked.

"A secret from me too!" I said angrily. "What can I tell you? I was sitting in a field after a thunderstorm. I felt something: powerful, disembodied presence. . . ."

"That's it."

"What's it?"

"What you met. A disembodied presence, a *being*, if you will."

I was angered by his acting as if he had a better line on it than I. "Okay, know-it-all, tell me more. What *kind* of disembodied being?"

"Chimerical."

81

Push was deriving great enjoyment from laying his cards down one at a time.

"Oh, imaginary," I said, disappointed that he couldn't do better than that, even if he was pissing me off.

"Not at all! I mean elusive! One jump ahead of you! Despite your convictions to the contrary, Mr. Getane, you are a fairly lazy man. So, your advancement depends on an ever-receding goal. Hence the chimera.

"The lure of its voice will take you through some pretty hairy desert. You will know great thirst. The end of your nose will get sunburnt. You'll be distracted by many mirages. Staying with them is up to you, but you'll have to accept the consequences. And you will find a few genuine oases that no one ever saw before. After you, no one will ever see them again."

"Tell me more about he good stuff," I suggested.

"You'll get an incredible tan."

"Ah-h. The houris will find me desirable."

"Sure. But that's not what you want."

"It isn't?"

"Nope. If that's what you wanted, you would've stayed in Tallahassee, and either patched things up with Ursula or started chasing Jo in earnest. But how many times have you thought about either one of them since you set off on this quixotic little tour? Once, or twice?"

"I see what you mean. Migod, am I going celibate?"

Push snickered. "Not if you can help it. Let's just say that getting laid is no longer of prime import, unless this being you're hunting turns out to be female."

"Thought you said it was disembodied."

"It is. But beings are capricious that way."

"So how . . ."

"You already know. Learn as you go, 'on-the-job training' they call it. If you blow it, figure out what blew it, get up and go for it some more. Every scrap of time can yield information, can be used for nourishment. Waste not, want not!"

Push looked at his bare wrist as if there was a watch on it. He shook his arm, then bent his wrist back so that the veins stood out. He held it up to his ear as if he were listening to his pulse. "Hup! Gotta go. Stop hallucinating me, so I can leave."

"Sure!" I said, though I wasn't. I closed my eyes and imagined a vacant banister. But when I opened them again, he was still there—a Push in Kerouac's clothing.

"Well? C'mon!" he said. "Scared I might be more real than you are?"

He began laughing and fading away at the same time. He turned translucent toward the end, trees and buildings behind him becoming visible through his body. Just before he utterly vanished, I saw him lick something from the palm of his hand.

A fragrant wind was blowing from the north. Frank's front wheel lined up with it like a weathercock.

The Natchez Trace was an ecologist's vision of a heavenly highway. From groves of oak and hickory jays screeched, mockingbirds yodeled, and green banks tumbled down to the road. In soft hollows between the hills, conifers congregated, lit their incense, dervished in the breeze. No crosswalks of signal lights slashed over this clean, narrow, two-lane road, no gas stations, billboards, Muckie's, Honest Injun Souvenirs, or litter lined the sides. There was just the woods.

And Frank's metal-and-wind song, the rare *whoosh* of passing cars, and a subtle but pervasive sense of things past.

For jays were not all that were calling back from in among the spreading branches and tangled leaves. Back in there, innumerable hooves, paws, moccasins, wooden wheels and boots had padded, rolled and walked for centuries gone. Here the Choctaw had bargained, fought, lost, been driven away. Here the Kaintuck boatmen had spat, drunk, guffawed on the trail north again to collect rafts for the trip down the Mississippi. Here "Old Hickory" had cussed his men down to the Battle of New Orleans. The traces of these passages were not only written as a crease worn in the cheek or brow of the earth, and now half-paved, half-buried under moss, grass, and fallen leaves . . . they seemed also suspended like motes in the air, ghosts of sound, just beyond the threshold of hearing.

Spellbound with history as it was, the Natchez Trace was a good road to take to the mythical kingdom of "Yoknapatawpha" (W. C. Faulkner, sole owner and proprietor). Yoknapatawpha was not the county's real name except in Faulkner's mind, but there it had proven real enough. Yoknapatawpha was simultaneously a geographical spot with actual citizens, drugstores, graves, and mailboxes, and a psychological place wherein that geography had become transfigured.

The small town where Faulkner lived and wrote was Oxford. In his writing it became Jefferson, the capital of the mythical Yoknapatawpha County. One town real, the other surreal but interfused with the first, taking raw material from it and giving back truth. A truth no longer exactly that of the earth, but something distilled from it.

And who was this Faulkner, this alchemist who had transformed one world into another and set up an imagic correspondence between the two?

Another Southern summer rainstorm gathered above me as I journeyed up the Trace. A light drizzle began heading ponderously towards a full downpour. I stopped and put my cheap plastic rainsuit on, over my leathers. I pulled out my roadmap. It was damp and beginning to fray, showing the fibers beneath the bright colors on the folds.

Hmm. If I turned off the Natchez now, I could take backroads quickly into Jefferson. I mean, Oxford.

The odd old towns I buzzed through were rustic with real rust, not tourist-trap claptrap imitation weathered iron and wood. A fine spray of rain and road dust jetted up from the front tire, gradually coating Frank and myself with a chocolate scum. The Mississippi road department had small triangular signs up, lettered with suggestions like: *Seatbelts? Check Mirrors, Drive Safely.* One redundant specimen read, *Read the Signs.* The last one said, *Be Courteous.* Its lettering had been almost obliterated by bullet holes of a sizable caliber.

Weary and wet, I drove slowly into Oxford around five. A fine gold and grey light played around the buildings. I stopped at a gas station and pulled the card Big Daddy had given me out of my wallet.

BEAR'S COSMETIC SUPPLY
HIGH gloss for HIGH times

Bear   698 Temple Ct.
Flemson   Oxford, Miss.

On a map taped up inside one window of the gas station I located the address, and went there without much difficulty. I switched Frank off and parked him at the curb. He sighed audibly, then began to hiss and ping at the rain.

The house was antebellum. At least, it looked as if a war had been fought in it. White paint and grey primer seemed to be chipping and falling from everything . . . the siding, shutters, even the columns that leaned toward each other on the sagging porch. What landscaping there had been was badly losing a counterattack from the seedier forces of Mother Nature.

I went up the steps, carefully testing them before I put down my full weight. The front door had a bronze doorknocker in the shape of a gargoyle doing a rude thing with its tongue. I let it thump back into place.

From inside came a massive, answering thump and jingle, but the door remained closed. It was unlatched. I pushed it open and looked around inside.

A fat man in Ole Miss gym shorts, bent over a set of weights, raised his face in alarm. He looked like the Pillsbury Doughboy, inflated a good 100 psi over. This mound of smooth flesh was topped off by a shock of dusty-yellow hair, a pair of gold-rimmed glasses perched on a beaklike nose, and a mist of perspiration. I noticed he was stand-up pressing all of sixty pounds. Pushing Mr. Universe.

"Hi! Guess you're Bear," I said, with the friendliest of smiles.

"Who the hell are you?" he demanded.

"Aha, good question. Steve Getane's the name; still figuring out the game. I'm passing through and looking for a place to crash."

"Well, I don't have park benches for no bums," he said, frowning as he waddled toward me. "This ain't no 'Crashpad'!"

"Guy in Jackson gave me your address. Big Daddy. Recommended I stop in."

"B. D.? Listen, I don't know what kind of a joke this is, but B. D.'s name ain't no kind of a recommendation around here!"

The door swung to and slammed in my face. A flake of paint fell off, fluttered, and coasted down to my feet.

I sighed. So much for the unwritten coast-to-coast code of hip hostelry; another revolutionary possibility biting the dust.

I cruised Ole Miss for a while, hoping a blonde goddess in a green convertible would stop and extend an invitation to come up to her place for a hot shower, warm brandy, and maybe a backrub. She stood me up.

So I hauled out my battered map and looked for one of those tiny triangles with ears that indicate a campground. Aha. There we go. If one impulse don't git it, git another. Push was right.

On the road west to Sardis Reservoir, I raced to catch up with the sun. There was still a light rain, but I didn't much care. Besides, it was raining light too, . . . a gold and green velvet light, reflecting and reflecting from all curves and angles of the verdant countryside, until the air seemed aglow with a soft, phosphorescent green. In which I rode bathed.

I was following my selected impulse straight into the heart of beauty, despite the faint but nagging sense of foreboding that was riding right behind me on the pillion.

I came to a place where kudzu vines were taking over. They had already engulfed a pasture, including its trees and fences, and were well on their way up the local phone poles. A sign poked up out of the omniverous, undulating green carpet like the hand of someone drowning at sea. With its last strength, it conveyed that Sardis Reservoir lay three miles to my right.

Sardis, I thought. Sartoris. I wonder if that's where he got it.

I took the turn. The side road wound in ever-tightening coils, forc
-ing me to drop to fourth gear, then third. The glorious light was fading
fast, and as it went, the strange sense of apprehension heightened.

Frank bumped and clattered across a cattle guard—one of those
ditches across a road covered with steel bars.

Then I saw it—a huge, shimmering expanse of lake, with clearings
on the shore nestled under dark trees. Unfortunately, there was also a
sign.

NO MOTORCYCLE OPERATION IN THIS AREA

Well, I thought . . . they just don't want bikers to run around
squirting noise pollution out of their tailpipes. But me, I'll just putt in
and shut down, then pitch my li'l tent so gently I won't even bend the
grass.

I stopped at an especially attractive spot and killed Frank. Then I
heard the sound of another engine. A car with its headlights off had
followed and was pulling in behind me. Suddenly its lights switched on,
and a spotlight as well. I was frozen in a harsh white glare, through which
the now visible rain fell like a thin curtain of parallel threads.

"Hold still, raht theyah," a deep, annoyed voice said.

I heard the buzz and crackle of a two-way radio and the voice saying something inaudible into it. Then a door slammed and a tall man
came swaggering into the light. He had a good five inches on my own six
feet. His outfit was resplendent: a dark brown serge uniform with silver
studs and ornaments; two loops of gold braid around one shoulder; a Bat-
man utility belt bulging with leather pouches and the handles of various
weaponry; glossy black boots, and a fawn-colored Stetson pushed back
from his forehead.

His face was long and coarse, something carved out of rosewood
with a hatchet. For all his height he hadn't much weight, his arms were
thin and hairless. There was something comically adolescent about his
swagger, but the thin-lipped expression of hate on his face was no
laughing matter. His nameplate read, *W. Jones.*

"Gimme some ID, freak," he said.

I knew then I was in for a hard time.

"Driver's license do?" I asked, struggling to sound polite.

He snatched it out of my hand and scrutinized it. Then he dug into me with those flinty, William S. Hart eyes. "Know how to read?" He
waited for the answer, forcing the humiliation. It seemed that my only
realistic option was to submit to it, and get out of this with as little
damage as possible.

"Yeah."

"Well straddle that 'sickle and foller me back up the road. I wanta show you somethin."

He was going to rub my face in that sign. I got back aboard, reluctantly, and started Frank up. The ranger got in his car and started up the hill. I wondered if I could outrun him. Maybe, but it would be hard to beat the radio.

I pulled in my clutch lever, and the cable broke. Right then! *Pwang.* I couldn't believe it. And if I couldn't, I was sure W. Jones would have a bit of trouble with it. His car circled back around.

"C'mon boy. Don't get me hot! Ah said to foller me out of here."

"I can't follow anybody anywhere. My clutch cable just broke."

"Godammit! Don't fuck with me!" He leaped from the car, his forehead knotted and his face darkened. "Show me that cable!"

The sight of a cable actually broken sent him the rest of the way up the wall.

"Off that sickle," he commanded. "Get off! Now go to the car, putcher hands on the roof, lean out and spread your legs."

"Wha?"

A shove plastered me up against the patrol car. I fetched my forehead a pretty good crack and it began throbbing painfully. I mechanically took the position. I couldn't believe this was happening. . . . He ran his hands roughly over my body and finished up with a hard slap on my balls. He grunted, disappointed at not finding a shive or anything he could beat me over the head with.

He grabbed me by the shoulder and spun me around. "OK, strip all the gear off that bike."

"Hey, for Chrissakes! All I did was pull in for a campsite! Believe me, I'm gonna split as soon as. . . ."

"You thinkin of resistin' an officer?"

He stood there smiling, hands on his hips. One hand caressed the handle of the sap that protruded from his belt. His meaning was clear. I untied the packs and took them off the bike.

"Open 'em and spread 'em out."

I unpacked clothing, food, and tools, and spread them on the ground. Then I stood back, arms folded, and watched soberly as W. Jones kicked his way through the clothes, opened food containers and dumped out their contents. Rain fell indifferently on everything. Droplets hitting his uniform vanished in dark blotches. Where they hit and clung to gun and badge, the shiny leather of boots and belt, they acquired a glittering suprareality.

After vandalizing my gear, Jones came back to stand before me, thumbs hooked in his gunbelt, savoring his power. "Well, freak," he conceded, "you hid your shit pretty good. It looks like Ah'll only be able to give you a ticket for operating your sickle in a restricted area. Of course, Ah'll be able to give you another for the same thing when you leave. And theyah's a fifty dollar fine for not cleaning up your campsite. Raht about now, Ah'd say yours looks pretty filthy. . . . And do go, freak, 'cos if you don't Ah'll see to it you have a long, unhappy stay. Don't much like bike bums around here. Understand?"

I nodded, biting my lip.

He wrote out the ticket. Then, he was gone.

I just stood there, letting the rain fall on my face. Then tried to concentrate on getting my gear together. I wound up jamming it all in packs to sort out later. I pitched the tent pretty fast, unrolled my bag inside, pulled off my clothes and crashed. Anger rose in waves from my body in a kind of delayed reaction, keeping me rigid with tension. I kept imagining I heard Jones' car pulling into the campsite again, headlights off. . . . No rest for the wary. It was very late when I finally dropped off.

Next morning I awoke early and went down to the lake. I went naked. Nothing was stirring at any of the other campsites. Cool air raised goosebumps on my flesh.

The lake was a pastel mirror of sunrise, surrounded by flawlessly reflected trees. Water was high—a concrete picnic table protruded above the surface like a diminutive Japanese arch. I waded out to it, each stride sending tremors through the reflected forest.

Yoknapatawpha, I thought. That was a Chickasaw word meaning "water flowing slow through the flatland."

I sat on a submerged bench near the old, mossy table, idly splashing myself with the cold water, and thinking. Here was one of the reigns of the world, masquerading as a force of justice and peace—in Jones' case, anyway. If he was no longer an officer of justice, then he had to take whatever cause and effect was lying around.

I could feel my anger, an equal and opposite reaction to his shoving. But I had submitted so often, not only to cops, but the control they symbolized, that a truly rebellious response had always seemed unthinkable. Might stay unthinkable, I thought. No!

When I finally got up from the bench and waded back to shore, I realized I'd stayed out too long. A middle-aged woman, dressed in a housecoat, baseball cap, and hiking boots, was busily producing clanking noises from behind the green shield of a Coleman. Her tent was a huge, brown pavilion, with a big Ford wagon parked outside.

Since I had no clothes, I figured the next best thing was to act as if I did. After all, that worked nine times out of ten for the emperor.

She looked up. I smiled and waved. She waved back with a spatula and returned to her work. I kept walking, but out of the corner of my eye I saw her suddenly freeze. The spatula fell to the ground. I kept walking. When I got to my tent, I pulled on a pair of cut-offs and cursed luridly. If she complained to the rangers, my cook was goosed for sure. But with an immobile motorcycle, there was nothing I could do but stay in place.

So, philosophically, I ate. Breakfast consisted of dates and coffee; not much else remained edible. Then I cleaned up the site and spread out my clothes to dry. There were dirty bootprints on most of it. Then I turned to Frank, with the busted cable poking forlornly above his handlebars. Thirteen miles in to Oxford for a new cable. Unless I could jury-rig something, I was in for a long walk or an aggravating hitchhike. I got out my tools.

I was in luck. The cable had snapped next to the lead ball on the end. It was an old cable; it might be stretched enough to give me slack to tie a knot in the end. I could pull it tight with pliers and use it in place of the lead ball.

While I worked, the woman in the housecoat and a man emerged from their brown tent. The man, muscular, with an omega of greying hair around the top of his head, saw me looking at them and waved in a noncommittal fashion. After they ate and cleaned up, they struck camp. There was nothing angry or hurried in their movements. Phew!

The clutch lever seemed to work well enough to get me into Oxford, where I could get a replacement, and get down to the business of exhuming William Faulkner. My clothes were still damp, so I let the sun work on them while I went for a walk. I took a footpath that went north, but stopped when I saw that it led right back up to the road. Other way. The couple in the Ford had departed. On the spot where the brown tent had been, a white square of paper fluttered under a stone. Curious, I picked it up. It read, "Thanks! You made my weekend!"

I continued to the south, meeting stiff resistance from the underbrush, and angled up to the road in search of a path. I wondered if the man from the brown tent knew what interesting enthusiasms the woman had. I figured he probably did.

I reached the road without finding a path and began to climb the embankment. Then I saw *him!* and instantly dropped, worming my way back down the bank. Nestled in a hollow on the other side of the road, W. Jones sat in his patrolcar. I didn't think he had seen me. He wasn't expecting me on foot; he was waiting for the sight and sound of a motor-cycle leaving a restricted area.

I sat on weeds and hard stones and tried to think. I wasn't too suc-cessful because of the anger singing along my nerves. Then I had the sort of inspiration that makes horns pop out on the foreheads of Dennis-the-Menace heroes in the Sunday funnies of your mind. As soon as I con-ceived the impulse, I knew I would go for it.

Back at camp. I struck the tent and packed all my gear as fast as I could, lashing it to Frank's patient back. My plan depended on speed. Green means GO! I sprinted back up the bank, far enough away from Jonesie's nook so that he couldn't see me.

I crossed the road, went up the hill, and around behind him. From my vantage above, I saw an arm in a brown sleeve languidly extend from the car window, stub a cigarette on the spotlight mount, then toss it on the ground. That butt joined a circle of half-a-dozen others. Some ranger, I thought. Just give me another fifteen minutes, honky!

I used three of them to go through the woods quietly, until I was above the cattle grate that Frank had rattled the previous night. That remembered rattle was the focus of my inspiration. Some of its bars were loose; the rest might need some encouragement. I spied an oak log with one white branch gleaming in the sun. Hard or rotten? I gripped it in both hands. It had been weathered into steel. I shoved against it with all my weight and it broke with a sharp CRACK that echoed through the woods. I hoped the sound would pass through Jones' unconscious like a pebble in a pond. Maybe I was asking a lot of his unconscious, but then I was sure there was a lot there to ask.

I slid down the hillside with my tool. The first three bars pried up easily. They were made of thick steel, shaped like railroad rails, eight to each side of the grate. The next two gave me trouble, the rest none at all. I reset them with their ends barely catching on the iron angle where they had been embedded in tar.

I left the row on the northbound side of the road intact. I had no intention of involving John Doe and the family Pinto in an episode with my bearpit. But I had to move fast if Jones was going to be the first to sample my little surprise. I pushed aside a moment of fear, and a clear ex-hilaration took its place. Past the point of no return.

Run through the woods! I moved twice as fast and yet more quiet-ly than before. I shadowed across the road, jumped and slid down the bank, and ran over to my bike. Frank started at the tickle of a button, something I had to thank the warm morning sun for.

Jones probably expected to hear me when I started up. I had news for him. My Hooker header didn't begin to cut in and trumpet until

4,000 rpm, and I intended on keeping it under 3,000 for a while. Slipping the clutch extravagantly, I putted down the footpath that led north and up to the road.

I went about a mile down the road, warming up the engine, memorizing the degrees of arc in each bend and every patch in the pavement. Then I stopped and turned. I cinched my helmet down, patted Frank on the tank, flexed my gloved hands. Then I took a huge bite of throttle.

"Here goes nothin!"

Frank cracked redline through the first three gears. The pipe lashed out a long stream of sound that flourished in the air. That howl was Jones' alarm clock; his nap was over!

Couldn't make it into fourth gear. I needed throttle play to slow for turns, high rpm's to jackrabbit out of them. But I knew that the curve around the camp, and past Jones' hangout, swept wide and long with an increasing radius . . . and I was into it right now! I kicked into fourth and flashed past Jones simultaneously. At this speed, he could see nothing that would confirm my identity, but he'd probably have a pretty good idea. As I passed him I felt, rather than saw, his rooflight come on and begin to revolve, and dust spurting from his rear wheels as he cranked up and came after me.

The grate! I swerved over to the intact rails, barely avoiding my own trap! A glance in the rear-views showed Jones in hot pursuit. I shot a look ahead, then glanced back as I heard a tremendous THUMP . . . and I had a vision of Jones' patrolcar veering across the road, front bumper five feet off the ground, front wheels canted inward at an improbable angle. Then sounds of shrieking rubber, metal, and breaking glass surged from behind to mingle with Frank's exhaust as we jetted away!

I had dared to counterattack the bogey! Intoxicating. But I'd only taken the first round. If my name came to be linked in a causal relationship to the crumpled patrolcar, I could be on the receiving end of a *bunch* of flak from the boys-in-brown. My plans had only taken me this far, but now I saw something else I had to have: an alibi.

Even though my instincts were to cut and run, the more I appeared a fugitive, the greater my chances of getting caught. It sounded crazy but it seemed true—the best method of getting away was to stay. So I headed for Oxford, to see if I could assemble an alibi. I probably only had a few minutes to play with while they tried to figure out what had happened, so I jacked Frank up to a hundred-and-ten.

I didn't have to slow until I reached town. A small but enthusiastic thunderstorm was squatting over Oxford. As soon as I zoomed into the outskirts of town, wet hell broke loose. Without a sprinkle of warning, I ran into a barrage of rain so intense it nearly blew me off the seat. Sheets of water and hail slammed against my faceshield and chest. Visibility dropped to the distance from the end of my nose to the faceshield. Not wanting to wind up as a hood ornament for some joker redballing through the deluge, I got over on the shoulder. As I putted along just short of stalling, Frank's rear end began to slew around in a sickening manner. I stopped, got off, and stared in disbelief as the rear tire squished down until the wheel sat on the rim. I had picked up a nail.

I made a brief try at cussing, but the situation simply outstripped my vocabulary. Cold rain trickled down my collar. When I raised my arms to adjust it, cold rain poured down my cuffs. "Goddammit Frank! Am I gonna have to change your name to Calamity Jane? How about Addie Bundren?"

It was obvious. I'd been cursed by something as soon as I'd come near Oxford. Almost as if the course of human events—here more than elsewhere—was subject to a force of destiny utterly opposed, or at best indifferent, to human will. At any odds, something calculated to induce despair. Did Faulkner, I wondered, simply report this force? Or did he create it?

I tried to get a grip on the situation. From my first time through, I remembered a motorcycle shop in town, just a couple blocks from my present location. Loaded, Frank was too heavy to push. But if I put him in first gear and walked along side playing with the clutch, and if the knot didn't pull out of the cable . . . . We made it. But by the time I walked under the sheet of water cascading from the eaves of the shop, I could feel two forces vying for dominance in my mind.

The first seemed kind of an inclusive despair, kith and kin to the psychic claustrophobia that had driven me from Tallahassee, echoed by the sensation of being caught within the walls of Cheney's apartment.

The second was the same kind of tough elation that I remembered learning from the Alabama bean farmer. That state of mind Push had been pushing . . . what did he call it? 'Goodbye to rains' was the phrase that kept cropping up. 'Reigns' too. What I'd felt when I'd decided to give Jones' energy back to him.

I put my will into arriving at the much more pleasurable and confident second state of mind, but the best I could do was a half-assed compromise between them.

As I squelched through the back door, I could hear someone thrashing around in the back of the shop, disentangling himself from his work. A wall clock above the counter clicked loudly, advancing itself one minute. On a sudden inspiration I climbed up on the counter, leaned over and set the clock back half-an-hour. Then I jumped down and stood in a gathering puddle on the floor.

A short, wizened man came around a partition, wiping his hands on a rag. His face was like a dried apple, with two strips of white, fuzzy fungus down the cheeks for sideburns. "Hee hee," he squeaked when he saw me. "Kinda damp outside, eh?"

"No," I said. "I'm a salesman for drip-dry leather clothes. You interested?"

"Hee hee hee," he said. "Don't let it rile you. We get pissant summer thunderstorms like this all the time. Hit'll be over in a minute, and hot again in an hour. What can I do for you?"

"Fix a flat and replace a clutch cable."

He glanced outside at the bike. "You drove in here like that?"

I shrugged modestly.

He looked up at the clock and seemed bewildered for a second. Then he scratched a sideburn with one greasy fingernail.

"Tell you what. I got one mechanic out with a broke leg and a high school boy that don't come on 'til three, but I might could fit you in. Come on back and check at five, if that suits you. That's right before we close."

"It does. You got a bathroom I can change in?"

"Yah. That door over in the corner. Now, don't change too much or I won't reckonize you when you come back. Hee hee."

Bizarre little man. I pushed Frank into the work area, got some clothes out that were only damp, and went in to change. On my way, I climbed up and switched the clock back. Well, I had my alibi. I also had the remainder of the afternoon to make myself look even more innocent; and perhaps get those coordinates on Faulkner....

It was as the apple-faced elf had prophesied. The rag-ends of the storm were quickly tearing up and blowing away. The entire town of Oxford looked like it had just emerged from a carwash. I walked past the Sonic drive-in, turned right, walked two blocks, and suddenly fell into a dream.

The set of *Intruder In The Dust*. Directly before me rose the heroic statue of a Confederate soldier on a pedestal. Behind him in the center of the square was the courthouse, resembling a train depot with its square facades and huge oblongs of dusty window. There was a live oak on the lawn, hundreds of years old, still used as a bulletin board for announcements and legal notices. The trunk was lumped and warted where the staples and nails of the past had been absorbed into the bark. Just as the messages themselves had been absorbed into the life of the county.

93

A row of benches facing outward from the east side were occupied by old men in sunglasses, suspenders, and Panama hats. They were mostly silent as they contemplated the slow eddy of activity around the square. They stretched their wattled necks forward like aged vultures, and leaned their chins on the heads of their canes.

The front steps of the courthouse had been worn low in the center by Manyfoot, the centipede of human history. In the building's cool interior, these same feet had turned the floor tile black, making even cracks between the squares indecipherable.

A woman in the offices of "Buddy East—Sheriff" took the ticket Jones had given me. She was a plump woman about forty, with face and figure as square as a series of stacked boxes. She *was* the Law. The bra under her prim blouse seemed as rigid and metallic as the front bumper on an old Cadillac.

Despite my (elaborately contrived) air of cheerful innocence as I paid the fine, her manner with me was cold, brittle, and *very* patient. She looked at me as if she were a commanding officer of the Salvation Army and I an unrepentant derelict caught drinking Sterno on the premises for the fortieth time.

Finally I burst out of the courthouse into fresh air. I stopped at the sight of the old men on the benches. A breeze came by, and they all nodded to it like so many dry stalks of harvested corn.

Yet I knew their unfocused eyes were simply cast back, wandering in the pasttime, where the roots of the bloom of now were entangled. I was struck by the thought that some of them probably had known Faulker personally. . . .

I picked out my man; or rather, my woman. She was the only female presence, and she sat on a bench by herself. Obviously she was an intruder upon this special zone of aged male reminiscence, yet through persistent reappearance had won a kind of acceptance. She was several circles in towards the center, but still attainable for an outsider like myself.

Unlike all the males, she was alert and alive in the present as well as the past. Her thin-brimmed black straw hat cast all her face into the shadow, except for an enormous nose that protruded aggressively into the sunlight. A receding chin emphasized the nose still further, as did a pair of glasses, perched on it like a strange insect of wire limbs and glass wings. Blue eyes shone behind the lenses, eyes I was sure had been unobtrusively watching me ever since I left the courthouse. As I walked up, she pretended interest in the patch of sidewalk just to my left.

"Good afternoon, ma'am," I said.

"Afternoon," she confirmed, looking up.

"My name's Steve Getane, ma'am. Could I talk to you some about your town?"

"Ah suppose," she said dryly. "Seems like you've got your heart set on it. My name is Louise Radclift, sir. Cleared up after the rain, eh? But it'll heat up again soon. . . ." I touched her extended hand, and she made room for me on the bench. I noted that a tear in the armpit seam of her floral print dress had been mended clumsily with brown thread. I glanced at her hands. Knobby fingers slanted at a bizarre angle from her palms—heavy arthritis.

Her eyes impaled me when I raised mine. "What is it you want to know about?" she asked in a severe voice.

"Well, a few things about Bill Faulkner."

"Mmmm-hmmm. Seems like every Yankee that comes through town, that's all they want to talk about. It's wuss than ever it was when he lived here."

"I ain't a Yankee!" I protested, sidling back toward my optional Southern accent. "I was born and raised in Florida!"

"Well then, you're just *almost* a Yankee," she conceded. "Go on and ask your questions. Maybe Ah can he'p you, maybe Ah cain't. Could be Ah'll have questions of my own to put to you, aftuh you'ah through with youahs."

"Hard to say just what I want. I don't think the truth of a man is something you get at with just questions and answers."

With a nod, Louise allowed this was true.

"Seems like I'll either get pulled to what I'm looking for by a kind of luck, or something I'll draw out of the whole picture of what happens to me in Oxford. Including, maybe, a few questions. . . ?" Her expression was resigned. "How well did you know him?"

"Tolerable well. Ah was a neighbor while we was growin up. Later, my husband used to do soil conservation work out near his farm, and we got to know him again.

"Hank had a steam-shovel and a ditch-digger, and both those machines fascinated him. He'd come out with his lunch in a knapsack and watch for hours. He said seein 'em machines chaw rocks all day without bustin gave him faith in hidden wheels. Hank said ever once in a while he'd say something like that, and the niggers would look at him funny. We all liked to hear about it, though. Y'could tell he was a man that thought about things."

"Did he ever talk to you or Hank about writing?"

"Oh gad no. He hated to do that wuss'n anything. Some mornin's I'd see him out in front of his house after breakfast. We'd stop and chat about, oh weather an crops an politics; but let a journalist or some other kind of busybody pop up to ask him about his life or writin, and he'd just stare 'em down with those little black eyes of his. Then he'd turn on his heel and stride back into his house without a word.''

Louise laid her fragile, gnarled hands on her knee. Her huge nostrils sniffed once, as if savoring a wind from a lost year. Her eyes focused dreamily on a patch of sky.

"Beats all how a man can give himself to something, then hate and love it both for the rest of his life. You know? An that goes for a woman, a piece of land, a job, or what-all. Writin shore gave Bill a hard time. He used to play checkers over at the courthouse, but he had to cut it out 'cos people were allus comin up to ask about writin. Even if that happened in the middle of a game, he'd still get up and walk off.''

"Which didn't endear him to the other players.''

"Nossir, it didn't. He had friends among the fishermen and hunters, though. Around the campfire, he always told the best stories. Later on he had a few problems. Publishin' essays favorin integration turned a lot of people agin him locally. They didn't know he had the vision to see it comin. After he explained it to me, I could see he was right. 'Course I had more sense than to go shooten my mouth off about it in town.''

"And all the time you knew him, he never talked to you about writing?''

"Oh, once or twice. He said it was like milking a bull to get money from novels. So when he needed cash-in-hand, he'd send out a coupla what they call *short* stories. Remember how he useta write 'em. He'd send a chest of cracked ice and a case of whiskey out to his farm. Then he'd go out, with a colored fella name of Jenkins that used to take care of him when he got drunk. They wouldn't come back into town until that chest of ice was all gone! Heh!''

I laughed with her, remembering hours of threading my way through Faulkner's lush jungles of prose, with the words like lianas and creepers incredibly, and at times magnificently, involved...almost swelling with life, frequently shifting before my eyes to reveal a new expanse of unsuspected meanings. It was amusing to imagine Faulkner downing a double belt of his favorite bourbon, rolling up his sleeves and plunging into the labyrinthine possibilities of a sentence.

"Ever read any of his books?''

Louise looked distinctly uneasy.

"Well now, I *began* several, just never got around to finishin any. He never would use his punctuation right. Some of those sentences just rattle on for *pages,* you know? He was a great one for commas and those semicolons. But he was pure hell on periods. Hank used to say that we oughta give him a book full of periods for Christmas."

Louise fell silent, and so did I. We watched people moving slowly in and out of stores around the square, a tangled procession of the faithful, weaving around the shrines of commerce.

"This square pretty much the way it was when he was here?"

"Yep. Matter of fact, sometimes when the moon is shinin just so, I swear I can 'most see him, walking down these streets, wearin that same old tweed jacket with them leather patches on the elbows. But he's been buried for years now, and his wife with him. Her body came back recently and almost nobody turned out to see her under. She never got any awards."

"He buried around here?"

"Oh yes, not more'n a mile away. Want to go see him?"

She didn't ask if I wanted to see the grave or the stone, but to see *him,* as if a tangible ghost were somehow available for comment. I chose my reply with care."

"Yes. I would like to see him."

Louise's eyes glittered behind her crystal lenses as she got stiffly up from the bench. "C'mon," she said. "We'll take my car."

I studied her as we drove to the graveyard in an antiquated, but carefully maintained Pontiac sedan. Her aged anteater's profile invited an impression of the ludicrous, but she held herself with a consummate dignity. She was getting old and she knew it. She was nobody's fool, and she knew that too. She was cautious of me but innately generous and willing to help. I liked her.

The crumbling light of late afternoon had a Vermeer-like quality that lent a strong and strange beauty to her features. It occurred to me then that old age was something of which I need not be afraid.

We drove slowly on a lane through the tombstones. Ironic twist on the old legend: here men had been sown and dragon's teeth had sprouted. We parked near a huge oak. Under its spreading branches, I saw a granite stone with FAULKNER etched on it in block letters. A weird, necromantic excitement mounted inside of me. Ah, tingle of the astrolabe.

The graveslab itself offered the legend, "Beloved, Go With God."

That shook me. What subterranean faith did this bespeak of a man whose troubled characters struggled for survival in an antagonistic, practically godless universe? Even the best of them were graceless, outcast, like saints in Hell, enduring only by a blind, deathless grip on the shreds of the last nobility in their souls. Perhaps "Go With God" was the message I was looking for, but it left me unsatisfied. I wanted his spirit to erupt then and there from the Mississippi clay, so I could demand: "How could this be your last word? How did this come to be written over you?"

I knew that spirit would only gaze at me with black, unfathomable eyes as I blurted the questions, then turn on his heel and stride back into the earth without a word.

I was startled from my reverie by the clash of shovels. Nearby, two black gravediggers were working on a new hole, their spades flashing in the sun as they flourished above the edge. Clots of red clay shot through the air. Their voices drifted to me.

"She gonna pay fo' it, hey?"

"Yah. Guess she wanted him in her ho' one las' time!"

Their laughter was low and delighted.

I turned to Louise Radclift.

"Well, I've seen it. But I don't know what to make of it. Might as well go."

She nodded. We walked to her car, drove slowly back out. Suddenly she stopped, pointing out the window to one stone among the hundreds, bearing another name that the flesh beneath it had forgotten long ago.

"That's where my husband's buried," she said. There was something tragic and caressing in her voice. I looked at her quickly, expecting an expression of grief. There was none. But under the folds and gathers of flesh I could almost discern an emotion that a younger, more toned face might have revealed more clearly, but less poignantly. In that final moment before we drove on, I saw a reluctant acceptance of fact mingled with a stubborn denial of defeat, and a love drawn so tenuous by the departure of the beloved that that love had either to become irrevocably strong, or crumble in upon itself in the despair of the faithless aged. This woman had chosen to make it strong and timeless. Not that those things that appear and vanish quickly in time—a flower, a glance or moment of unspoken poetry—do not have their own beauty and worth, but a human can have both these things and achieve something that goes beyond them, reaching down into the well of the timeless real from which both flowers and instants of unspoken poetry spring.

"My God," I thought, "she still loves him!" In that instant I began to feel and understand something about Faulkner and these people of whom he wrote—that the gauntlet of death and betrayal and pain, of the violation of honor and the decay of ideals, through which his characters moved, formed not a repudiation of the human soul, the human heart, but a tremendous challenge to it. And even someone overwhelmed by this wave of awesome darkness, if he denies defeat with his last strength, achieves his victory.

I gradually became aware that Louise Radclift was talking.

"...brought that movie to town! One of the few things he did that made him popular as well as famous. All folks talked about for months. That store where the murder was? Right over there. That quicksand pit where they threw the body is near a bridge five or six miles from here."

We circled the square.

"Now. Down that street is the *Oxford Eagle*. Some years ago they ran a special edition. Had reprints in it of everything Bill'd written for the paper and most of what they'd written about him. Saw 'em advertising to sell copies of that edition last week. You go down there, you just might be able to get one."

"Sounds good."

She slid the old Pontiac into a parking space and turned off the engine. We looked at each other for a second; then we touched hands.

"Thanks," I said. "You've shown me something, and not just about Faulkner."

"What do y'mean?" she said.

I felt embarrassed. "Love," I told her. "The love you keep alive both for him and your husband. I don't think I've quite seen or felt it this way, this clearly before."

She nodded and squinted. Something twitching at the corners of her mouth suggested a smile of inner amusement. I suddenly saw that she had been studying me as much as I her.

"Wal," she said, "enjoyed showing you around. And as it turns out, Ah don't have any questions Ah need to ask you."

"Goodbye," I said. "Take care of yourself Mrs. Radclift."

"That's what Ah've bin doin! Goodbye, Mr. Getane. Have a nice vacation."

I clomped down the sidewalk towards the *Eagle*. A few neon signs attached to venerable storefronts tried for an air of modernity and failed utterly.

As I walked, through a smudged plate window, a photograph of William Faulkner caught my eye. And another, and another. One entire wall of this shop was devoted to photographs of him! A veritable montage of *cartes de visite*.

I saw no one inside. Very carefully, I pushed open the door. I feared arousing some tourist-gouging shopkeeper who'd try to sell me a packet of Faulkner Fotos, very nice, only $15.00. As I eased myself in, a bell tacked to the door frame emitted the tiniest of tinkles. There were all sorts of framed prints inside; only one wall was devoted to Faulkner. Some shots of local sports heroes had been autographed. There was a desk covered with papers, a floor covered with heel marks and dust, and a coatrack from which a faded umbrella swung.

A thick curtain had been drawn back from the entrance to the second half of the shop. Back in the shadows I could only see one thing, a huge bellows camera mounted on a tripod. Its varnished wood and brass fittings gave the impression that it was quite an antique. Perhaps it was even Civil War vintage, like the collodion plate cameras used by Brady and Gardner. It stood there like a single emphatic, if forlorn, exhibit in a photographic museum.

I was turning back to the wall of Faulkner photographs when a man surprised me by emerging from the dark back room. He wore black, baggy trousers, a stiff-looking white shirt and a maroon bow tie. He had the lantern jaw, square shoulders, and slim hips of a once athletic and handsome body. He moved with something of an athlete's confidence, something of an old man's care, chagrined that he must exercise it.

I knew at once he was the photographer from his eyes. Though they were rheumy with years, something alert and almost predatory radiated from them. Perhaps, I thought, this was the kind of vision that came from regarding the world with a view toward snaring those moth-winged instants when the reality of someone or something truly shows itself...in the proper light, at the proper time, and once only.

"Ah," he said. "Afternoon. And getting hot outside, eh?"

I wondered gloomily if every conversation around here began with a reference to the weather. Oh well. If you can't lick 'em....

"Yeah. Does it cool off at night, or just keep getting hotter until August, when everything melts?"

I didn't pay much attention to what I was saying, even less to his reply. I was becoming increasingly captivated by the photographs.

It was quite a collection, beginning with a rakish and jaunty young Faulkner in his Canadian R.A.F. uniform. Then in shirtsleeves, ready to fish. Outside of Rowan Oak, a relaxed family man. Jumping a thoroughbred over a split-rail fence. Faulkner on the set of *Intruder in the Dust*. Faulkner amused, Faulkner melancholy. In the center was a large portrait of him in his favorite, final role—the accomplished writer and country squire. The outfit was impeccable: black top hat, red jacket, white jodhpurs, clipped military mustache. The pose was stiffly ceremonial and unyielding. There was a vast sadness and weariness about the eyes.

I felt I could almost perceive the life force that moved between these images, these slices of light out of time. I had the impression that remnants of Faulkner's passage on this planet were before me now, even more so than in the Oxford cemetery. Not words, not the most carefully produced painting, can evoke a moment of lost time as strongly as a good photograph. And these were good.

"I'm Colonel Cofield, son." His eyes noticed me noticing the signature at the corner of a matte board. Those eyes missed nothing.

"You took all of these?" He nodded. "You must've known him a long time." There was envy in my voice, for that experience.

"It's not how long you know someone that makes it possible to photograph him," the Colonel reproved. "It's how well. I knew him both well and long. You've read some of his short stories? I helped him mail the first ones off. Look up here."

He pointed at a framed page from the *Saturday Evening Post.* It bore the illustration of a pair of WWI planes poised in stalls, amid spectacular explosions, about fifteen feet above the English Channel. Under this romantic misconception of a dogfight, a line of elegant script announced, " 'Thrift'—by William Faulkner."

"Not many people think to ask," the Colonel said, "but that's the first one he ever sold. Concerns a Scottish pilot who goes to war. All he leaves behind is one cow, that neighbors are to take care of for him. Now, while all his mates are drinking and playing poker, he's scrimping on every bit of his pay. To send home for the cow, y'know...."

The Colonel saw that I was only lending him one ear. My attention had been snagged by the photos again. This time I was looking at two framed halftones, one hung above the other. The upper one was a three-quarter profile of Faulkner himself, shot in a studio with hard light and printed medium contrast. The one beneath it was taken from the same angle, but it was a picture of a bronze bust of Faulkner, which had obviously used the upper photograph as a study.

The pair of photographs produced a fascinating reverberation bewteen art forms. A Faulkner had lived; his body had reflected light; a camera had trapped a moment of it. A bust was made after this photograph, and another picture had been taken of that. Now these hung together on the stage, while the original source of the image had tiptoed off into the wings, down the stairs, out the alley. Gone into the rain-haunted night.

I looked back and forth between the two images, pursuing the echo between the flesh and the bronze, convinced that this reverberation had some sort of secret to yield.

"Ah. You notice that." Colonel Cofield was pleased. "In that bust, something so different from the actual flesh...." He gestured in the air with his long, slim hands, "as if the sculptor were moving the head through time in two directions at once, making him both older and younger."

Something clicked in my perceptions. These two views, one interpretive and one strictly representational, crisscrosssed at the man. Gazing at them together was like experiencing the parallax view in astronomy, where a given star is viewed from two different points simultaneously, to estimate its distance and magnitude.

The photograph of the actual flesh reported a compact skull with a high forehead, tilted at an angle of defiance. Yet the mask of muscle and skin seemed to have slipped on the aquiline bone, drawn downward by weariness, hangover, age, and vision. Sags around the jawline and eye suggested that the earth had begun to finally assert its proprietorship, through the imperative of gravity. Flesh must be returned to the clay from which it has been borrowed; the consciousness within that has struggled to achieve its vision, purpose, or statement—moving with or against the current of time—must in the end surrender that body back to the earth.

But the vision of the sculptor had nullified the earth, had held the steadily beckoning hand of mortality at bay. On the face of the bust the wrinkles and lines of experience remained, the messages of time were still written into what had been the smooth tablet of young flesh. But these lines were drawn back against the bone, not down, and revealed the profile of an indelible Faulkner who had escaped from time into a personification of his own vision. I saw that he had not existed utterly *as* the flesh, but as an energy and an understanding and a will somewhere within and beneath it, surfacing in his written art, in a piece of sculpture, in the minds and hearts of those who knew him...and, I began to believe, somewhere above and beyond that plot in the Oxford cemetery where the irrevocable earth seemed to be having the last word.

Colonel Cofield also had become rapt in contemplation of the photographs. Looking at him, I saw his flesh also succumbing to that same insistent downward pressure of bedrock and soil.

He and Louise Radclift were different in that where Louise had a natural warmth and vitality to which she added dignity and reserve, the Colonel seemed to possess an innate aristocratic poise that he sought to modify with a democratic friendliness. But they were alike in this respect: they were both old people whose wills to *be* had at last worn through to the surface of their lives.

Then I realized that the Colonel's fascination with the photographs—he had to have seen them thousands of times—had its roots in a rich understanding. These three Faulkners: the photograph, the sculpture, and the invisible consciousness (a consciousness *still* creating its effects, thus endowed with being in the present and the future) were one and the same! And the strength and wounded beauty praised by the sculptor's hand had been found in Faulkner's face not despite his mortality, but rather precisely because he had existed within that haunted flesh. He had thought, acted, created and endured under the intolerable sensation of open eyes, the joy and burden of love and the shadow and pain of unlove, advancing age, beckoning death...in a world that could not but fail to satisfy him.

It was not just her innate spirit or heart, but both interacting with this life and the death it embraced, that had given Louise Radclift the timeless love that had so shocked me in the Oxford cemetery. It was spirit and flesh joined that gave the earth the chance to create the phenomenon of human presence: presences, that could then themselves proceed to create their own significance and strange beauty, just as Radclift and Cofield and Faulkner had. I felt staggered by this magnificent adventure that we were all on together. I could feel myself on the verge of some great understanding, that would bring me closer than ever to the object of my search.

"Read this."

The Colonel pointed to a yellow index card. Lines of poetry had been hand-printed on it in India ink.

> "...a voice telling me that work I must,
> for everything will be the same
> when I am dead a thousand years.
> I wish I were a bust, all head."

"He got his wish, didn't he?" the Colonel smiled ruefully. "Y'know," he said, " we delight in telling such exquisite lies about ourselves. A photographer must see more of that than anyone."

I nodded.

"People want shots from their 'good' side only, with their pimples brushed out and halos dodged in. We try to purchase enticing visions of ourselves at the expense of our true lives, our true flesh. In many ways, Bill was no different."

He indicated the portrait of the country squire, dressed to kill. "Ole Count No-count. But these," he pointed to the profile and the sculpture that had been taken from it, "show something more at the *core*. Bill was a man of principle. If one of his friends was under fire from the entire world, Bill was the kind of man who would go and stand beside him. In fact, if Bill had been St. Peter, I think there would have been four crosses on Calvary."

"I suspect that's true," I said.

My gaze wandered out the window to the streets of Oxford. I was shaken from my speculations by a clock on a shopfront across the street. I saw—with a start— that it read five-to-five. I felt like a swimmer surfacing rapidly after a deep dive.

"Colonel, I'm sorry," I said. "I want to talk with you a great deal more, but I've got to get my motorcycle out of a shop. You've already given me a lot to think about. Maybe I'll be able to make it back at some point."

"Well" he extended one tremulous hand and patted me awkwardly on the shoulder, "I've enjoyed talking to you too, son. I always enjoy talking with people who want to understand about Bill. A lot of people in this town never knew what a good man they had living among them. Many still don't. You've got to do this..." (with the wink of a wise eye, the Colonel bent his elbow rapidly several times as he raised an imaginary shot glass to his lips) "...with a man a couple times, before you find out what he's really like."

"Well Colonel, if I come back and I'm not on my way to the slammer, we'll have to do *this*..." (I bent my elbow in a conspiratorial salute) "...a couple times together."

"Look me up!" he chuckled.

"I will, sir. Goodbye."

"Goodbye sir!"

VI.
The
Empress
Reversed

I walked rapidly back through Oxford, checking all approaches to the motorcycle shop for lurking patrolcars. The coast was clear.

The desire to get it on and get it gone sparked and burned. Since I didn't have the contemplation-time to do it justice, I jammed all of my recent experience into the darkroom of my mind, to sort out later. It'd be interesting to see what my subconscious did with it.

Frank sat outside the shop on his centerstand, looking sleek, sassy and ready to roll.

Inside, the fuzzy elf was busily tidying up his cash drawer. "Aha! You made it," he said. "I was all set to write you a note telling you what pawn shop to pick up your bike at. Hee!"

"Good thing you didn't," I said. "Or I would've had to leave a note telling your wife what hospital to pick *you* up at. Hee-hee."

"I'm not married," he deadpanned.

"I can't understand why."

He rooted around on the counter, and handed me a yellow worksheet and bill. "Tire patch and clutch cable, with installation, comes to $15.57."

I gave him a fifty, and as he counted out my change he impressed me with his ability to whip small bills out of the drawer. I was particularly impressed by the extra ten bucks I received, in fives. I decided I'd been burned by enough Honda partsmen to keep it.

"Gettin' kind of late," he said. "Where you plannen' on spendin' the night?"

Something in the look in his small, twinkling eyes made me retreat into fantasy. "I'm staying in town with a friend," I told him. "Bear Flemson. Know him?"

"Yeah," he said, unenthusiastically. About the same way I'd respond to the same question.

"And after that, I'm off back home to Miami. So, thanks for the work on my putt. So long!"

"Long enough. Hee hee hee! Don't get it bit by no crockigators!"

Shaking my head, I went outside. As Frank warmed up, I checked the tire. Firm. The clutch cable was adjusted perfectly, and had graphite grease running well down into the housing. He'd done it right.

I realized I didn't want to keep the old fruit's ten bucks. But if I gave it back now, I'd have to admit I'd originally intended to keep it. Then I thought about Push's rap on achieving freedom via follow-through on selected impulse. A bit of embarrassment was a small price to pay.

I swung off the bike and went back into the shop. The man was closing windows and turning off lights. "Here," I said. "You gave me too much. I just decided not to keep it."

He stared at me, astonished.

"Bye now," I said. "Watch out for them allidiles."

Then I hopped on Frank and tooled off to the edge of town, where I pulled over and paused. Whither? The answer wasn't long in coming. My best move was one I'd be unlikely to make, were I guilty of stacking a ranger's patrolcar. I turned my front wheel towards Sardis Reservoir.

Frank ran well, and the air was fragrant. I passed the kudzu, the turn, the same curves . . . then came to a place where black tire marks veered off the road into a patch of torn earth, and on into a tree that bore a terrific gouge in its trunk. Bits of metal, glass, and paint glittered in the late afternoon sun.

Even though the loosened bars had been replaced, red cones and a pair of sawhorses directed traffic to the intact side of the cattle grate. There was no sign of Jonesie's car. I looked around no more than any curious passer-by, then went on in search of a campsite. Going by my old site, looking at the view out over the shimmering water, I heaved a sigh of regret. But going back down there again would've been just a little *too* brazen.

The road over the dam gave me an even better view of the lake. It was much larger than I had thought. Even though the air was clear, the farther shore was not visible. Things were like that, sometimes. The more ways you looked at them the bigger they got.

Another campsite. To my surprise, the sign by the entrance gave grudging permission for motorcycles to enter.

At first, I didn't want to. The place was packed with huge, obscene-looking rec vehicles and trailers. I had a revulsion for the way these artifacts of technological opulence destroyed the very beauty they allegedly came to observe. But there was less of a crowd at the north end of the camp, and I went over to explore. I found a grove of young pines, up to their adolescent, coniferous ankles in castoff needles. Perfect.

Another reason for selecting this spot: it was a stoned throw away from a circle of tents I mistook for a snookery of girl scouts. I'd always had a weak-spot in my libido for these cookie-pushing cuties, ever since I'd visited a cousin who was throwing a slumber party for her senior troop. I was in the early throes of puberty at the time, and the glimpse of a few pearly thighs formed the stuff of depraved fantasies for an entire summer.

The sky was becoming overcast. A cool evening breeze had begun to mutter Druidic wisdom in my circle of pines. I pitched my tent, then cooked my poor bhikku's dinner of brown rice from the one sack left unravaged by Jones, and laced it with Tamari soy.

I sat with my back to a tree and spooned in the warm food. On the dusty road that went past the nearest tents, I watched laughing, delighted children hold footraces. A few adults had gathered nearby, rooting for winners and losers with a hearty impartiality. Hard to say which of them was having a better time. But I had to give up my affectionate vision of a snookery of girl scouts. I didn't realize who these people were until they left the twilit road, and began to assemble in the center of their circle of tents. I heard the clash of unfolding chairs and a preacher's opening exhortations. Then I knew—I had camped alongside a coven of Baptists.

There was a silence, then they began to sing. These were not the polished harmonies and cadences of a practiced choir, but the simple, strong harmonies of voices gathered from farms, garages, kitchens and stores. If anything, I had an anti-theistic background, but these working people and their children singing praise to the good they found in their lives, spellbound me with their beauty, their uncomplicated sincerity.

I wondered what Carl Wiggins in Jackson would've thought.

The sound rose up in a gentle column, librarian sopranos on the top, bass mechanics rolling on the bottom. The column spread out through the trees like a mist, and settled back down with a drifting fall like a rain of cottonwood seeds.

HE'S THE LILY OF THE VALLEY
ITS BRIGHT NEW MORNING STAR

Footsteps crunched up in the pine needles behind me. The footsteps stopped. I didn't *want* to turn—fearing I would see, what I in fact saw, when I forced myself to do it—a young, burly ranger in his brown uniform and Baden-Powell hat, his thumbs hooked over the buckle of a thick, black belt. The crescent of shadow from the hat's wide brim obscured most of his face, but he seemed to be staring at me with accusation.

"Ungg-g," I said. "Ah, hello."

"Hello hotshot, why you so antsy? You sitting on a sandspur, or what?"

"*Push?* Dammit! You scared the crap out of me again!"

"Just what you need."

He looked over my head at the congregation, and gazed at it for a second.

"Ah-h-h yes. God's glee club gets it on."

I looked at him sharply. "Are you snide and insensitive to human beauty all the time? Or just when you want to impress me with your ability to get crude?"

"Just joking," he apologized. "Actually, the singing fills me with so much reverence and awe, it makes me want to leap up, rush out, and get involved in holy work of some sort."

His tone was so serious it was hard to tell whether he was just taking his mocking to a deeper level, or revealing, at long last, his true nature. Demonic? I wondered. Was it just the presence of the congregation that made me think of the flip-side of their reality? Or had I been for the past week or so in the process of bargaining with Mephistopheles? I remembered how I had feared him the first time we met.

I watched him suspiciously as he circled around me. This put his back to the west, his body between me and the congregation, and his face into deeper shadow than before. The only way I could still recognize him was by his eyes, golden and faintly glowing in the shadows of a green dusk.

He pulled out the tails of his shirt and sat cross-legged about ten feet away. It had been a bullish market for the impulses of Steve Getane these past few days. I felt heady with aggressive confidence. It was time to shift the offensive in my relationship with Push to *his* turf for a spell. It was important for me to find out exactly where he stood on some things. "Push?" I said. "C'mon, give. Are you for or against what these Baptists are doing? Whose side are you on?"

"Whose side am I on?" Push feigned surprise at the question. I say *feigned* because he was such a competent actor; I had no doubt that he could seem any way he chose, for reasons of his own.

"I'm on the side of perception. Asking me whether I'm for or against anything you humans are up to is ludicrous."

He blinked several times and leaned toward me. "Besides, you don't want my answer for itself. You're looking for someone to reinforce your feeling about them." He indicated the Baptist congregation with a jerk of his head, and his voice took on brisk, Madison Avenue disapproval. "That's a chancy trend, chum. Contradictory, searchwise."

IT'S LOVE THAT'S SINGING IN MY SONG

"Remember? You're the one who wanted to cast off all social conditionings, of culture or culture-counter, and leave all your past minds behind to chase something fresh and strange. That right?" Push's voice began to carry a mocking edge of scorn. "Or did you just drop your hip student fantasies to chase some of Kerouac's old fantasies, and drop his to chase some of B.D.'s fantasies about Faulkner's fantasies? Aren't you just trying to find out where I stand, so you can edge over to the same place?"

"NO!" I yelled back at him. "Just because I'm after your slant on something, doesn't mean I'm not putting together what I learn in my own way! Learning from others doesn't have to mean the same thing as having them decide who I am for me! I'm not the same person who used to let that happen."

"No, you're not," Push agreed, mildly. "Just checking. Still, watch out for that tendency. You'll be tempted to reach for it again. Respond as you have, and you'll be safe. You won't need anyone else's opinion to validate how you feel about some singing."

OH COME, COME IN BLESSING, EMMANUEL

"You got that?" Push asked. "Let's try it out." He leaned toward me, spreading his hands as if he were painting an image in midair. "Jones' patrolcar. Now, you really stuck your noodle up a wilecat's ass on that one."

"Now hold on, Pushkin baby. Ain't you the same dude who urged me to follow my impulses?"

"Yep. Now I'm jumping on ahead and urging you to look at the way you pick 'em. For instance, you could've walked up and kissed Jones on the nose. That would've challenged his bastardized authority game and demonstrated your courage just as effectively. But no, you had to kick the hornet's nest for all you were worth. Do you have any idea how many cops are after you?"

"No-o-o," I said, suddenly sobered. "Did he get hurt?"

"Interesting it should occur to you to ask. No, he didn't get hurt too badly, though he did take a sizeable bite out of his steering wheel. He was very surprised."

"Good," I said.

"Don't get me wrong," Push continued. "I enjoyed seeing Jones get what was coming to him. Now, you've got more of the same coming to you. Maybe I'll enjoy watching *that* get delivered. The point is, because of past episodes between bikers and rangers here, there's a dangerous edge between them. You found out about it soon enough after you got here. But instead of walking away, you did something that might aggravate the problem for years. Giving the energy eddy another boost. More innocent bikers than you may inherit worse experiences than yours as a result. So you perpetuate and propagate it. Now, if that's what you meant to have happen, I've got nothing more to say. But if it isn't, then you're a fool, because that's a logical and obvious consequence of what you did."

What about the logical and obvious consequences of Jones, and the others like him, learning you can't shove people around without getting shoved back some day?"

"Ah," Push said. "Which is *more* logical and obvious?" When I didn't answer, Push continued. "Ignoring the effects of what you create is not the same thing as escaping them. Freedom isn't a *carte blanche* for self-expression in a vacuum. It is a *quality* of being that operates in the sphere of cause-and-effect. That's where it makes its living. That means it must choose what will nourish it. Freedom has to be responsible for its own maintenance."

"What about impulses, and the willed violation of conditioning?" I demanded.

"That's a phase, an adolescent phase. You caught on fast and went a long way in a short time. But if you stayed in a state of opposition to your old mind, you'd still be trapped in it, making it more real than it has to be. Believe me, you're ready to go on.

"You may have thought you were showing your freedom to Jones, and in one way you did. But in a larger sense, you surrendered it when you stooped to fight him in an arena he defined. Think about that while you run from cops for the next couple weeks. You used your freedom in such a way as to put it, and potentially even your life, in danger.

"The biggest part of any act is shaping the consequences, not just letting them happen. An act, especially a creative act, is a seed; consequences are that act in bloom. Any fool can act; it takes an artist of life to act in such a way that the consequences nourish his original aim.

"Most humans do not reach this stage. That is why their limited freedom is bound about with law and conditioning, moral and custom. Without these they are lost. Even their rebellions against these reins on them tends to be selfish, unimaginative, and shortsighted. They need restraints so they won't damage themselves or others excessively, and lose what little freedom they have.

"If you want to say goodbye to these reins, you will have to expand yourself in understanding of the structure of reality and the nature of choice. You'll have to take responsibility for the creation of a world within the world where you find yourself."

WHOSE ALMIGHTY HAND LEADS FORTH IN BEAUTY

"I'll mull that over," I said.

"See?" Push said. "You're already doing it. By the time it comes, you'll be ready." The golden lights in his eyes danced.

"What comes?"

"Your appointment."

"Appointment? With whom?"

"Whom do you think?"

I put my head down and thought. The disembodied presence, of course! My storm star! I remembered that sensation of contact with *something other* . . . . I lifted my head to tell Push that I knew, but he was already gone.

A form was still there at a distance, but it was no longer his. His hat had become the peaked roof of a large tent near the center of the Baptist encampment. His shirt had become that tent's sides and walls. Where his eyes had been, I saw two glowing lanterns hung on the poles of the entrance awning.

And as I watched, a girl in a long white nightie came out of the tent, and stood on tiptoe to blow them out, one by one.

I had had on overfull day. Moving slowly, I crawled into my tent and collapsed, fully clothed, on the sleeping bag. The silence was full, dark and unbroken.

Morning. I stretched, yawned, then wormed back out of my nylon tent. No butterfly wings just yet.

Figured I'd make coffee, clean up, pack, and get off to an early start. While my water heated, a strong voice blunted by southern accents began to bludgeon through the air. Next door, the preacher was getting off to an early start as well.

". . . and ONCE you've LOST it, it's GONE FO'EVAH! THE DEVIL IS CONSTANTLY LOOKING FOR WAYS TO DECEIVE YOU!"

As the preacher ranted on, it became clear that he was exhorting the girls to hang on to their maidenheads until they could swap them for a ring, and telling the boys to keep their hands to themselves. Not *too* close, of course.

I signed, and thought "A new be-attitude I give you: blessed are they who pick and choose over what they hear, for they shall be called the ones who know their own minds."

The coffee was bitter but good. It jacked me into enough energy so that my packing went quickly. I left my scrub gear for last, and went down to the camp faucet for a washup and a cold shave. Nearby, a giant Winnebago was rumbling with the signs of imminent departure. Their campfire was still burning.

I was going to hassle them for their slovenly woodsmanship, but the ground was so wet there was no danger of it spreading. It'd leave less of a mess if it burned itself out.

The tapwater was cold and made my razor tug painfully at the stubble. I cussed myself for not saving a bit of what I'd heated to make coffee. Still, I would've made it through shaving without cutting myself if a big, green, Corps of Engineers patrolcar had not chosen that moment to stop at the road into the camp. At my distance it was hard to tell, but it looked as if the ranger's careful scrutiny of the campground had come to rest at the point where my motorcycle protruded from the grove of young pines.

"Oh *shit*," I said. I had a strong sense that the powers-that-be were closing in.

The Winnebago, waddling down the road past the patrolcar gave me the inspiration of a way out. Create . . . a diversion. I hefted my can of shaving cream and smiled.

As I strolled back toward my site, I passed the fire the r/v occupants had left behind. The shaving cream slid out from the folds of my towel to land in the coals with a soft plop. I kept walking, but as soon as I entered my little copse, I quickly stashed the rest of my gear and suited up to ride.

The pressurized can went off like a small bomb. A spray of dust and ash burst up, and a white whirling shard of metal sailed out of the fire to clank down among the tents of the Baptist encampment. The preacher stopped in mid-spiel and everyone turned their heads.

The ranger's car suddenly materialized by the scattered fire. A handful of people gathered. They gestured energetically in the direction the Winnebago had taken. The car spun around and shot out of the campground. It accelerated purposefully up the road to the north.

Me 'n Frank putted out of my copse looking—I hoped—

singularly unhurried. I turned south at the road. It seemed advisable to put on some miles.

Didn't stop until Lula, where I had breakfast in a roadside cafe. The outside was pleasantly weathered, the inside worn but clean, and crammed with good smells. A Michelob bottle on my table was doubling as a vase. When I sniffed the weary rose it held, a petal fell to my table.

I got my hands on a local paper that had been abandoned on the next table. It had nothing on the stacking of Jones' car, much less any whodunit speculations or words on the search for a suspect. Which didn't mean a dragnet of sorts wasn't flung out; it was quite possible that the authorities weren't airing the embarrassing news until they had some good news to go with it. I sighed. Push was right. Consequences.

Consequences. Mechanically, I chomped my way through hot country ham, hotcakes, grits. They began to disappear in more ways than one. As I ate, I thought, and as I thought, the cafe around me began to waver and dissolve.

Instead, I became only conscious of those illumined points of recent experience that had become my inner stars. The lines I was drawing between them fitted together in a glowing geometry of the consciousness, almost a neon effect on a black field, with the star of that *presence* I pursued in the center.

Like physical stars, these points of realization might not be seen steadily; they could be eclipsed by clouds of distraction, confusion, or pain. When that great central star was occluded, then my inner astrolabe navigated by the three nearest it in magnitude, which triangulated and fixed the location of the center star, even when it had vanished from me, or I from it. The names of these three *felt* like the progressively freer states which Push had described with the phrases goodbye-to-rains, goodbye-to-reigns, goodbye-to-reins.

I wanted to bring down that pattern I saw forming above me, so I could feel its knowledge and power radiating out through me . . . . But I couldn't quite reach it from where I was. Well, if the mountain wasn't coming to Mohammed, then it looked as if Mohammed was going to have to hike. That meant utterly letting go of the last of what I had known, launching myself across a threshold . . . an even greater leap of faith towards that evanescent *presence*.

It was time. That was the "appointment" Push had mentioned. A few more things were required. The first of them was a decision right now. I made it. It was the same decision as before, in the rain-wet pasture, looking at the storm, when I hadn't even known I was making a decision . . . . At a greater magnitude, now.

I came to. I was pushing the last bits of grits around on my plate with my fork. I felt good. I thought I ought to do something to commemorate this moment.

There was my glass of orange juice, sitting untasted by my plate. I picked up the petal that had dropped from the rose, and floated it on top of the juice. They looked nice together, the golden liquid and the velvet piece of dark red. I raised the glass, toasted the moment, and drank it down.

I crossed the Mississippi on route 49. My first glimpse of the Big River! Disappointment. Instead of the roiling, boiling daddywater of legend and song, ole mile-wide, hard-assed pounder to the sea, I saw a narrow muddy streak.

Arkansas was so flat, the highway turns so long and winding after the unrelenting undulations of miss Miss.; it was terrific terrain to stretch and run. And did we ever! Frank sang his sweet street song, while the short yellow lines blipped by, keeping time. We zigged and zagged all over Eastern Arkansas, unreasonably happy, drunk in the notion of motion itself. We swung miles away from any coherent or constant direction, sometimes emerging at crossroads we had first seen hours earlier. One thing was sure, any rangers on my trail would go cross-eyed before they tracked me down.

I'd left most of the summer southern rains on the east side of the Mississippi. Here, only a few stray grey cumulus clouds floated overhead. The Luftwaffe . . . . Hup! Whuzzat? Bogeys coming in at 10 o'clock, Frank! Strafing with deadly raindrops! Take evasive action! Barrel-roll through this S-curve, soar up the hill. Then! A full-power dive down the other side, cutting across the trajectory of a big, twin engine Junkers, *just in time.*

Naturally, all these maneuvers took gas as well as time. I stopped for my second refill of the day at a station in the quaint little town of Cotton Plant. As I drove in under the awning, the Junkers buzzed in overhead like we'd been towing it on a rope. While Frank got gassed and the station briefly rained on, I turned to the attendant.

"Y'know, I brought this cloud with me from Mississippi. Gimme fi' dollahs and I'll leave. . . ."

"Hell no! We need it. First rain we've had all month."

"Well then! Gimme twenny dollahs and I'll stay!"

That was it, the last gasp of the deluge. In the sky, there were only a few rags of grey left, with a blunt sun tearing slowly through one of 'em. And a black strip of road knifing through wet, green fields. And Frank 'n me jamming down it, giddy with the exhilaration of acceleration.

We zoomed around a nondescript hill, and, POOF, the city of Little Rock materialized before us. Approaching from the north, the city just appears like that. No outskirts to crawl up under, no suburbs, just countryside and countryside and boom, you are there.

We drove slowly through Little Rock and out the other side. No campsite in sight. All the fields and forests were properly fenced off with barbed wire. The real estate folks had been at their Stratego again.

Finally, south of town, I found a place where the right-of-way for a new highway had sliced right through a sixty-foot hill, as if the road were the anal fold between two stone buttocks. I spotted my site— a stand of trees atop the western rump. Now, as for getting up there . . . .

We clattered and bounced over the chunks of exploded rock. A muddy ditch barred the way. I got off and heaved stones into the ditch until I had a bridge, then roared and jolted across and straight on up the steep slope until I was among my trees.

I noticed that certain places were starting to feel more "right" than others. This one felt very right.

I shut down and proceeded to make camp by the available light, which wasn't much, since night was descending with the speed and assurance of an anvil tossed out a twelfth-story window.

Stretched out in my little tent, wiggling my toes in the coolness, I waited for the advent of sleep. I heard the cry of nightbirds, sharp and random as the flicker of fireflies. I tried to synchronize with the birdcries, bidding one nerve or limb or portion of my body to relax, sleep, each time I heard a call echo in under my trees. Then I did the same thing with thoughts, associations, small physical awarenesses, soothing and soothing my brain in time to the random music of the birds.

I felt as if I'd achieved some form of magical state, my mind floated by itself. Sleep came so imperceptibly I was hardly aware that it had happened. If it *was* sleep.

A wind rustled the tent flap, peeled it back and entered, and that wind was in the shape of a woman.

My last waking thought, and the one that had been hardest to extinguish had been of good ole Tallahassee Jo, how sweet and delightful it would be to lie in her arms, to become slowly nourished by her warm and loving friendship, and her ripe womanliness, . . . how in my decision to hike to the mountain, she, and what she represented to me, would be the hardest thing to leave behind.

The wind that was in the shape of a woman had a scent of jasmine, delicate in the air around her. She was coolly naked. There was a whisper of fabric from my bed as she lay down beside me. I did not move for a long time, although the kiss of her cool, silken flesh was against me, thigh to thigh, arm to arm. Her breath was soft and fragrant as a cat's. I felt a hand descend on my forehead, insubstantial as fog, leaving cool sparks that danced under my eyelids as her fingertips caressed my face. The touch of those hands came to know me intimately, like the hands of the blind.

I reached for her. Where we touched, our forms melted together, interpenetrating like two mists flowing smoothly into one another, the particles uttering soft explosions of music as they contacted, creating a sensual song timed to the rhythmical undulation of our mingling. That was our whole universe, while it lasted.

Eventually, we passed completely through each other. I heard my name called, and the sound of the voice that uttered it was rich and satiated.

Jo? I thought back. I heard a faint, answering giggle that trailed off into silence. Then the fabric rustled, the tent flap opened, and she was gone. Outside, I heard the wind pulsing in a kind of vast soft breathing, with the light rasp of a purr in the tall grass.

The next morning I bounded up happy and zapped, as if the remnant of some astral nectar still flowed in my veins. After a very leisurely breaking of camp, and a few moments of staring in disbelief at the rocky slope I had charged up the previous night (I mustabin *crazy!*), I set off again.

Next stop, Hot Springs National Park, Ark., where I stopped to reconnoiter with the inner astrolabe.

A hundred yards from the place I pulled over, a tepid creek flowed between grassy, littered banks. A bunch of small fry in shorts and bathing suits were clustered there, collectively brandishing a fishing pole and attempting to achieve a cast. A wad of dough and a chunk of hot dog swung wildly from the hook. Nearby, a pair of pudgy middle-aged folk reclined in aluminum arm chairs, sipping from styrofoam cups of wine.

Just upstream, around a bend, I saw a small sign planted in the bank.

NO SWIMMING OR FISHING
This Stream Polluted!

I turned around and walked back to the people in the lawn chairs. "Those your kids?" I asked.

The man looked up. His face was round and red, and there were deep creases in his forehead. "What's it to you?" he said.

"There's a sign upriver. Says this creek is polluted."

116

He snorted and looked away. "Don't look polluted to me."

Not this way.

After blasting away from Hot Springs, from its gaggle of hotels, souvenir shops and bars, I drove past a big lake named Ouachita. Finally I got away from people and buildings and phone lines, and cruised down a winding two lane road with the smells of the Ozarks forests pouring down from both sides.

The appointment! The appointment! I could feel it approaching; I could feel myself approaching it, with a greater sense of urgency.

At length, I came to a small country burg called "Y" City, named for the fork in the road. Six or seven old houses were scattered around the fork, quietly peeling in the sun. Unlike the buildings of Hot Springs, these seemed to belong to the place where they had been built. One was a store, and a freshly painted sign asserted with pride that it contained a dairy bar.

No one, I thought, could resist going into a place like this for a milkshake. I didn't.

In a short time I sat on a stool inside, performing a natural act with a large metal tumbler of fresh raspberry shake. I was just wiping my mouth, and wondering if I could get a search clue or a dab of local color, or both, by striking up a conversation with the elderly waitress, when I heard the distant wail of a siren. I stiffened automatically. Then, I remembered wryly what Push had said about running from cops for the next couple of weeks. I put a bill on the counter to cover the shake, and went outside. The siren got louder. Suddenly a black '57 Ford sedan whipped into view, coming from the road that curved away to the south. The screech of a four-wheel drift and the roar of high-performance drowned out the pursuing siren momentarily. I caught a glimpse of the driver. He was young, with long blonde hair combed straight back from his forehead and plastered to his scalp, and a T-shirt with sleeves rolled to the armpits. He steered expertly out of the skid, glanced over one shoulder, and accelerated. He swerved around a startled tourist station wagon that had stopped dead in its tracks, and POW! he was gone.

In a second, a howling patrolcar screamed around the same curve. Inside, two Stetson-hatted cops looked stern and extremely irritated. Their car went into a similar skid, but instead of steering out of it, spun around in several circles. They screeched to a halt, both cops now looking dizzy as well as irritated. Then their car lunged clumsily down the road after the Ford.

I noticed that the elderly waitress had followed me out of the dairy bar. She clapped her hands together in glee. "That Todd boy can drive, cain't he?" she said.

"Yes ma'am," I said. "Seems like he can."

She studied me a moment. "That siren made you kinda nervous, didn't it?"

"Everything makes me nervous," I said.

She just nodded and looked shrewd.

"Well, I'd best be on my way now."

"I figured you would be," she said.

"I finished the shake," I pointed out.

"I know," she said.

"Goodbye," I said.

She nodded. "Stay out of trouble."

"I intend to."

"Lawd knows, don't we all," she said. Then she ascended the steps and went through the screen door of the dairy bar, shaking her head over the mystery of human intentions.

I didn't want to follow the Blonde Otter—as I had christened him—down the road he had taken in his Ford, pursued by the heat. I didn't want to see him trapped by the inevitable roadblock and caught. I preferred to remember him as I had seen him flashing by, brilliantly, if briefly, free.

So I went south, then west, down a road that wound between the lesser Ozarks. Overhead flew a large black bird, bigger than a crow, that seemed to be going to Mena, too.

That's the town where we both wound up. I squatted on the curb by my motorcycle, checking the roadmap, and my feathered fellow-traveler flapped away to the north. My options did not look very optional. The map showed one road into Mena, and one road out. But something nagged at me. I felt that a different move was called for. The appointment Push had told me about seemed imminent. For one thing, I was becoming dominated by a sense of the surreal, as if everything around me, although normal in every recognizable way, was still imbued with a buzzing, crackling electricity.

I putted slowly through town, looking for the sign of an alternative. I got one. It was painted green, and bolted to a long metal pole. "Queen Wilhelmena State Park" it read, and an arrow pointed up a street that led to the north. I bumped over railroad tracks, passed a few stores, and wandered into a residential section. That didn't seem too promising, but I kept on. Soon I found the houses falling away as the road wound higher up the hill. Then I realized that it was not a hill, but an immense ridge. I could see it rising and reaching for miles ahead of me. This was great. It felt right. A road so scenic and intriguing that a photograph of it could have been used as a symbol for all roads up mountains everywhere. And it hadn't even been mentioned on my map!

The dark green expanse of the Ozarks stretched away from the ridge on every side. Because of the height, and lateness of the hour, I was getting rapidly chilled. I took a turn off to a vista point so I could put on my jacket. One car was already there: a bulbous old black Ford. A young, blonde man leaned against the hood, taking in the view to the east, while he puffed on a cigarette. It was him, the Blonde Otter.

I drove right up and jumped off Frank. I walked over to him, my hand extended. "You got away!" I said.

He looked startled. He made no motion towards my hand.

"I was in the dairy bar at Y City when you blasted around the curve. It was beautiful! What's your name?"

He slitted his eyes and regarded me suspiciously. I was aware that I had made a mistake. "Mitch," he said slowly. "Mitch Yokam."

"The lady at the dairy bar said your name was Todd."

He sighed and looked away. "That old bat doesn't know what she's about."

"If you don't know each other, how come you know she's an old bat?" I blathered. Oops. I was just getting myeslf deeper into trouble with him. I tried to clear things up. "Listen, I'm not anyone you need to worry about. Look at my bike. It's got Florida plates, and it's loaded with camping gear. If I was at all related to the heat, would I come up this clumsily and try to get you to give yourself away?"

He smiled reluctantly. "Guess that's true," he allowed. "But they *are* pretty clumsy. I've been gettin' away right regular for the past three years."

"I hope I can match that." I said.

"You got a reason to try?"

"Not much. Just helped an obnoxious ranger stack his shark in Mississippi. I didn't know whether they were on to me or not, but I still had to light out. I'm happy I made it this far."

He looked me over again, and I could feel his awareness probing, almost as if I were bathed in a ray from his forehead. I checked him out, too. He was tall and thin, with angular shoulders and a narrow smoker's chest. He had a triangular face, with a broad forehead, and a narrow, almost feminine jaw. There were acne scars on his cheeks. His brown eyes were hard, but not ugly. When I tried to look into them, I felt as if my gaze were bouncing back from a mirror or a shield.

"Wanna smoke something to celebrate?" he asked.

"Is a big wheel round?"

"That's what I thought you'd say." He reached through the window into his glove compartment, and brought out a baggie and a pack of

Job rolling papers. Despite the cool wind blowing across the ridge, he rolled a one-paper joint with no difficulty. When it was lit, I smelled the incense-like aroma of a really good grade.

"I had a romantic notion that you were running moonshine," I said, "But I guess the stuff in your tank rustled more than it sloshed."

"You're about right," he said. "But I've already ditched it."

"That was quick. Quite quick. How did you get away?"

"Easy. Got enough of a lead to duck down a dirt sideroad. I waited 'til they went by, then doubled back. I know a couple of back ways around Mena, so I probably passed you while you were tangled up in town."

"Sounds reasonable. You must be a local boy."

He laughed. "Don't I look it? The only time I've spent away was a hitch in 'Nam, practically. Thought I was going off on a big patriotic adventure. I was, too, for about a week. Three years later, I graduated with V.D. and a D.D."

"Doctor of Dentistry?" I queried, puzzled.

"Dishonorable Discharge. I was making more loot on the black market than even my colonel. He decided to eliminate the competition." He shrugged. "Beats getting fragged. But when I came back I couldn't get any work; so I set up a little import business with a buddy who was a recon pilot. We do okay. My granpappy used to run a still in these hills during Prohibition, so I see myself as carrying on with the family business."

"But in a place this small, aren't you known?"

"Sure. That's one of the other services I perform. The local preachers hold me up as an example of the pitfalls of youth.

"But I'm thinking of getting out of the weed import racket anyhow. It's not like it used to be. Greedheads are taking over the distribution from the missionaries. You know what I mean? And a lot of the customers are just blowing their heads out with it. Not enough respect, all the way around. That puts bad energy back into the Marijuana Deva. Then she can't do anything with you. The way I see it, the stuff is meant to be used as a catalyst."

He leaned back against his car with all the existential aplomb of a hillbilly James Dean. Who read Oriental philosophy, and Alan Chadwick.

I leaned against the car too. I had to. We had smoked some righteous herb. I was stoned, but not precisely as I had ever known it before. My mind seemed stronger, larger, more capable of assimilating the drug effect than it ever had before, more able to turn the perception cast free and the energy released to its own purposes. Like the search.

The sense of the surreal that had begun in Mena grew. Close at hand, the scenery seemed exceptionally alive and writhing with detail. In the distance, it was misty and amorphous, like a soft fog that had arbitrarily formed itself into hills. My appointment seemed very close.

"It's getting dark," I observed.

"Might as well get stoned," he said.

"We are stoned. Very stoned."

"Might as well get stoneder."

"No more for me thanks," I said. "I'm on a diet."

"Well, it *is* my diet," he said. "Green and leafy vegetables build your body nine ways. Medicinal properties too. A pipeload of *Kif* will keep your thing stiff."

"Uh-huh." I was confused by what Mitch or Todd or . . . Push! was putting out now, seeming to contradict what he had just said about the respect due a potent catalyst. That was what made me think of Push; challenging me with paradox was right up his alley. But I could detect none of Push's characteristic light in this man's eyes.

I didn't have time to mess around. It was time to get moving.

"There someplace you're supposed to be?" He had noticed my agitation.

"Seems that way," I said.

"Well, keep the rollin' side down," he said. "Nice jawin' with ya." He took my hand this time.

"Ditto," I said. "Thanks for the herb. Keep your power dry. I hope you keep getting away forever."

He saluted me with a forefinger to the eyebrow as I shot away. It was hard to adjust to the road as it wound tighter and climbed higher. But soon I fell into the rhythm of the curves and achieved the concentration necessary to maintain my speed.

Then I came to a place where my path led off the road, simply, abruptly, and just like that. This was the place of my appointment. Another high overlook, this one facing west.

I pulled off my helmet and walked to the edge. At this point, the ridge fell away to an incredible panorama of mist-filled valleys and rolling green hills. Scattered lakes gleamed at a distance. The sky was full of restless grey clouds that seemed barely able to contain the coiling force of something latent and explosive. I felt as though I were inside a Van Gogh vision of a gathering storm.

And then, entering a silence suddenly. It is strange that I associate no sounds with the experience, as if what happened next were soundless, or an experience so demanding that I had no awareness left for sound. I had an overpowering sense of the *presence*, much stronger than I had felt in Tallahassee. Hairs rose on the back of my neck. My body felt like an empty shell, bathed inside and out with electricity.

A wind swept up the slope, flattening grass before it. Reaching me, it beat against my body as though demanding entrance. I allowed it. The air moved through me in silvery sheets of flame. I closed my eyes. Images began to come and go, like cards raised before a mental eye and flicked away before I could more than glimpse them. I concentrated on holding one. It vibrated rapidly, then gradually jelled into a scene. It was very dreamlike. It seemed that I was simultaneously within the figure I observed, *and* observing him from the outside.

I see, and am, a traveler on a forest path. I wear a tattered cloak of some rough, grey material. On my head is a wide-brimmed hat with a seashell fastened to it. In the traveler's hand is a thick staff with one green bud sprouting from the end. Moisture that may be rain, sweat, or tears glitters in the stubble on my cheeks.

As I watch, a figure clothed in black, wearing a hood with no eye-holes, steps forth from the trees. This figure circles me several times with a weird, gliding motion, then squats and shuffles in a circle, laying ten blue stones on the ground. The figure hands the traveler another stone and gestures toward the circle on the ground.

I step into it, and everything changes.

The forest, the path, and the black cloaked figure have vanished. I am in the presence of a lady, feeling altogether scruffy and disreputable before her regal poise. She sits in a carved chair by a creek that collects into a pool near her feet. Behind her, tall European cypress wave in the wind. Before her there is a small garden of ripe, golden wheat, ready to harvest. Her robe is deep green, embroidered with gold thread in the design of three interlocking rings. On her head is a silver tiara with twelve prongs, a white diamond set at the tip of each.

She is fair, her features obviously refined and aristocratic. But as I gaze at her I seem to recognize the faces of Jo, Joyce, Ursula, Miss Crystall, my mother, and many other women I'd known or just glimpsed on the street and somehow remembered. Their faces appeared briefly projected on the features of this lady, then became reabsorbed and lost in hers . . . just as the emotions that any woman had ever aroused in me seemed ultimately aimed at this one.

But in the end it was still her face at which I stared, cool, aloof, and perfect.

Her eyes were on me, powerful and alive, and it seemed that she was trying to reassure me with them. I could see the deep, receding energy of thought in those eyes, the web of thoughts of control and shaping, civilization and culture; and there were songs there, music and poetry dedicated to her by men who loved no other but her.

She was the incarnation, the tangible form of these thoughts and dreams, or else the source of their emanation and their final destiny.

I could stay with her if I wished. There was that invitation written in her eyes. I might not always see her, but her influences and her graces would be guiding me as I accomplished myself in her service. But if I did stay with her, there would be something further that remained unknown, a doubt or mystery unresolved. It was something connected with the fact that, no matter how well I served her, she would never allow herself to be reached by one who served.

I indicated my desire to go further. This was connected to my search for the being. She herself was the strongest manifestation of that energy and understanding that I had yet seen, but I felt that she herself was not the object of my search.

She waited for me to say the name of the being that I sought. I didn't know any name . . . but then, I realized that I did. No sounds came out of my mouth, but the thought of the name, the impulse to say it, was enough. "Goodbye-To-Rains."

Her eyes vanished. The sockets were like the empty black holes in a mask. She rose from the chair, removed the tiara and shook down her hair. Before I could move to halt the sacrilege, she had raised up the hem of her embroidered gown, and lay down on her back. Her thighs were exquisitely white, with faint, blue veins like subterranean rivers. She beckoned to me with one hand, while she spread open the lips of her sex with the fingers of the other. The eyeless eyes watched like holes in a skull.

I approached her numbly, not wanting to, yet compelled by my decision. She beckoned again. I got down on my knees between her thighs, and suddenly I was inside her. *All* of me.

I was inside a cold, rocky tunnel, not much wider than my body. It was the shaft of a cave, filled with a deep impenetrable darkness I could almost taste. The passage was low as well as narrow, so I had to lay my cheek against the clammy rock. The feeling of confinement was unbearable. I began to writhe forward like a snake. Darkness, and the vast, cold weight of the encircling rock, filled me with a mounting terror. I jerked my head up, and cracked it painfully against the ceiling. The passage went on forever. It was becoming hard to breathe.

I felt that I crawled toward my death. Or, perhaps, that I was already dead, and was now crawling through my grave. Perhaps it did go on forever. I raised my head and bumped it again, just as painfully. The rock was *hard*, as real as any rock had ever been. I felt my own groans and pants as vibrations in the air. It seemed to me that there were other echoes rebounding from the walls, as if this were a passageway and there were others behind me, as well as before.

At last, my exploring fingers felt no walls! At last, one arm raised cautiously over my head, I could rise to my knees, then my feet!

I spread my arms out, and encountered nothing. Only the ground was there, smooth and solid beneath my feet. I moved carefully onward. A yellow light flared, as if a torch had been lit behind me. I did not turn, because the rock wall suddenly illuminated before me was astoundingly covered with the forms of leaping, flying beasts—bison, mammoth, tigers, reindeer, wild ass, weasels, condors, owls, rabbit, fish, and countless others—all fleeing outward from the cave as though eager to escape their imagery and take on flesh. Continuing the panorama was a series of crudely styled leaves from many different types of vegetation, and following these, a series of black and orange dots in differing combination. As I gazed at the dots, I realized that they referred to simple mathematical relationships that became more complex as they were welded together.

And then I saw, at the end of the cave, on a ledge of his own about fifteen feet above the floor, a strange watching figure. It leaned forward, with its front paws out, and one hind foot raised in a kind of prancing posture. The figure had a round animal chest, like a horse, but a man's legs and feet. The tail was a full brush, like a fox or wolf. Under the tail, a large penis swung with the motion of the dance. The front paws were broad and flat, clawed like the paws of a bear.

Its head was the most bizarre. There, the antlers, skull, and ears of a stag blended into the nose, chin, and long beard of an old man. The eyes were marked by a series of concentric rings, like a pair of targets. These eyes steadily regarded the cavern and all it contained. They were hypnotic and penetrating, like a sorcerer's.

For all its strangeness, something in the demeanor of the figure seemed familiar. I thought, here is a primordial and ancient Push, closer to the core, a more essential manifestation than the forms I've seen.

In this cave one might study, explore and meditate, coming to grips with knowledge beneath and above the human sphere and responsible for its existence on the plane of matter. Here again I could remain forever, probing into the realities, the spheres, the histories and futures generated by this set of possibilities, this set of understandings willed into existence.

The being, Goodbye-To-Rains, had been here. I could taste the traces of his presence *between* everything I saw. But the actual being, the consciousness itself, did not seem to be present. I looked around, but there was only one passageway to the cavern, the one by which I had entered. There was no one, and nothing, to tell me what to do.

Not enough, not enough! I shouted. Where is what I came for?

No sounds came from my mouth, but my thoughts had been heard. From the wall of the cave, the shamanistic figure regarded me intently. My right arm twitched, and I remembered the eleventh blue stone I had been given. I still had it. I raised my arm, and with all my strength, hurled the stone at the figure on the wall.

It all vanished . . . the cave, the wall, and whatever I had been using for a body. The only thing that remained was the light that had shot out of the blackness to illumine everything. I was conscious that the light moved through all spectra, and much further than I could grasp. I was cast adrift in a vast sea of energy, woven with dimensions that revolved about and within each other. I saw that it was filled with an immense significance that I could never contain. In fact, the effort of my consciousness to represent to itself the things it perceived as energy, or a sea of dimensions, was a presumption that bordered on blasphemy.

The only awareness that could ever encompass that vast expanse of being was if that vastness were aware of itself. And as I thought that, I saw that it was so. The wonder!

This imponderable, infinitely marvelous sea could know itself, love itself! It gloried in taking on whatever form it chose, and even the aspects that I could perceive, were formed more by the limits of my perception than by any constraint on the abilities of the sea to manifest. Sometimes, it conformed to patterns it had already set in motion. Sometimes, it erupted from them, able to willfully forget itself and cast a portion of its being out from its consciousness . . . endowing that portion with a consciousness of its own, for the purpose of making an experiment in a newly conceived dimension.

My own origin seemed related to a process of that sort. A natural path for my splinter of consciousness to take would be to explore the variables in several dimensions . . . then enter a purification until I could merge again with what I now beheld . . . gradually dissolving my current selfhood, as I moved deeper and deeper, back into the warmth and understanding and love of that vast being.

The picture was of a crystal hailstone, dissolving into a sea from which it had once been drawn by evaporation.

I yearned for that rosy consummation, to begin the rigorous process of surrender and dissolution. But I held on to those limits which—I saw now—defined me. To my shock, I saw that the essence of Goodbye-To-Rains was not to be found in this fashion.

How, then? All my being formed this question.

The knowledge was displayed for me against a panorama of understandings contained within the vastness. It was like a melody that I instinctively recognized. As soon as I felt the opening chords, that part of the song already within me awakened, and I found I could continue the music on my own.

The theme that I recognized was the search for Goodbye-To-Rains.

I began to follow the internal demands of the music. The process was interior, psychological, and once begun, self-perpetuating. It was a chain reaction, with a logical consequence of fast, irrevocable steps. I had initiated it with a tremendous act of will, so it gathered momentum rapidly, much faster than the core of my consciousness was prepared for.

The process that was now playing me had begun to make things disappear. First, awareness of any being or reality outside of myself went away. Then, vanishing in rapid succession were thoughts, feelings, memories, and soon awareness of any datum, however insignificant. My last self image was of a child closing his eyes, putting his hands over his ears, and holding his breath. Then there was a final, ultimate step in the destruction of conditioning and association that I had begun once, long ago, in a place I could no longer remember.

I could no longer remember beginning this process. The sense of waiting for an outcome vanished too.

FOR THERE WAS NOTHING.

I had arrived at a BLACKNESS emptier than any blackness could be! EMPTINESS devoid of history, future, or even a present. There was nothing to feel, think, or remember. Only a DESOLATION and a SILENCE astronomically beyond the terror of the senses in the cave . . . !

It is impossible to say it. More impossible than description of the vast being. Any adjective or symbol attached to that void alters it from the absolute emptiness that it was.

The spark of awareness left to me tried to retch upon the blackness, to scream and struggle against the horror of it. But there was no scream and NOTHING to struggle against. NOTHING NOTHING NOTHING.

But a recoil, and a falling.

A fall to consciousness.

And a return to my body, lying face down in the long grass at the edge of the slope. My hands were clenched in the dirt and roots of the grass. The muscles were rigid and the knuckles white. It took several minutes of concentration, of looking at the fingers and willing them to be mine, before they opened. When they did, the pain was excruciating.

VII.
Seven
of Wands

I had kept the appointment. I had seen that . . . nothing was at the end of my search. I felt as though a wind had seized me and flung me up against a rock, then down into a bottomless chasm. This was unendurable. It went past sadness, beyond despair.

So much had ridden on the content of this revelation; I had burned all my bridges behind me. Now, I saw that a dark emptiness lay ahead. My body was shaking in fear and loathing of the mind that had returned to it, and the memory it contained. The body feared its own death, but the place I had seen was like the threshold to the extinction of consciousness itself, and *immense* was the fear that that inspired!

I sat up clumsily. How could I, how could anyone continue past this point? Everything I did from this time on would be a farce, a pretense, to hide the horror of the emptiness from myself and others. The wind was gone now, and the grasses stood stiff and still. I felt a brooding, negative power, as if I could sweep them out of existence with a thought.

I walked to the motorcycle, my body moving jerkily, like a marionette with stretched and broken strings. Started the thing. I leaned forward on the handlebars, to rest for a moment. Then drove off.

I no longer had a place to go. And I did not care. Whatever happened, was fine.

A few miles further up the ridge, near the top of the mountain, I came to Queen Wilhelmena State Park and turned in. I was near collapse, and indifferent as to whether I camped, or just fell over on the road. But my body still seemed to want to take care of itself, just from a kind of momentum.

I found a place by itself under the trees and away from the main campsites. With what felt like my last strength, I put a flat rock under the kickstand and dragged out my sleeping bag. With my boots and clothes still on, leaning back against the trunk of a tree, I pulled the bag halfway up my body and fell asleep.

I awoke sometime in the middle of the night. The air was cool, quiet and clear. Off to the east I saw a strange, hard light that glowed, then pulsed strongly, illuminating an entire valley for a brief second. It did this several times before I realized I was watching a lightning storm from a point *above* the thunderhead. Eerily, the top of the cloud flared like the abdomen of a giant firefly, then a short bright streak arced between the bottom of the cloud and the earth.

My hair and face were wet and cold. The sleeping bag was soggy. Nearby, I could see the motorcycle lying on its side, blown off the kickstand. Fumbling noises came from that direction, as if a small animal was rooting through my packs. I didn't care. I had no energy to care. I went back to sleep.

Warmth against my face. I heard footsteps. My eyes opened. It was morning, and the sun was well up. A bald man, wearing scrubbed denim jeans and a white muslin shirt was walking past me. He strode with vigor and purpose, his chest was thrust out like someone who took an almost theatrical delight in breathing the air. In his hand he carried a thin, dead branch that had been blown from a tree. He poked the ground with it as he walked.

Ahead of him, a golden retriever frisked happily through the leaves, towards my fallen bike. It sniffed around my packs, then raised a leg and pissed on them. The man stopped and watched, evidently amused. Then he saw me, observing both of them.

"Siddhartha!" he shouted. "Cut that out!"

The dog looked at him, waited until it had finished pissing, then romped back towards its master. He grabbed it by the collar.

"Sorry," he said to me. "He didn't know what he was doing."

But you did, I thought silently. Now, go away. Leave me alone.

He walked up. "Looks like you spent a hard night, brother." I had no response. "Want some help putting your bike back up?" His eyes, brown with very clear whites, sparkled with vibrancy and enthusiasm.

"No," I said.

"Oh. Like to do things yourself, eh?" He put his hands on his hips and looked down at me, sizing me up. His gaze traveled slowly from my disheveled hair and unshaven face to the wet and muddy sleeping bag.

"Tell you what," he said. "After you get things straightened out here, come on down the road to our campsite. We'll share our breakfast with you." His voice was gentle but firm, like a forebearing parent with a wayward child. "See you in about ten minutes. Siddy!" he called. Then he stode off, with that subtly ostentacious, self-confident air. The dog ran after him.

The sleeping bag was getting hot and sticky. I pushed it off and stood up. Dizzy. I looked at the bike. There was a dent in the tank, and gas had leaked out through the filler cap. My food pack was opened, and the remnants of what it contained had been scattered. I put my hands under the seat and tank, and with a grunt of effort heaved it upright. I put the stone back under the kickstand.

Had to crap. I walked down the road to the washroom, past the campsite of the bald man and his dog. And a woman. She was tall, vegetarian thin, and had a Nordic face that was topped by a helmet of short, champagne-colored hair. She wore a pair of hotpants, cut on a line from her crotch to her hip-bone, and a T-shirt tie-dyed in green and blue. She was cursing in Swedish, thumping on a two-burner alcohol stove. The bald man was reading to her from a booklet of instructions. When he saw me approach, he gave me a big smile of welcome. This changed to a frown when I kept walking.

The washroom was brown-painted brick. Its smooth concrete floor smelled faintly of piss and disinfectant. After the crap, as I was leaving, I caught a glimpse of my face in the mirror . . . . I looked impossibly old and tired, with red-rimmed eyes staring out of a haunted face.

He stood by the road on my way back. I didn't meet his eyes. He touched my arm. "I thought you were coming to breakfast, brother," he said.

I looked at him then. What you think is a very provisional reality, buster, I thought at him. I shook his hand off.

"Hey c'mon," he said. "My wife's already cooking for three. We're happy to share, and you look like you could use a good meal. Join us."

His insistence engulfed my indifference. He hauled me over to their campsite and sat me down on a log. His wife gave me a big smile. She had dazzling teeth.

"I'm Jerry, and this is Sigrid." He waited for me to introduce myself.

I didn't.

Jerry and Sigrid exchanged a significant glance.

"We're both from the Avatar Institute in San Francisco," Jerry said. "We're on our way to work in a drug abuse clinic in Atlanta, but we set aside this month for digging on the countryside before we go back to work." He made an expansive gesture that took in the mountains, the valleys, the trees, and the rows of recreational vehicles parked under them. "So, where you from?"

I shook my head and grimaced. "Who cares?"

"What do you mean, 'who cares'?" His eyebrows came together slightly. He glanced at his wife as if to share some private reaction, but she had suddenly begun to put all her energy into a furious stirring of pancake batter. Her nipples made small circles under the thin stuff of her shirt.

"I mean, why care?"

There was a dark pressure inside me—the memory of that ultimate end of things. It was forcing itself out through my thoughts, into my words. I didn't want that, didn't want to show others the shadow I'd found behind and before and within what we were and did. Why paralyze them too? But if he kept probing and pulling on me, trying to drag me out into his reality, I wouldn't be able to help myself. The speaking would happen.

"I care," he said seriously. "Because that's the kind of person I decided I was going to be. And I aint coming on like some salvationist Pollyanna, I been there. I used to shoot junk, and then I shot a pusher. I've done time for both of those. But I pulled out of my dive with help from some good people, and training in psychology, Zen meditation, hatha yoga, massage, macrobiotics, you name it. Now I'm a professional counselor and pretty good at my work. I can practically smell the way somebody is bumming out. And when I do, I go in after him, because that's what somebody did for me."

His eyes sparkled, his face became thoughtful. "Now I'm just guessing, mind, but I'll lay odds your problem is with amphetamines. I bet you've been doing 'em up for at least a year.

I sat and stared at my feet. What was I looking at? I felt surrounded by what I saw as the shadow of his professional lie. He was just like all the others, surrounded by those suffering minds they had seduced or coerced into believing in them. Feeding off of the blind hope of the suffering. I saw the shadow behind that. I saw a temptation to give in, to let him take charge, and tell me that my visions were bad dreams, and my understandings distorted. And I saw the shadow behind *that*.

Sigrid slid a plateful of steaming pancakes onto my knee. She put her hand on my shoulder, and let it remain there for a comforting moment before taking it away. She had mistaken my silence.

I looked down at the pancakes. Rivulets of melted butter and syrup trickled enticingly across the crust. I took the plate and put it on the ground. Siddhartha, the golden retriever, leaped up to investigate.

"You're still a junkie, Jerry," I said. "Only now your fix is having people choose you for a teacher. I can't eat your food," I added slowly. "It's not real."

Jerry's hands tightened convulsively. His jaw worked.

His wife pointed her spatula at me. "Dot's not a smart vay to act ven someone's trying to help you!" she said. Anger danced and spun in her eyes.

"If that wasn't his number I dialed," I said, "why did he answer?"

Her eyes flared. "Get out!" she said. "Ve are sorry he invited you. Take your bullshit away!"

Jerry tried to restrain and soothe her, but I was already on my way. "Hey, adios partner," he called after me. "Hope you learn to take as good as you give someday."

As I drove away, the event that had just transpired with these two people stayed in the front of my mind. By what right did I spread my poison?

I headed north, then west, on another road my map hadn't mentioned.

Long rails of cloud slid across the sky, as if a prison door were being slammed on the sun. Bars of shadow fell across the land. This prison the earth was in—a bubble of assumptions, looped and crossed with chains of wistful thinking . . . all hung on nothing. But minds still clung to the chains and bars, at the same time they desperately closed their eyes to them. And did one who saw the prison become more free? Or did the happy inmate know a greater freedom than the frustrated escapist?

Happy inmates. Perhaps there were some, but I could never be one again. The dead end of my search for freedom and Goodbye-To-Rains was seared into the center of my consciousness.

I coasted many miles downhill, falling from Rich Mountain with the ignition switched off. Silent and deadly, the banshee of the Ozarks came to the plains of Oklahoma.

Several towns. Boarded windows. People moving with unnatural slowness. Drive on. Motion distracted me. The wind in my face, the necessity of accelerating, turning and braking, occupied all of my body and some of my attention, kept me from turning back into myself and facing that paralyzing memory. The memory of the blindness of knowledge, the meaninglessness of action, the ultimate claustrophobia of being.

Light receded. A huge blue and red sign reared up against the sky. "STEAK" it asserted, in seven-foot neon letters. I hadn't eaten since Y City. I stopped.

Inside, clumps of cleanly dressed people, men with wet hair and women in sprayed bouffants, were scattered among the tables, quietly feeding. The girl behind the counter seemed to be staring through me, at a point just beyond where I stood. No emotion, no feeling, so much as flickered on her face as she mechanically took my order, my money, and handed me a receipt. I picked a table. It seemed that silence fell across the other tables as I walked through them, and as I sat down, that the tables around me fell silent.

The food, when it arrived, was inedible. It smelled and looked all right . . . the steak was still sizzling from the broiler, the salad was fresh, wisps of steam floated from the melting butter in the baked potato. But I couldn't eat it, couldn't raise my hands to saw off a bite, couldn't bear to place it in my mouth. I didn't care. I had stopped to eat at the suggestion of habit only. I drank the glass of water, got up and went outside.

I got on the motorcycle. Before I put on my helmet, I felt a strange sensation in my back, and turned around. Everyone in the restaurant was staring out the window at me. The bland, expressionless faces seemed flat, unreal, pasted on a sea of shadows. A shudder of fear and nausea ran down my spine.

Following the suntracks, choosing roads without choosing them. I didn't care how narrow or unmarked they were or where they led; the main thing was to keep moving.

Fields full of weeds behind rusty barbed wire fences. A line of phone poles with single crossbars marched over the horizon like the gibbets of a mass crucifixion. The air was jaundiced with death of sun.

A small town. White buildings jammed together in the space of a few acres. No motion, light, or sound, within or around the homes. No barking dogs, singing birds, or children playing in the streets. Where were they? At the side of the road, I removed my helmet and listened. Windscythe, windsigh . . . .

And faint, distant singing. I putted slowly onward. The singing grew louder, but between phrases of the song, the wind still gasped and sighed. Outside the anonymous church from which the singing came, I stopped to buckle on my helmet. The hymn and the sound of the organ rose, then went silent.

I imagined myself inside the church, hearing a motorcycle pass, pause, then roar and fade.

The sun was balanced on the rim of the world. Like the center of a cobweb, it gathered the yellow strands of light into itself. The brown sides of broken barns threw cliffs of darkness across the weeds. By the side of the road, a scaffold of rotted timbers exalted a windmill with rusty blades, like a cog in a decayed machine that had, long ago, hummed in communion between heaven and earth.

The wind pulled me westward, first into the sun, then into deepening night.

Stars began to burn through the steel-blue sky like the tips of acetylene torches.

My body was hypnotized by lights moving through darkness, by the roar and rhythm of motion, by the vacuum of thought and purpose in which I moved.

I moved on through another edge of night and day, driven by a single desire. My body was trying to run away from my mind and the seed of dark knowledge that burned within.

In the early light of morning, at a rivulet that came down a canyon wall, I stopped and splashed my face with cold water that tasted of minerals. My body thought to rest, but when I closed my eyes I was jolted by visions of short, shaggy men who drove bison over the edge of the canyon and clambered wildly down the walls, to cavort and chant around the corpses, and cut slabs of flesh with long, crude knives. I stood over their bones . . . .

Moving, moving, moving. I became a needle, piercing the wind. Everything was pared away. I became cold and stretched by the wind, like the high cirrus overhead, in which floated the eroded bone of a moon.

Endless fields. Huge black birds, that I now recognized as ravens, rose from barbed wire fences at my approach. Things changed. The fields became the cracked desolation of eroded land, where the raw, natural forces showed themselves more nakedly. Hard light reflected from facets of red, crumbling earth. A faint pungence of sage, tiny desert flowers, and rodent droppings hovered over the barrenness.

I wanted to press forward until my last strength had been spent in motion, and then fall.

I was well into the next night when that happened. I thought I was in New Mexico, but wasn't sure. I'd taken so many turns, gone such distances without reading signs. . . . A jouncing path up a long abandoned road, and a flat place near a dry creekbed were the last things I saw in the glare of my headlight.

In the distance, the sound of running water ululated between banks of darkness.

Morning bleakened my little corner of desert. There was a dog barking. And barking. I burrowed my head deeper into the bag. For a while I faded out of consciousness, but the furious yapping and barking dragged me back. The son-of-a-bitch had been at it, nonstop, for half an hour. The frost that had settled in my limbs during the night was gradually replaced by a red tide of anger. It's hard to maintain a dignified metaphysical despair when something is irritating the hell out of you. I ripped off the bag, leaped up, and ran toward the creek. The dog was on the other side. "Rowf!" I yelled. "Arf! Arf! Af!" The dog froze for a second in pure astonishment, then tore off through the brush with his tail between his legs.

"Not bad," a deep, amused voice said behind me. "Now, if you can fetch, you've got yourself a job."

I whirled, and saw a tall man standing by my crumpled sleeping bag. He wore a red flannel shirt, open at the neck, with the sleeves rolled up to the elbows, a pair of well-worn corduroy pants and lace-up boots. A circle of bone swung around his neck on a piece of leather thong. His black hair was short and well cut, fitting itself to his round face, high cheekbones, and generally Germanic appearance, or what *would* have been a Germanic appearance, were it not for his dark olive complexion. But the thing I noticed first, last, and almost continuously while noticing other things about him, was his mustache. It erupted enthusiastically from his upper lip, divided like a black waterfall around his mouth and the briar pipe it held, then plunged majestically to a curling finale several inches below his chin.

His face was intelligent, and interesting for the features of the various races mingled there, but the mustache was arresting and downright coercive. It forced one to notice him, to watch while he took the pipe out of his mouth, even to admire the way he laid the broad palm of one hand upon it and stroked it in thought. Though he was young, probably under thirty, the mustache gave him something of a patriarchal aspect.

We regarded each other for some moments in silence.

"You know," he said, "if I didn't see that motorcycle sitting there, I'd think you were some mad rock prospector who just wandered in from the desert."

"Yeah," I said. "Where'd you come from?"

"My cabin. Up the creek. I heard the dog, and thought I'd mosey down and see what the ruckus was about."

"Satisfied?" I wanted to get rid of him, get back on my bike—even though I still reeled with weariness—and try again to ride until I disappeared.

He put the pipe back in his mouth and shook his head. "Nope. It interests me that the dog barked at you so long. He usually doesn't waste words. Something about you really set him off." He raised one eyebrow, looked me up and down, and tapped his teeth with the pipe. "You sure look like hell," he said.

"Figures," I muttered. I didn't feel like my voice was my own. For one thing, my tongue felt thick and dry. But mainly, I had no interest in talking to anyone. I was too weary to intercept the habit.

"Why?" he asked.

"Dropped by the place on my way here," I mumbled.

"Oh. How was it?"

"You wouldn't really care to know."

"Sure I would," he said. "I'm a metaphysical voyeur."

My body had run out of things to say, so I just stood there, stupid and quiet, waiting for him to leave.

"Why don't you come up to my cabin, and get yourself cleaned up and fed," he said cheerily. "I'll swap you that in return for satisfying my curiosity about who you are and what you're up to."

"I'm not interested in getting saved," I said flatly.

"Gott!" He laughed. "Why would I want to mess with that? Last time I tried to save somebody, I wound up with my ass in *their* sling. Taught me a good lesson."

VIII.
Six
of Swords

By a variety of measures, playing on my sapped will, encouraging my growling stomach—which had about decided that it wasn't going to take any more shit from my demented brain—he got me up to his cabin. He gave me some food I little noted nor long remembered, and watched approvingly as I keeled over on a long bench covered with cushions.

It was midafternoon when I awoke. I lay there quietly, looking around the cabin. It was a small, but comfortable enough place, with an aggressively hand-hewn look. Peeled logs formed the framing members and rafters; the siding was rough-sawn planks. A lantern swung from a peg over my head. From other pegs were suspended, a lever-action Winchester .32 Special with a look of well-oiled use, a tight coil of climbing rope, and a straw cowboy hat with the crown busted out. A bookshelf at my feet began, on the first row, with Ezra Pound's *Guide to Kulcher*, wandered through numerous volumes on Oriental philosophy, notably Confucius and Lao Tze, and wound up with selections from Hiedigger and Nietzsche. The next two shelves were lawbooks. On top of the bookcase was a deer skull with a thick candle jammed into one eye socket.

I stretched and sat up. The kitchen was at the other side of the cabin. It sported a large wood-burning stove in blue enamel, and a sink with a hand-operated pump at one side. I went to the open front door. The man was hoeing his garden. A girl wearing striped overalls, but no shirt or shoes, was helping him. There were regular, metallic *tinks* as their hoes hit small stones.

136

Hard, clear sunlight reflected from their sweaty bodies as they worked. Then the girl noticed me in the doorway, and told the man, "He's up." He saw me and waved. Then he told the girl, "I'll go to town now. Will you do the goats?" She nodded. He put down his hoe, kissed her on the lips, and walked to the cabin.

"Ah!" he said. "He is not dead, but has risen! Feeling better now?"

I shrugged.

"Good. I've got some business in Santa Fe. You should come; we can talk on the way. You still owe me for breakfast, remember?"

I shrugged.

"You do that a lot, don't you?"

I could have told him that I was half-paralyzed with disinterest in everything, and that a shrug was the most eloquent expression I had. But I remained silent. He could ride me around, feed me, find me places to sleep to his heart's content. I didn't much care. When he got tired and stopped, I would continue my headlong flight away from the knowledge. And if he poked and pried and prodded and coaxed until I told him about it, then he would get what was coming to him.

His truck was a clean Ford half-ton with a four-speed. A huge wad of sage was tucked behind the visor, filling the cab with a sweet, spicy smell.

We jolted down a mile of rough, unpaved road, passing the place where I had crashed the previous night..

"Where's my motorcycle?"

"I pushed it into one end of my goatshed while you were asleep," he answered. "Do you know where you are?" I shook my head. "The Embudo River, near the place where it joins the Rio Grande."

"My name's Art Saruthaz," he continued. "If you wonder about the name, I'm half-Persian and half-German. I was conceived on a yacht near Greece, and born in a taxi in Hungary." He glanced at me out of the corners of his eyes. "I came to this country ten years ago, got through law school in New England, got out, and moved here."

The expression on his face, the tilt of his head, even the tone of his voice all radiated optimism, strength, and self-satisfaction. The voice especially . . . it was strong, cultivated, and slightly impressed with itself. Despite that, he managed to come off as extremely direct and sincere. He irritated the hell out of me.

"A lawyer and a farmer," I said. "An organic professional. How hip. You do your briefs on the back of a shovel with a piece of coal?"

He laughed. "No," he said. "I do 'em in petroglyphs on sandstone! But really, I don't live this way to impress anyone. It's just that

I've found out something by watching my classmates grow to commute to the arenas of power in their rolling status. In a chaotic world, most people are so desperate for respectability, that as soon as they get their hands on a little they immediately become insufferable.

"I don't want to get sucked into that. Another thing, I find it interesting to work for people who ordinarily would just get chewed up and spat out in the courts. Around here, that means small farmers. I can relate to them better and defend them better if I share some of their lifestyle. In any event, they can never afford to pay me much, so I have to farm to eat!"

He eyed me as I slouched in one corner of his cab. "So. Why don't you tell me about yourself?"

"I'd rather not."

"Why?"

"Because I don't want it to damage what you're doing."

He seemed to find that idea amusing.

We drove on in silence to Santa Fe. The buildings we passed ran the gamut from 20th century psuedo-Spanish, to real adobe. Soon we were in the old part of town, where aged buildings with tile roofs, and crumbling beige plaster on the outside walls, leaned over the narrow streets. There was a flowing crowd of Chicano residents and Anglo tourists, but somehow the buildings, reaching back into time, gave the impression of a warm and uncrowded space.

"Okay," Art said. "If you want to roam as the roamers do, the old square with the Palace of the Governors is off to your right. Also the local authentic kitsch emporiums. I'll pick you up here in an hour."

"I'm not interested."

"Well, my friend, you really don't have a choice. I'm here to see about a job, and I don't think your radiant expression and cheerful manner will help me much." He leaned over and opened the door.

So I went for a walk. It was either that, or sit on the sidewalk for an hour until he came back.

The Santa Fe square's most outstanding feature was a monument to the conquerors of the savages.

Some shops, adjacent to the square, had the macabre taste to prop full-size paper-mache Indian mannequins before their storefronts, like so many elaborately rouged corpses lined up for a body count. This sociological fart was beaten on its way to the bottom of the barrel by a jewelry store with a live one. Some poor Navajo grandfather, dressed in "genuwine" injun garb, sat in a special section between the cases. He squatted behind a rope in a square of sunlight, with his jewelry tools and a jug of water. The management had thoughtfully provided everything but a sign saying, "Please Don't Feed The Indian." Still, every tourist coming into the shop could see that *these* bracelets and squash blossom necklaces were the real buffalo chip.

I stopped going into stores and tried a few art galleries. Most of the work in them was so malproportioned and two-dimensional, it was impossible to guess what it might be doing in an "art" gallery, save as a joke with the pricetag for a punchline.

But in the basement of the last one I entered, I came across a series of paintings being crated. There was nothing left but the title tags on the wall, and one final painting which the clerk was lifting from its hook—a work executed with considerable talent.

I had noted that (interesting oddity) all of the title tags still up bore the word "wall" somewhere in them.

This last painting actually portrayed a wall, of huge stone blocks, as massive and endless as the Wall of China. It ran across a scene of the desert of the American Southwest, at that hour in the late afternoon when pastel shadows begin to ooze from wounds in the rock.

Near this massive wall, a plump, middle-aged man was sprawled. He wore an Hawaiian print shirt, a pair of Bermuda shorts, and white shoes. His limbs were contorted, and his fingers raked the sand in agony. This was understandable, since, perched on his chest, a huge mosquito-like figure had rammed its probiscis through the man's eye socket and down into his brain cavity.

The body plates of this giant insect had a metallic lacquer that stood out in surreal contrast to the dusty hues of the rest of the painting.

In the foreground, a woman, by age and appearance the man's wife, was taking a snapshot of the scene with a Kodak Instamatic. Her expression was one of vapid absorption, as if at any moment she were going to say, "Turn your head a little to the left, dear."

The work's title was *Picnic by the Wall.*

"Why take that down?" I asked.

The clerk, a young, thin white man with thick glasses held together by odd bits of wire, shrugged. "Manager said to. Yesterday some old biddy came in to get out of the sun. When she saw this painting, she threw up on the carpet and fainted. We've gotten negative comments on it before, but nothing like what we heard when she came to."

The clerk wrapped the painting in brown paper, taped the corners, and inserted it into a wooden crate. "So the manager said, since this guy's new stuff hasn't sold well, we should just pack it all up and ship it back. I don't know where we're going to send it, though; this guy's got a lot of different addresses. He moves around."

I thought about the painting all the way back to my rendezvous with Art. The tourist symbolism was obvious and easy. Less obvious, but of greater impact on me, was the identity of the bizarre guest lunching on the tourist's innards. I had realized, with a swift stab of rapport, that it was the artist. The sardonic rage of the artist's attack suggested that the acids of his contempt took effect in two directions at once. For if that giant, stinging insect was more real than its symbolic victim, it was also considerably more grotesque.

The implications, for me, of that metallic wasp of the tourist's doom, were too obvious to dwell on.

The truck was sitting at the curb when I got there. Art sat very quietly in the cab, his back straight, eyes focused on the street ahead of him. I looked in that direction but saw nothing unusual. I got in the cab and shut the door.

" 'Scuse me a moment," Art said. "I'm sitting here marveling."

"At what?"

"I'd rather not explain. I'd rather sit here and marvel."

About fifteen seconds went by; then he started the truck. Santa Fe was a diminishing memory in the rear views before he spoke again. "Looks like I'm getting a job," he said. "The ACLU wanted to hire a rep for the local Pueblos, and I think I'm it."

Art tugged at his mustache, and stared out through the windshield like a man who has just been coronated emperor of his own life. I saw that he belonged to himself and his home, to his work, his times, and his society. All his relations with these things were imbued with the fullest characteristics of his personality and his purposes. He had chosen them.

He made the vacuum in which I floated seem even more barren and cold by contrast. But I was full of one thing. The memory of what I had seen was a dark, constant pressure at the back of my skull. Its light of shadows revealed a lack of meaning in everything, including Art, sitting at the steering wheel of his truck, sublime with confidence. I envied . . . no! hated him for the success of his lie, for pretending to *be* with such aplomb!

"Art?" I said. "I have a thing to tell you . . . ."

I began with Tallahassee. The cushy situation, infused with the swelling dissatisfaction that rose to a crescendo the day I met Tallulah Crystall. The tearing of the photographs, the tearing of the umbilicals that bound me to the reality where I had been shaped . . . .

We stopped at a Mexican restaurant, but my narrative only paused for a moment. While Art ordered for both of us, I continued to talk. I told him about the energy of that strange and marvelous *presence*, that afternoon after the thunderstorm in the rain-wet field, my awe, and burning desire to pursue it. Hitting the road, following the urgings of the astrolabe of my heart. The ways that my perceptions began to change. My frightening visions and conversations with Push.

We ate tacos, burritos, frijoles, I didn't much notice or care.

Push, a belligerent apparition with a complex charm. I did not know that his demonic aspect would prove his strongest, as he lured me ever further into a psychic trap.

I was blinded by the exciting sensation of prying further into a rich understanding of my experience, wherein everything seemed marvelously linked to everything else. I was drawn by a spontaneous discovery of clues and patterns, by the *quality* of the energy that flowed between myself and Joyce, Big Daddy, Cheney, Radclift, Colonel Cofield, Faulkner, and even the Baptist encampment. All of it was significant, all of it led, suggested, directed.

On the rough drive back to the cabin, I told him how my strivings, and the promptings of Push, had helped me to destroy the remnants of my conditioning and move on into the freedom of following my impulses. Which made it possible for me to at last abandon myself to that one grand impulse, my search for that disembodied *presence*. The growing sense of appointment and my oath in the cafe in Lula to keep that appointment.

Inside the cabin, Art lit a kerosene lamp. We sat knee to knee, I on the bench and he on a chair facing me, smoking his pipe. His only visible reaction had been a smile at my description of Push, but I knew that he was caught up in my story. There was a rhythm and momentum in my voice now, a steadily growing force. My words formed a psychic vector, heading like an arrow toward the center of that dark memory. It was like driving toward a mountain at night—a huge, undefined black shape that gradually reaches up to blot out the stars.

Mena. The journey up the long ridge, the ceremonial herb from the thin blonde man. Moving on, and stopping at that point of view where I knew it would all begin. The appointment.

The traveler, the cloaked figure, the blue stones. The regal woman, and the impulse to go further. The cave within and through her. The images, the forms of understanding, the watching figure of the Shaman. And the impulse to go further, expressed in the thrown stone that tore through into the vision of the vast, oceanic being, in all its grandeur. And yet the need to go further still, somewhere else, in order to complete the melody, the process, called The Search For Goodbye-To-Rains.

Then I stopped talking.

I couldn't say it! All the time I had spoken of the visions, I could *see* them erupting from the shadows of the cabin and streaming like wisps of half-formed colored smoke across the face of Art Saruthaz. I stared into his eyes in a frenzy to explain. But the inspired stream of words dried up abruptly when I reached the threshold of that place of desolation. My fear of invoking that vision was far stronger than my urge to communicate it. It came anyway. It swelled out from the center of the pupils of my eyes, flared into the cabin like a dark rose in sudden bloom, then vanished.

I leaned back on the bench, shaken, one hand over my eyes to press that knowledge back in.

Art sat still for a while, staring at the lantern flame and sucking on his pipe. Then he turned the bowl upside down and tapped it into an ashtray. He got up.

"Well," he said, "you can unroll your bag there on the bench. I'm turning in right now. Big day tomorrow."

"*WHAT?*" My shout was shrill and breaking. "I showed you what it comes to; I showed you what it all comes to! You saw! And that's all you've got to say . . .?!"

He looked at me soberly. "You are a visionary, Steve. You invited a vision, and you got precisely what you asked for. Instead of just freaking out, why don't you realize that, and deal with it? If you want any sympathy, you'll find it in the dictionary between symmetry and symptom. Goodnight."

He left me sitting there.

I watched him walk to a bed at the back of the cabin, where there was a lump under the blankets, a spray of dark hair on the pillows, and a pair of striped overalls in a pile on the floor. I finally got it together to blow out the lantern and lie down, but my rage and frustration at the way Art Saruthaz had received my communication kept me awake for a long time.

So did the thumps and sleepy giggles that came from his end of the cabin.

Next morning, before I realized what I was doing, I was fondling a set of hairy goat tits. Art had plucked me out of bed at the crack of dawn to lead down the footpath to the goatshed. The air was cold, and smelt of dank clay and willows. To the east, sunrise was a thin band of incandescent pastels at the edge of the indigo hemisphere that soared overhead.

The goats were already milling and bleating for their grain. Art put the smaller doe into a stock on the rough-hewn milking table. The goat didn't seem to mind. She cheerfully snuffled and chomped through her pail of feed.

"Steve, this is Sheba. She's dumb, patient, happy, and she's got big tits. One of these days, I'm gonna run her for Miss New Mexico. Anyway, she's the easiest one to milk. Here's your bucket. Go to it."

"Now wait a minute," I said. "I never . . . ."

"It's as easy as jerking off. Just use your thumb and first two fingers. Brush her with the back of your hand, then start at the top of the teat and squeeze down. Get a gentle rhythm going, and try to land most of the squirts in the bucket. Your first time, that last isn't important, but it does give you something to aim for."

He put one hand on my shoulder, and I sat mechanically on the low stool. "I'll be back in a minute, if you have any problems," he said. "I've got to go scratch some itchy chickens."

I sat there, quiet, brooding, and utterly apathetic. By themselves, it seemed, my hands reached out and began to work clumsily on the goat. I didn't get anything at first, but soon splashes and splatters of milk were running down my pantlegs, and down the sides of the bucket. There was something warm, vibrant, and attractive about the scene . . . the cozy space full of lantern-light, and the smells of piss, straw, goat's breath, sweet grain, and fresh milk. But it seemed an invocation of that black memory, and a small motion of will could make it all disappear. The goat kicked, nearly upsetting the pail. Art walked in the door. "Here," he said. "I'll finish."

He took over the stool and expertly stripped the udders. The goat looked relieved. He let her down from the table and led the other doe up. He glanced at me standing in the corner with my hands jammed in my pockets.

"On the south side of the cabin there's some fir and cedar logs, and a nice double-bitted axe hanging under the eaves. When you chop wood you get warm twice; once when you cut it and again when you burn it."

"No," I said. "I'm splitting."

Oh?" he said. "Before breakfast? Very unwise. Ungrateful, too. Here I've fed you twice, given you a place to stay, and you won't even help with the chores. All you've done is tell me a long, involved story you don't even know the ending to yet. I'm not trying to keep you here, mind. Just get the *quid pro quo* straightened out. If you really want to charge off and drive into nothing until you fall over, that's your business. But I think you ought to settle your bills first. Besides, if splitting's what you're into, there's nothing quite like splitting firewood." He grinned under his mustache, and his eyes twinkled at me in the dim light of the shed.

I set my jaw and walked back to the cabin. That man sure made it hard to be apathetic. The axe hung from two nails, bracketing the handle just under the head. The edges were keen, the hickory handle polished smooth from much use. The ground underfoot was spongy with layers of chips and shavings. Near a sawing-buck, a number of short logs were piled. I put one on a broad, flat stump evidently used for the purpose, swung the axe high over my head, and put my shoulder into the swing as it came down. There was a nice, satisfying ka-CHUNK, and the log split in half. I chopped a lot of wood. Art came and got an armload. I didn't look at him. After a while, smoke began to rise from the chimney on the cabin roof.

"Chow!" Art yelled from the window. I toyed with the idea of just jumping on my motorcycle and leaving. But the morning air was still cold, and my stomach growled an enthusiastic objection. I had worked up one hell of an appetite. Maybe after breakfast.

When I sat on the bench, the girl shoved a plate, bearing an omelet full of fresh vegetables and goatcheese, into my hand. She was a young, comely Chicano lady, who seemed to take care of all necessary communication with her luminous dark eyes. In this instance, I saw a warm love for Art, and a mild curiosity about me. She retired with her breakfast to the bed at the back of the cabin, and picked up a paperback: *The Journal of Albion Moonlight*, by Patchen.

Art poured me a cup of coffee from the huge speckled pot on the stove.

"Sufi dancing at da Gama Center today," he said.

"Soufflé dancing?" I echoed, between bites. That was an odd image.

"*Sufi,*" Art corrected. "Sufism is a Moslem mystical sect. One thing it's into is a kind of spiritual square dancing. I'm sure you've heard of whirling dervishes; they're Sufis.

"Da Gama Center is a spiritual commune on a mountain east of Taos, dedicated to the multidenominational pursuit of religious ecstasy. Every Sunday they put on a Sufi dance for the locals and everybody comes. It's the closest thing to a church the freaks around here have . . . the Sufi Church of St. Dionysius the Emancipator, I call it. There's a lot of freaks in Northern New Mexico, you know. It's a hangout for old Beatniks and disenchanted hippies who came here to maintain their ethnic purity. Anyway, da Gama's where I'm going today. You're welcome to come too, provided you can tear yourself away from your angst."

He grinned, challenging me.

"No," I said. "I'm leaving."

"Well," he said. "You might find that hard to do. I'm afraid the goats got into your motorcycle. They munched up your spark plug wires and had a pretty fair start on your seat, before I stopped them this morning. I'll pay for the damage and get it running again, but it'll be tomorrow before anything can be done. So you might as well come. Besides, I don't want you hanging around here to curdle the milk."

I shrugged and slumped back onto the bench. My only emotion was an irritation with the pushy ways of Art Saruthaz, but my apathy by far outweighed it.

We headed north, the Rio Grande gorge to our left, the Sangre de Cristo Mountains to our right. When we could see it, the river was a foaming stampede of water, whispering and singing over glistening rocks.

Art was in a chatty mood. "You know, the ACLU man said that what cinched the job for me was not so much my regular qualifications as my sense of humor." He twirled one end of his mustache around a finger. "Maybe the best way to illustrate what he meant is to tell you a story. It's my turn, anyway. . . .

"This takes place at the time of the first Spanish conquistadores that got up this way, around 1541. When they made it into New Mexico, they were very disappointed to find mud pueblos instead of fabled golden cities. They consoled themselves by sacking what they *did* find. The Indians thought that, for uninvited guests, this was rather poor behavior, and they protested. Vigorously. The Spanish swatted them down and ignored them, as they continued to cast around the countryside for the gold that was never there. In the process, they acquired an Indian slave they nicknamed 'El Turco.'

"El Turco observed the power of his new masters, their curious behavior, and the bottomless greed behind it. After carefully considering which side he wanted to be on, he made them an offer. He told the Spaniards that there was, indeed, a marvelous city of gold, called Quivira. It lay many miles to the northeast, but he, El Turco, could lead them to it.

"Enthusiasm and greed renewed, the Spanish mounted an expedition that spring. They marched northeast for over a month, penetrating deeply into the plains of Kansas. There they found the grass huts of some poor plains Indians, and a vast quantity of buffalo chips. No gold. First they got discouraged; then they got angry; finally they accosted El Turco. 'Ah,' he said, 'the city lay just ahead.' Only a few more days of travel, and they would find wealth beyond their wildest dreams. Naturally they kept on. Naturally, they didn't find it.

145

"El Turco stuck to his story. He wasn't about to nip a good joke in the bud. Francisco Coronado, however, was. Particularly once he began to suspect how much the joke was on him. He nipped El Turco in the bud.

"Right up until the end, the Indian insisted that the city existed, but without his help they'd never find it. Thus, he masterfully set up a tension between the conquistadores' worst fear, being taken for fools by an Indian, and their greatest hope, getting their paws on the gold. In the end their fear won out, as he probably knew it would. Perhaps he considered his life a small price to pay for such a good joke. In any event, he was right about one thing: without his help, they never *did* find it!"

Art chuckled. I remained silent. He glanced at me with one raised eyebrow.

"Just a couple years back," he continued, "a New York, real estate development company came out here to throw up a Sunbelt version of the American Dream. They bought large tracts of land from the Indians and began to encrust it right away with their version of reality: pools, tennis courts, luxury homes, a shopping center and a golf course. 3½ acre sites! Models open!

"But as usual, they forged ahead with their big money schemes without really getting to know the culture and the land they were trying to exploit. If they had, they would've found out that water is of fantastic importance around here. Even farmers have their water carefully alloted. Water rights are equal in importance to land deeds, and they can be bought and sold separately.

"Can you guess what happened? The Indians sold the land at a good price, but somehow the subject of water rights never came up. And when, eventually, it did come up, they had decided not to sell them."

I repressed a smile.

"Now I'm not just telling you these things to show you how far out my sense of a good joke is. I want to share something, explain something, and ask you something. What I want to explain is that the New Mexican Indians were conquered politically, economically, and devastated culturally. Your redoubtable Kit Carson destroyed their orchards, confiscated their fields, torched their villages, and then herded the survivors together for a forced march in the dead of winter up to a concentration camp—that was a cesspool of disease!—called Bosque Redondo. That journey was called the Long Walk, and it makes the Bataan Death March look like an Easter Parade!

"But despite that, despite the fact that they had their entire universe smashed, tortured, and beaten into the ground, despite the fact that they had their reality torn apart and thrown to the winds in a *very* graphic fashion, and have been forced to adopt unfamiliar ways in a strange land, there's quite a few Indians around here who haven't lost their ability to appreciate a good joke, or to play one. They still have the healing medicine of their humor.

"Now, what I wanted to ask you was: where's yours?"

I had nothing to say. I didn't want to do it, but I thought about his question all the way up to da Gama.

A few miles east of Taos, we drove through a soft rain of cotton-wood seeds and turned onto a dirt road that switched back and forth up the mountain. We passed fields of rocky sand and fragrant sage, and further up, stands of pinon and ponderosa pine. At length the road expired in a dusty lot full of vans, trucks, and battered cars.

A wooden hand, mounted on a post, pointed out a path that led up through the trees.

We followed it a short distance, and emerged at the lower end of a meadow that extended magnificently up the mountainside. At the top of the meadow a large, domed building was silhouetted against the forest. The building had two wings extending from the sides of the central dome. It looked like a giant, Tibetan lama's hat perched on the mountain's forehead.

"Nice theatre, eh?" Art said, "the way you get aimed toward the best view."

We walked up a well-worn footpath to the dome. Clumps of hairy young people were gathered near the building, under the trees. They were dressed for the most part in sandals and loose, flowing clothing with a mideastern flair. A few faces turned in our direction. A beautiful blonde woman, wearing a white caftan and an incredible tan, called to Art. He waved and walked toward her.

I continued on the path. It was a relief to be freed of the pressure of his presence.

The building's Oriental bearing in the cowpoke wilds of America was startling, particularly when one saw how it had been built. The lower walls were constructed entirely of adobe, but the upper part was a Buckminster Fuller-certifiable geodesic dome, made of plywood panels on 2 x 4 frames. The entrance way was a cool, shadowy tunnel with a packed clay floor. On low wooden shelves at the sides were strange musical instruments: long narrow drums and short, wasp-waisted ones; a mandolin with a giraffe-like neck; zithers, dulcimers, tiny hand cymbals; and an autoharp. Then the tunnel opened up into the main dome.

Here the flooring was of smooth fir planks, with a central hexagon of flagstones. Eight diamond shapes of light fell from skylights in the roof arching overhead.

In one of those diamonds of light stood a thin woman. She wore only a pair of loose cotton trousers held up by a knotted cord. Her body was in superb condition. Every time she moved, arabesques of muscle rippled across her chest and belly. There was not an ounce of extra flesh anywhere on her. Her breasts were so small, high and firm that I had originally mistaken her for a man, but the large brown coins of nipples made me look closer and realize my mistake. It was impossible to guess her age. Her narrow, youthful body rose to a face so weathered and lined that it looked like it led the body through time at an advance of several decades. Her hair was curly and uncut, and stood out from her head in all directions, like an explosion of brown protein. For all its lines, her face bore an expression of wistful amusement, and her black eyes had an energy in them that almost audibly crackled.

She looked like a cross between a ballerina, a yogi, and a brown dandelion. This, I later found out, was Nasrudi.

The only other person in the dome was a young girl who stood demurely at the woman's side. She was dressed in a light blue shift of voluminous dimensions, with part of its hem raised and knotted about her hips as a kind of girdle. Her long, black hair was twisted into two braids; a small feather was tied by a leather thong to the end of each.

"This is the walk of water," she said to the woman. The thin, brown woman began a slow, quiet beat with her fingertips on the drum that she held at the curve above her hip. The girl moved in long, smooth strides around the flagstone hexagon. In rhythm with her walk, she swung her hands in symbolic motions, evocative of the rise of moisture to the heavens and its fall to earth. For a moment the dance almost hypnotized me; I could almost *hear* the cascade of water between drumbeats, but then I was able to fight down the illusion and deny it.

The dome began to fill. Perhaps a hundred people, answering to the most fantastic descriptions of people anywhere in the country at that time, gathered around the hexagon.

Nasrudi had stopped playing for the girl, and was using the attention her dance had drawn to organize the crowd. She described and illustrated the motions she wished them to perform, the steps for the men, the steps for the women, and the differing chants for each. Then she and two male drummers that joined her in the center began to tap out their beat.

In a short time the dancers were whirling happily in a maelstrom of their own energy. I was seized by a desire to join them, but paralyzed by an inability to believe in what they were doing, in what anyone was doing. I had become an outcaste of my own volition, obsessed with a cynical distrust of all I observed, a loathing for my own paralysis, and a weird, shamed longing for the safe and sane state of normalcy from which I had severed myself.

At that point, I flung myself into the crowd of dancers and tried desperately to belong to them! I forced myself to make eye contact, to twist and bend to the rhythm, but my movements were clumsy and stiff. It seemed that all whom my eyes met turned their eyes away, to shut themselves off from the spectacle of my clumsy and desperate efforts. I stopped trying to dance and headed for the door.

Outside, it felt easier to breathe.

From inside came the sound of the drums, the shuffling feet, and a shout, *"La illaha el il Allah!"* I hurried away. A path suggested itself. It lead into the forest of ponderosa. The air was thick with the smell of pinesap, and the warmth of midday. A bluebird yodeled in the distance.

I came to a clearing, where the circular foundation of a building had been laid out in adobe. The bricks wore the same beige hue as the surrounding dirt, which suggested that the earth was growing the building out of itself, a natural formation on the rise. Across the clearing, up among the trees, I spotted the lodge poles and smoke flap of a tipi. I headed for it. I needed a quiet place to rest and think, to concentrate on blotting out the memory of the search for Goodbye-To-Rains, to focus my attention on escaping back into life.

I couldn't find a path that led to it, so I forced my way through the trees. The tipi was made of large, tanned hides, stitched together with gut. A Navajo sun symbol was painted on the side, in blue. I presumed that the tipi's occupants would be down at the Sufi dance; so I opened the doorflap and stepped in. I was wrong. A man sat there, naked, in the lotus position, under a wedge of light that fell through the smokehole. He was about forty, square-faced and deeply tanned, with a vee of dark skin at the base of his neck, pointing down his chest. The line on his red-blond hair had receded about as far as a hairline could, leaving a narrow fringe over each ear. As if to balance this asperity with abundance, a thick beard jutted from his chin and curled in amiable confusion with the hair on his chest. His eyes were a pale, high-altitude blue, like the New Mexican sky at midday.

As he watched me enter his tipi, the man's face was absolutely expressionless, but not frozen or unkind. When I saw him, I made as if to turn and go, but he stopped me with an upraised hand. He reached into the pile of clothing in front of him, taking out a rapidograph and a spiral notebook. Flipping it to a blank page, he wrote in spidery script.

"No. You came to the right place. I am John. Tell Nasrudi I've checked you out, and it's OK."

"What?" I said.

"You are here to work," he wrote.

There was no punctuation after this to indicate whether it was a question, a statement, or an imperative. I motioned that he give me the pen. I made all three signs after the sentence and handed it back to him. He nodded.

"Fine," he wrote below. "The agreement is to work for two weeks. We feed you. You can participate in all ceremonies and *seshins*. You must observe all rules for order. Afterwards, if you want to stay longer, a meeting will be held to consider this."

I looked up, astonished. Evidently I had stumbled into the process by which prospective entrants to da Gama Center were screened. It suddenly seemed desirable to allow the process to continue. It was as if life itself were reaching out for me, drawing me into an alternative to my desperate flight from the dark memory. Here, perhaps, among the residents of da Gama, I might be able to escape it.

I looked at John, and nodded my acceptance.

He wrote at the bottom of the page, "Tell Nasrudi that John has seen you. She will give you additional information."

Then he bowed once from the waist, with his folded hands raised to his forehead. It was clear that the interview had just been concluded. As I left the tipi, I looked back at him. The reflection of light from the walls of tanned skin made him seem encased in a pyramid of shadow and gold light.

I made my way back down towards the dome. Clumps and couples of people were scattered under the trees again. The dance had ended, though the thump and throb of the drums still floated from the main building.

Art Saruthaz sat on an outcrop of rock, flanked by the girl in the caftan. I realized, when I saw him, that I had another reason for moving to da Gama. He was the only one, right now, who could know what I ran from, and why. It was essential for me to believe that he could not know, and continue to be such a powerful and disturbing presence.

He was talking to the girl with animation. She seemed to be listening with rapt, even worshipful, attention. Art saw me approach.

"Steven! I wondered what happened to you."

I faced him. "If you'd listened last night, you'd know what is happening to me all the time. Let's just say I made myself scarce."

He smiled. Disarmingly, I'm sure he thought. "Well, it's a good thing you made yourself present. Time to buzz down the mountain and take care of bizz."

"No," I said, "I'm staying." It gave me an inordinate pleasure to see him surprised. "Ah," I said. "You listened that time."

His mouth twisted in a sardonic expression, and his grey eyes regarded me gravely.

"What are you going to use for gear?" I shrugged. "I see. Well, walk with me down to the truck at least. We've got to figure out what to do about your bike and so on." He kissed the girl goodbye with approximately the same warm technique he had used on the Chicana who helped him with his garden.

"I have no plans," I informed him on our way to the truck. He shrugged. When we got there, he took a sleeping bag stuffed into a nylon sack out from behind the seat, and a toothbrush and a flashlight from the glove comparment. He slipped these last two articles into the bag.

"Here," he said.

"Don't want 'em."

"Look," he said testily. "It gets cold up here. You've got enough problems without frostbite and halitosis." He slammed the bag into my chest so forcefully that I had to grab it to keep from falling down.

"Maybe in a couple days I'll come by and give myself the opportunity to not-listen to you some more. And see if you've learned to hide from yourself as well as the people you despise."

I flinched. He jumped in his truck, slammed the door, and started the engine.

I watched him drive off with feelings that could only be described as mixed.

"Yeah! I'm Nasrudi, most of the time anyway! To work, huh? I guess you've already talked to John then. No, he's not a mute. He's taken a vow of silence. He's done well with chastity and poverty, so I guess he's givin 'em all a whirl. Only opens his mouth these days to eat and chant. If you like, we can stick you in his tipi. If you don't bug him to talk, he won't even know you're there.

You know how to mix adobe? You'll learn. I love getting someone else to do it. Gives me more time to teach yoga. Know any of that? Good. You mix adobe and I'll teach you yoga. It's great for headaches, backaches, any other kind of ache you got. Don't worry, after a day of mixing adobe, you'll have plenty. Don't thank me, teaching that is my work, getting the kundalini of the world flowing like a mountain stream. I'll help your schedule do that too, right now if you want. All you have to do is get into the flow of things here. Rise at 5:30, go to the meditation chamber under the north wing, and you'll get to hear John chant his sutra. He's got a lovely voice. Then there's meditation and breakfast until 7:30. Work on the new building goes until 11:30, yoga lesson until

12:30, lunch, then more work until 6:00. Supper. All food, by the way, is the finest vegetarian cuisine. The least we can do, while we're working you to death, is to keep from poisoning you.

"After supper you get to hang out, play, do anything you want . . . though probably you'll prefer to sleep. If you're not used to it, the first few days of working in high altitude can ruin you. Oh yeah, I should tell you about the 'glitch,' which is our affectionate little nickname for Rocky Mountain dysentery; closest thing da Gama has to an initiation ceremony."

Minutes past sunrise. From far away came a high, thin ringing. The bell made a silver sliver of a sound, that slipped easily and without pain between my eyebrows. It rekindled the fire in the brazier of my cranium. The glow rose; my eyes became open and lit; fog began to pour out of my ears. It took a couple minutes for me to remember who and where I was.

The inside of the tipi was like a dark cave. Quiet John was already up and gone, his bag and blankets folded on the spot where he slept. I folded mine exactly the same way, put on my clothes, and stepped out into the milky light of a new day.

I walked north with quick, shivering steps, hugging myself from the cold. When I burst from the forest into the high mountain meadow that held the dome, it was like walking into the nave of a vast cathedral. To my right, hot white light sang around the peaks of the mountain, like the first high, held note of a choir. To the left patches of glowing pastel—like the light that falls through stained glass—pursued purple shadows across the lowland plains, and into the Rio Grande Gorge.

The earthen colors of the main building were just beginning to come alive in the sunlight. From different points of the compass, cloaked figures were gliding toward it across the meadow. I followed . . . aware of an acute inner yearning to have and hold the knowledge that they moved toward with such a sure desire. I followed them down the brick steps that went under the north wing to a low chamber, where the hard packed clay was covered with a cracked, off-white plaster.

A small, square altar reposed in the center. A cross of sun fell from an upper window onto the altar, illuminating a glass vase of mountain flowers.

Quiet John knelt by it, his ass resting on a small hard pillow held between his heels. He sat motionless in a roughwoven serape, the strong features of his face brought out by the faint light in such a way as to give him the appearance of a desert ascetic from some dead century. He looked as if he held some deep and timeless secret in the cracked and worn hands that rested between his thighs. He looked as if he could give me what I so desperately wanted and needed—an alternative.

He waited until the people were settled. Then he struck a small gong, and began to chant the "Prajna Paramita Sutra" in a resonant basso profundo. I recognized it instantly. This was the sutra that taught emptiness of the senses and the unreality of everything—enlightenment or nonenlightenment, suffering or pleasure. "Form is emptiness, emptiness is the form"

HERE, TOO? After the chant came a long meditation, during which I backpedaled from my memory of the form of emptiness. The harder I struggled, the closer it came.

I was feeling fairly dissociated by breakfast time, and feeling less hope about the ability of da Gama to fill my void, or at least distract me from it.

The kitchen and serving space was a two-story, octagonal structure behind the main dome. A wire ran from it to the top of the dome, bearing a tattered line of Tibetan prayer flags, like so many good intentions hung out to dry. The kitchen, a warm cocoon of organic carpentry, was full of the smell of coffee and tea, pans of scrambled eggs mixed with spinach and spices, hot fresh biscuits and honey.

The faces around me, whether rapt in a small inner ecstasy, stern with discipline, or lit from within with friendliness and compassion, seemed animated in their various roles with conviction and fervor. I could not believe in their reality, but at the same time, I envied them bitterly for what they seemed to have.

I almost expected the food to echo as it fell into me. It was only after I had attracted a number of significant stares that I realized I had eaten many times more than my share.

I took my half-empty plate back into the kitchen again, and went down to where the work-people were assembling at the foundations of the new building. I was surprised to see Quiet John as the foreman. Perhaps a dozen others, vegetarian thin, with Old Testament beards and New Testament eyes, were gathered around a fire when I arrived. John handed out sheets of paper from his notebook, outlining the day's activities in his neat script. There was a moment of collective silence as we read; then we went to work.

Nasrudi appeared briefly, to help with the adobe mortar mixing that was my assignment. She showed me how to mix the red clay with dirt and water in a broad trough, chopping and turning it with a hoe. Her tight, thin body bent enthusiastically to her work.

"There you go!" she said, handing me the tool. "Soon you'll have your basic hoe-hoe-hoe down good enough to try out for Santa

Claus. Don't forget to smile as you do it. That's very important.''

Work went on with a will after Nasrudi was gone, but everyone seemed strangely silent and intent. Normal workman's banter seemed contrary to rule or custom. I couldn't take it. I needed something to keep me on the surface of life, on the physical, so that I would not fall back into the black hole at the center of my mind.

I attempted a small joke, to break the eerie silence and ingratiate myself with the people around me.

"Hoe-hoe-hoe," I said, as I chopped in my trough. "HOE-HOE-HOE!"

I was immediately reproved by Mesquite, a young man in his late teens, with a scrawny beard, and the tight, possessed expression of the true believer.

"John wants work to be a meditation," he said. "That's why we communicate just vibrationally as much as possible. He has written that we should put our highest spiritual attention into the laying of every brick."

Several hairy heads nodded agreement. John himself fixed me with those high-altitude blue eyes of his and smiled, not unkindly. I found something interesting at the bottom of my trough and spent a great deal of time looking at it.

Work was only interrupted by the arrival of a Pueblo Indian mason named Jimmie. His face was itself the color and texture of an old adobe brick—he had to be at least seventy years old—but he moved with the supple energy of a man much younger. He wore a complete Anglo cowboy outfit: five-gallon hat, Western shirt, bolo tie, dress jeans, and a pair of boots with toes so sharp they looked like they could slash tires. But a hawk feather fluttered in his hatband, his long black hair hung in braids past his shoulders, and the heels had been knocked off his boots. He greeted everyone with a thoroughness that indicated he had all the time in the world; then he rolled up sleeves, took off his tie, and began laying brick faster than anyone had yet attempted.

I got a closer look at him when he came to check the mortar. Under heavy, tortoise-like lids, his eyes were brown and liquid as those of a deer. I looked into them, in search of that humor that Art had told me about, but all I saw was an inner *presence* that reminded me of what I had once followed, and I hastily averted my eyes.

Jimmie lingered over the trough, rubbing a pinch of the mix betwen thumb and forefinger.

" 'im need a bit more clay," he informed me gravely. "Turn 'im longer too, please, huh?"

Then he went back to his bricks.

As make-work for my consciousness, a kind of mental fix, I set myself to figuring out the political infrastructure of da Gama. A community meeting on the evening of the third day gave me a chance to crystallize my impressions.

The main division was between full-time residents of the Center, and visiting workers like myself. The residents were the Elect, the Holy Few, whereas the workers were considered—both by the Elect and the workers themselves—to be a motley band of aspiring interlopers, blessed to the extent that they contributed money and time to the Center, but otherwise regarded with a compassionate disdain.

This spiritual pecking order dictated that there be a hierarchy within both divisions. Foremost among the Elect was Winbhag Dass, a tall Cocoa Beach ex-surfer, who had spent years in India acquiring local color, bacilli, and assorted mystical doctrines and chants. He subsequently employed this expertise by acting as a tour guide for famous disenchanted American psychologists who came to India to snuggle up to the Real Thing. This, plus the fact that he was enormously photogenic, had won him honorable mention in national magazine articles exploring the new wave in American spirituality. He had a voice like a bass foghorn, and an impressive wardrobe of authentic holyman garb, straight from the New Delhi Goodwill. He was not one of the founders of da Gama, and had no real authority over anyone, but he was a main attraction, a cock of the walk. And he never let anyone forget it, particularly during the meeting.

After Winbhag came Quiet John, who frequently outgunned him by not deigning to write a note of reply, and Sarai, one of the wealthy lady founders of the Center, an adept at the spiritual art of looking through visitors as if they weren't there.

The pecking order went on down through the twenty men and women of the Elect, all effectively rated by their ability to put the others in their relative place. This yoga of putting others in their place had been developed to a fine art. It involved a posture of unassailable humility and righteousness on the part of the placer, while he or she gravely informed the placee of their shortcomings. The yoga became complex when the placee attempted to reverse the roles, by informing the placer that his humility and righteousness was actually a mask for massive insecurity, as proven by the compulsion to lash out in arbitrary judgement. Both of these moves were trumped by the transcendentalists, who sat silently in a corner, overseeing the proceedings with a benign contempt. As you might imagine, the meeting went on for some time.

The hierarchy of the underdogs, the visiting workers, who numbered about eighteen, was based simply on who had been there the longest. Mesquite had no real competition. He was the sparsely bearded young man with the severe case of zeal. A year previously, he had attatched his sidecar to Winbhag's juggernaut, and now dressed like him, wore his hair the same way, and shivered with worshipful ecstasy whenever Winbhag came near or spoke. The rest seemed content with their plebian status, content to labor without complaint for the eventual privilege of joining the patricians. Many had strong religious disciplines of various sorts—fasting, yoga, meditation—to hasten the day and hour of that consummation.

Two did not fit at all. Nasrudi was a maverick, a psychic acrobat who seemed to leap about the various status agreements without paying the slightest attention to them. She was regarded as amusing, but rather lacking in spiritual focus and depth. Despite this grave flaw, she seemed more interested than anyone else in sharing what little she knew, because it was she who organized both the public Sufi dances and the yoga classes.

The other one who did not fit was . . . me. I did not fit because I could not fit into the humble dedication of those working towards their dissolution in the vast being, or the spiritual assurance of the Elect, or the starry fascination of anyone's disciple, or the blithe abandon of Nasrudi. To me, we were all ants crawling along the convoluted twistings of the knot. It didn't matter which strand we chose; each inevitably led into the others, and they all went nowhere.

A point of view uniquely my own, but I really didn't want it either. Much as I tried to pretend my judgments of the da Gama Cosmic Follies were objective and impartial, I knew that my cynical distrust was primarily based on envy. I mightily resented those who seemed to be succeeding at da Gama, because I had chosen it out of fear rather than love; "sophisticated" contempt was my way of bringing them all down to my level. I was becoming the metallic wasp, whose only form of self-expression lay in its sting. I ground my teeth at feeling such a mechanism operating inside me, but I could not stop it, any more than I could exorcise that dark vision at the core of my mind from which it all came.

By the end of the third day, when it became obvious that interaction with da Gama was not going to save me, I felt like a swimmer caught in a tidal whirlpool, clawing with broken fingernails at a shore that would not receive me. The swirling, dark water sawed at my resistance.

IX.
Death

Tea-time at the adobe works. Two Center women came through the trees with a tray of cakes and a steaming pot of tea. We all gathered around a fire built up from scraps of wood. Workers swung down from beams, appeared in the doorways of half-finished walls, and approached with their empty cups in hand. I'd just finished pouring my tea through the strainer, when a shout came from the main path into the clearing.

"Hot damn! HOT CHAI!"

Two dudes whom I'd never seen at da Gama before came swinging toward us with long, rangy strides. One was tall and lanky, with a bandit mustache and shock of unruly, sunburnt hair. His face was so pocked and weatherbeaten it looked like a broken-off chunk of cliff. His companion was short, round faced, and probably hammering on the doors of fifty. His tan was as dark as the lanky younger man's, and contrasted pleasantly with a clipped grey beard and remnants of grey hair. A tiny gold earring glittered in his left ear. Both radiated a durable insouciance. The Duke and the Dauphin, I thought to myself.

They introduced themselves as Burt and Ben, then helped themselves to some tea. Mesquite looked askance, but John quietly indicated it was all right.

Burt, the lanky one with the face like Mt. Rushmore prior to carving, said, "It's a helluva walk up this mountain. The least you guys could do, in return for the pleasure of our company, is fire up a joint." He looked hopefully around the circle, but no one moved. "Ben," he said

157

sadly, "looks like we'll have to smoke yours."

Ben looked irritated. He fished a joint out of the pouch tied to his belt, lit it, and passed it reluctantly to Burt. Burt took an enthusiastic toke that consumed nearly a fourth of the cigarette. Ben reached for it surreptitiously, and Burt just as casually moved it further out of reach. Then he took a second toke of equal magnitude. "Goldurnit!" Ben exploded. "You fucken Bogart! Pass it, already!"

Burt gave him a crooked, unabashed grin, took his third toke, and passed it to me. "Shore," he said affably.

"We're throwin a surprise party tonight," Ben announced, as I tried out their herb. "We hiked up to engrave an invite for whoever wants to come."

"Who's the surprise for?" someone asked.

"For us, mostly," Ben said. "We didn't even know we was gonna have a party until about an hour ago. Then this fool here ran into Melba with the truck, and I had to finish her off with my rifle. So, its gonna be a barbecue pig feast if you guys can tear yourselfs away from your lettuce sandwiches."

"Sounds pretty decadent," Mesquite said. Pork was not holy.

"Naw," Burt said. "Sleazy's what we're goin for. Little live music, little cold beer, hot grub, good dope. Decadent's more like a party I went to last week, up in Arroyo Hondo. We were all buzzin on pharmaceuticals, man, and who should show up but the fucken *Banditos!* Talk about your heavies. They were all swaggerin around with those hairtrigger six-guns strapped on. . . .Whooo-oo, jump back! You know what I mean?"

"Banditos?" I asked. Their dope was strong, but I knew it would not remove the edge from what devoured me inside. Maybe sharing some of their bright and crazy reality would.

"Yeah," Burt explained. He leaned forward and scratched his nose with one yellow fingernail. "They're a bunch of New York toughies that sat around watching TV too long, got off on it, and figured they'd come out West and take a stab at bein Billy the Kid. Literally."

"They're like a bunch of bikers, only on horses," Ben put in.

"That's about right. They hang out in the hills, living on deer and what they can steal. They all wear those stinky old buckskins that they only take off once or twice a year. They like to get drunk and shoot each other. Every once in a while, for entertainment, they ride to town and rob a jewelry store or something, buy more booze, and ride off to their hideouts again."

"Don't the local cops get excited over that?" someone asked.

"Naw," Ben said. "They figure as long as the Banditos go on

shooting each other, they won't have to mess with it. The fuzz around here only gets agitated around elections. The rest of the time, they just kick back and collect dust.''

"And graft," Burt added.

"Are you kidding?" Ben said. "From who? For what? The only organized crime in New Mexico just stopped for lunch on its way to Las Vegas."

The scuttlebutt went on for some time. During the course of it, and later, talking to people who knew them, I found out that Ben and Burt were oldtime Sausalito beatniks, who'd fled the deluge of tourism that destroyed the atmosphere they'd helped create. They now lived on Bison Tennial Commune, five miles down the mountain from da Gama, and were renowned throughout the state as a pair of incorrigible characters.

In any event, they opened up another avenue of escape for me, and I eagerly seized it. The chance to give myself over to the Party had been offered to me in Tallahassee, and again by Big Daddy's clan in Jackson. I'd turned it down both times, from a misplaced sense of obligation to the search, and the questions I'd asked. Well that search had taken me to a place I could not endure, and da Gama's spirituality had not proved anesthetic to the memory. But if I boogied long enough and hard enough, I might be able to bury forever the drives for freedom and a deeper perception that had turned me into an outcaste whose vision corroded all he looked upon.

As soon as work ended that day, I was off down the mountain. A few others, facing the withering disapproval of Mesquite, had decided to come too...but they all wanted to shower and change. I couldn't wait for that, so I went on ahead alone.

After a long walk, I reached a side road branching off toward a creek. A small, hand-lettered sign requested: *Please Don't Pollute! Drinkin' Water.* I passed a big flatbed truck, laden with the stripped carapaces of old cars; then came to a long adobe ranchhouse with a tile roof. From behind the house came the rollicking sounds of live rock 'n roll.

A few others were there, scattered across a back yard that extended without hesitation into several square miles of desert. A low plywood stage had been set up against the back wall of the house, and a band's equipment distributed on top of it. Lettering on the front of the bass drum announced, *Viva Banana and the Pealers.* A thin girl—NY hip thin, not ugly thin—wearing a brief black top, jeans and wedgies, was talking to a beefy Chicano man who sat at the electric piano. I admired her animation and energy, the way her short brown hair shagged over high cheekbones, the full sensuous curve of her lower lip. The Chicano, in his handsome macho twenties, kept sniffing his nostrils as though he had an allergy or a bad cold.

She strolled back to a mike snapping her fingers to a beat, nodded to the guitarists and the drummer, and launched into a high-powered version of "Johnny B. Goode." I sat to the sidelines and watched.

People materialized from everywhere, gathered in a clearing before the stage, and began to dance. The band jammed on their theme. The guitarists looked as if at any moment smoke would begin pouring from their fingertips. The keyboard man stood up, kicked over his stool and proceeded to go beserk. The dark lady grabbed her mike and performed a convincing fellatio on it while she belted out the final verse. The entire band swung, hovered around a single note, then plunged into their next song.

I watched spellbound as the music exploded out over the desert. I thought of Tallahassee Jo and the Pastime. This scene was the mad and careless lifestyle I'd left behind; I *had* to get back to it! I got up to dance, not because I wanted to, but because I felt that if I didn't do it now, soon I would be unable.

With a dry mouth and sweaty hands I tried to concentrate on the beat, but again the music was like quicksilver and my fear-stiffened body too clumsy to grasp it. I felt as if my last chance to return to normalcy was ebbing....*Keep trying!* One beat ahead or behind, I could find no rhythm or continuity within myself to match to the music. I knew all watching the dance must be laughing at me now, thinking me drunk.

Then el Chicano rang down the curtain with triumphant flourishes on his piano, accompanied by a crescendo of thumps from the drums. "We gotta stop fer a minnit!" he yelled, waving his arms over his head. "I got sweat under mah wings! And I gots to powder mah nose! Yah!"

I staggered away from the stage and into the crowd. There was one now; the few onlookers of a few minutes before had multiplied like loaves and fishes. There were old-timers, hobo hippies, road gypsies, squareheads, farm-types, bozos, whores and high priestesses, winos and belly dancers, all notified by the grassroots grapevine that a good time was waiting to be had. They were dressed in recycled army fatigues, embroidered denims, Bedouin robes, blue collar outfits (OshKosh B'gosh, Ben Davis, Union Made, Plenty Tough), House of Levi's latest styles, leathers, and granma's best dress, as they danced and laughed around the tables where they placed their offerings of food. Bearded, baubled, and beaded men smoked, drank, cussed and discussed. Small eddies of people gathered around a joint, a bottle, or an idea, then plunged back into the meandering current. It looked like a good party.

I drifted around it like a ghost, dipping lightly into conversations, songs, brief contacts, drifting on. I never found a place I could trust myself to stay, a relation that my clumsiness and desperation would not ruin.

An immense yellow parachute was rigged as an awning at one end of the house. Under it, spitted sections of pig sweated beads of fat into pits of glowing charcoal. The lady lead singer was there, sipping on a Coors, joking with the fat man who brushed sauce on the joints of meat.

"Hello," I said to her. "You sound really good." Those were my words, but underneath them I was saying acknowledge me, reach out to me, let me be a part of what you are doing, help me escape myself!

"Thanks," she said carelessly. It was probably her fiftieth compliment since leaving the stage.

"Uh, what's your name?" I said stupidly.

"Viva. It's on the drum."

"Oh yeah. Well, I wanted to tell you that you're really good."

"Thanks." She studied me for an instant. I hid inside my eyes hoping that she would not see my strangeness. "Well, time for the next set," she said. "Enjoy."

I moved some distance away from the crowd, sat down, and things got critical inside. I was not even conscious that the fluid oozing slowly down my face was made of tears. All I knew was that my body was a thin husk wrapped around an awesome and horrible nothingness, and that that shell, with the last feelings left to it, was riddled with the leprosy of despair. My gaze wandered over the jagged horseshoe of people clustered around the band.

A tall figure with an Olympian mustache reared up out of a small group that had been sitting by the awning. He waved, and strode toward me. It was Art Saruthaz. He came on like a ship, the prow of his indomitable vibration cutting through the mellow, fuzzy atmosphere, trailing a wake of startled faces behind him.

"*Eco, homo!*" he said. "How are you getting on?"

"I'm off," I said, my voice catching, the words sounding strange. "Getting off, further off...."

He sat down beside me, reached into the pocket of his leather vest and pulled out his pipe. He shot me a sidelong glance as he filled and lit it.

"Christ! Not through feeling sorry for yourself yet? Thought you were tougher! I thought you'd be way past this stage by now."

"What *stage?* I've gone crazy. I burned my ties to life to chase something that doesn't exist, and now I can't get back. It's killing me! I can't relate to anything; all I can do is throw this dark venom on it...!"

"Well, naturally!" Art said. "You've got unfinished business with the goal of your search. You actually found what you were looking for, you know. But instead of recognizing and dealing with it, you let yourself freak out and miss the point. You ran away. But no matter how far you run or what you run to, you'll always have that unfinished business hanging on you until you take care of it. It's just too basic to ignore. Your life will become an increasingly silly, hypocritical game until you take care of it."

"I can't take care of anything! What does it take to make you understand? I was led into a psychic disaster! I'm damaged! I'm like one of those accident victims that can't remember how to walk and has to move by crawling...."

"Then crawl, goddammit!" Art lost his patience. "Life is worth it! Crawl back to that vision that still sucks up all your attention, get on your feet and face it! Look, fear is beside the point, though it's hardly inappropriate that far into the unknown. But you rejected everyone else's solutions, rejected the standardized realities that the world has to offer, and sailed your head into uncharted seas. You're living dangerously and that's beautiful! Don't give up now! Don't piss and moan and try to scramble back. Stake out the space where you find yourself and see what you can make of it."

"How? If you've got the solution for all this, stop fucking around and tell me!"

He laughed, suddenly and uproariously.

"The solution! The right idea! What a sublime, idiotic fantasy! Ha. I tell you, my friend, I've got *my* way . . . where's yours? Unless you can create it for yourself it'll never be anything you can keep, or even have in the first place!

"This despair you're flaunting, in the hopes it will take you off the hook, is nothing more than the tantrum of a lost child! Someone who demands things be given from the outside and refuses to take responsibility for himself. A child who grows up into a victim by insisting on his right to continue living that way. But you *chose* to cut your cords to that childish world. You chose to search for the world of a creator! The power you produced for yourself, when you made the oath to do that, is the power you need to *complete* the transition.

"You found the world of a creator, and your efforts to pretend that you're still a suffering child, a victim, just won't wash anymore. It's your resistance, a last-ditch attempt to block out your new being. A child is someone to whom things happen; a creator is someone *by* whom things happen! Once you've achieved that freedom, truth is not something that you find or have given to you any more. It's something you must make. Until, at last, truth is something that you *become!*"

I was knocked off balance, out of my self-pity, as Art relentlessly hammered home the things that had been waiting for me to understand. I didn't understand just yet. I was still recovering from the victim's game of exaggerated fear that Art had caught me in. As he continued to talk, suddenly liberated energy blasted free inside me and rushed from one end of my body to the other, like light in a laser crystal. I jumped to my feet and took in a deep breath that went right down to my heels.

"AHHHHHHHH!" I yelled at the top of my lungs. The music stopped, the crowd turned. Art began laughing again.

I had to move, express the energy somehow, or it would blow the top of my head off. I ran, out toward the road. As I passed the flatbed truck, I could just hear Art's voice as he made an explanation to the crowd.

"He had to go to the head pretty bad. The glitch . . . ."

I ran up the hill until I could run no further. I felt dizzy. All the doubt, dissociation and paranoia that I'd experienced since the vision jangled around me, whirling through my mind like bonds of barbed wire with points that tore. But in the center grew the awareness that I had the ability to create a choice, and the priceless opportunity to do so. I aimed that awareness at the black hole in my mind, the memory of the EMPTINESS. . . . And as my body stood there on the road, panting for breath, I said, *I choose to be!*

I did not sleep much that night. I lay on my back in John's tipi, looking at the stars through the smoke hole, listening to the wind struggle in the trees, like an animal with its foot caught in a trap, tearing itself free to go soaring across the mountains.

The thoughts within and around me were clear, strong, crystalline. I felt I could almost reach out and touch them as they dangled and spun around me in the darkness.

"Truth is not something that you find or have given to you anymore. It is something you must make. Until, at last, it is someting that you become."

"You will have to expand yourself in understanding of the basic structure of reality and the nature of choice. You will have to take responsibility for the creation of a world within the world where you find yourself."

I was infused again with the confident power I had felt that morning in Mississippi, in that coffeeshop in Lula, where I had sworn to follow the path of the stars, and the trace of that *presence,* to the end of the appointment and beyond if necessary, . . . and what had I found? As Art Saruthaz asserted, had I arrived at precisely the goal of my search?

Metaphorically, I stood on my own two feet and peered back into my memory, gazing at that spot of utter desolation . . .

> through the freedom of goodbye to rains
> allowing the physical forces of the earth of which I
> was a part to flow without prejudice or interruption
> which I understood

> through the freedom of goodbye to reigns
> loosing the grip of desire and fear by which the pat-
> terns and institutions of other men controlled me
> which I understood

> through the freedom of goodbye to reins
> the liberation from the maze of conditioning that
> had formed the definition of the old myself
> which I understood

. . . and beyond the place where those numberless souls abandoned or cast aside their own creativity and individuation to dissolve in the Source, in the womb of that vast being from which they had been drawn. If done for love and as a completion, a worthy path. But the one I had chosen led on, into. . . .

I began to perceive it. That which had—so unnecessarily!—filled me with such shock and fear. That incredible NOTHINGNESS was simply my own, uncreated space. It was the most precious thing there could ever be for me: a universe of my own, interpenetrating all other universes. A realm of my own possibilities.

To be *and* not to be, I thought. We already are the answer to Hamlet's question.

Between word and act lay uncreated space, between breaths, between the intention of one moment and the tempered intention of the next. Thus Faulkner, for example, was able to interpenetrate the world of his own special significance with the elements of the world where he found himself. To fuse Oxford with Jefferson. To infuse flesh with the spirit of creativity. That had made it possible for Radclift and Cofield and Faulkner to become fully human, to become themselves. And I.

In each of us there was a point at the heart like the sun, glowing with the innate power of choice, of understanding, of love. Of hate, confusion, and despair. What was chosen shone out through the clumsy beauty of the flesh, manifesting each creator's special nature in the words, the works, and the relations of his lives.

Enactment of this understanding was the swordstroke through the knot!

The next day began as a thin line of grey light under the tipi's edge. I hadn't undressed, so when I heard the high, distant tinkle of the bell, I stood up immediately and went outside. I could see the white shape of the bellringer fluttering in the shadows of the forest. I followed the shape and the sound down the path, towards the dome and the meditation room.

Then my feet slowed on the path. There was no longer a point in joining the diligent seekers of any other enlightenment. I had mine.

Pleasantly startled by this turn of mental events, I dawdled, dangled, stood on the trail and stretched. A bit down the hill, I spotted a rusty old pickup lounging by a neat stack of firewood. A sleazy, don't-care saxophone started a solo in my mind as I walked down to the truck, got in, and banged the don't-fit door behind me. I gazed out over the plains of the Rio Grande Gorge and lost myself in vision for a moment. . . .

Then I snapped back to that place, that point in time, that truck cab with its smells of old grease and rotting leather, its peeling paint and broken glass, the erupting seat springs that jabbed me in the ass. I put my forehead on the steering wheel to think.

A faint suggestion of woodsmoke and coffee in the air, drifted down from the kitchen, and in through the smashed side window of the truck.

This moment was most real. Compared to it, all the past events, forces, and personages, even my galaxy of former thoughts, seemed vague and dreamlike. My only true possession was the *Now!* within me, trembling like a droplet on the tip of a leaf.

I remembered my choice to *be* on that dusty, twilit road last night. Make it again, make it again! Moving with the slow steady pulse of breathing, into the more rapid alternation of heartbeat. And always, between, the precious silence.

This moment, this choice to be present and absent within it, this motion from one to the next is not only my only possession, it is me. I accept and choose this life, this body, this mind, this world in which I find myself, and take responsibility for them. But even more, I accept and take charge of my uncreated space, for this is the realm where I shall become.

Welcome! I greet myself, stretching my limbs as I get out of the truck cab. I am like someone awakened from troubled dreams, or a child in a body he has just recognized as his own. Welcome! I am here now, and ready to be who I am.

The door of the truck banged and sagged behind me.

I strode merrily up the hill. I felt light and energetic, each lungful of air bouying me up. Ahead of me was the righteous warmth of the kitchen, where, my nose now knew for sure, there was coffee steaming on the hot stove, coffee fragrance filling the space between walls and ceiling and floor, and coffee aroma getting down on its hands and knees to crawl out under the door. Now, that's my kind of sutra, I thought, the coffee sermon.

I pulled open the thick door and entered. There I found Sarai, one of the upwardly mobile, spiritually aware folk who'd founded da Gama Center. She bustled about, preparing breakfast. "Bustled" is the word, because she wore a swaddled girdle that made her ass stick out, but more than that, her motions were quick and aggressive as she got de job done....BANG that pot's ready, CLATTER these dishes are stacked, and so forth. She had grey eyes, grey hair, and radiant health. She also had a perpetually beatific expression coupled with the aforementioned knack of staring through workers and visitors, as if they were so many glass dolls before her enlightened gaze.

In spite of her usual frosty calm, this morning she seemed a bit frantic. Perhaps behind schedule, not keeping the beat of the music of the spheres.

I asked her if there was anything I could do to help. She ignored me. I asked her twice more, with similar results. Then, as she was passing me with a bowl full of fruit, I stuck out my foot. She had a nice trip. The bowl sailed across the kitchen, scattering fruit as it went, and Sarai sprawled out full length on the floor.

She got up to face me quickly, holding one elbow, grey eyes filled with white fire. "Why did you do that?!" she demanded.

"Do what?"

"Trip me! Are you trying to pretend you didn't?"

"Don't be silly," I told her. "If I wasn't here the three times I offered to help, I don't see how I could've possibly been here to trip you." Then I broke eye contact with her, which was getting pretty intense anyway, and went outside.

It was a while before the noises of breakfast preparation took up

166

again, and when they did, they were a bit louder than before.

I watched the New Mexican land become slowly drenched in daylight. Ah yes, I thought. The earth is my co-creator. The Goodbye Terrains....In the late dawn, women in their flowing clothing drifted down from the forests like extras from Maxfield Parrish's dreams. Their Oriental finery seemed frequently affected, but there were times when it achieved a rare beauty.

Breakfast consisted of stacks of whole wheat pancakes drenched in butter, molasses and honey, bowls of chopped bananas, apples, dates, grapes, and peaches, topped with yogurt and shredded coconut. The coffee was delicious.

"Nice breakfast, Sarai," I said.

"Thank you," she said.

All morning I gamboled through da Gama, bursting with power and delight in it. I gloried in making my mark wherever and on whomever I chose, boisterously high on my youth and good spirits.

Lunch, after that breakfast, was disappointing. As I emerged from the kitchen with my plate of leaves, I spied Quiet John sitting on a split log at the south side of the building.

"Howdy, John! Can you hear the hummingbirds fart yet?"

He looked at me with a glint in his eye, and waved me over to him. I stepped over to the log and plopped down.

"I want to talk to you about the ruckus you were raising around the work site this morning," he said.

I eyed him suspiciously. "I thought you'd taken a vow of silence."

"Never took no vow," he said. His gaze came back at mine steadily...strong, kind, and imperturbable. I had the feeling that I was being trumped. He took a deep breath and his posture subtly straightened. "It seemed like I needed to remind you—work is a meditation."

"Dingleberries! Listen, I've just gotten to the point where I can handle some of the rotten vibes from some of your *saints* around here, and I was feeling loud and happy. Loud happiness is just as spiritual a quality as keeping a sober nose to the fucking grindstone! Anyway, I didn't feel like suppressing it, so I didn't. And I won't."

"You workers," John said patiently, "have been hired in return for certain benefits; while you are here you must live by certain agreements."

"Horseflop! The workers came here of their own free will as a service to you and what you supposedly represent: the renewed spiritual life of this country. But it's a con! Instead of nourishing and instructing us, your Elect just uses us as a captive audience for the biggest Holier-Than-Thou trip I've ever seen. Except maybe for Nasrudi. She cares. But as far as being hired, shit, we're not even being *fed* enough, considering the energy we consume in a working day." I flourished my plate of leaves. "And are you people grateful? No! You just try to keep us orderly, so we can channel our extra energy into being envious of you!"

John reacted with neither anger nor confusion. He just regarded me steadily.

"I don't really mean that," I confessed. "Just blowing off a little charge from this wasp head I got into when I first came out here.... I had a great breakfast this morning."

"Ah," John said. "I can see you've been through a change. Care to tell me about it?"

I looked him straight in the eye. "I've become a creator."

John eyed me back for a second, then looked off into the forest as if he were seeing his response written between the trees. "You're part right about the workers," he said. "I pretty much find them more interesting than some of the yo-yo's up here that have been genuflecting to their own egos for years."

He looked back at me. "But you talk of creating, creating experience. Aren't you aware that every individual in this place is creating his or her own experience, just as much as you are? Whether they know it themselves or not? We selected this environment, and we recreate it continuously among ourselves by maintaining its agreements...with all their virtues *and* vices. We have a right to it just as it is. Rules and formulas have a purpose in maintaining a special reality for those who desire and need it.

"This is a meditative space. There are many places where a person can be boisterous, only a few where he is helped to be meditative."

"Oh-oh." I said. "*Click.* Someone else once told me that freedom is not a *carte blanche* for self-expression in a vacuum. So. What else can be said about that? Morality is nothing more or less than metaphysical courtesy to your co-creators."

"Mmmm." John agreed. "Don't get me wrong. I'm not trying to wring an apology out of you. Just watching you blast through a change has jarred a lot of people out of their ruts, and that's good. I'm one of them. Sarai is another. Our creativity is benefitting from yours, just as yours has from ours. However, in this place a little disruptive input goes a long way. The agreements that hold da Gama together are a good bit more fragile than you might suppose."

I picked up the inference. "So you want me to leave?"

168

He nodded.

I thought about that. "I'd like to stay two more days. There's a couple of things around here I'd like to check out before I go, if that's all right with you. Promise not to rock the boat any more than I absolutely have to."

John nodded his agreement. "You'll want to confirm this change, so you'll be able to draw strength from it in the future. Your generation is going to start inheriting the planet pretty quickly now. You're going to need to bring to bear every strength you can on it. You're going to need to remember the promise of this time."

"That's what I want. Something that will survive outside a spiritual hothouse, a rarified environment. Something that travels well...into bars, street corners, or insurance agencies. Used bookstores and public restrooms. Something that will make it on into the future, too."

"Nietzsche says," he quoted, "that 'I would not believe in a God that could not laugh and sing, and dance too.'"

Nasrudi surprised me by leaning out of the window over our heads. "Now I," she said, "would not believe in a God who could not fly. From this I conclude that He should have feathers."

That afternoon, while working, I felt someone's eyes on me. I turned, and it was Jimmie, the Pueblo mason. He lowered his eyes as soon as I met them directly, but not before I saw some of that same shocking quality of *presence* I had remarked before. Something damned similar to what I had chased two-thirds of the way across the country.

He wandered away during a lull in the work that afternoon. I noticed and followed. At length, I saw him standing between two trees, his back to me, looking out towards the west. He reached into a beaded pouch on his belt and took out a cylindrical object. He stretched out his arms and made a circular motion in the air.

"Hello, my fren," he said. Then he turned around and looked at me. I supposed he had heard me approach. He was smiling, but that was hardly anything new. The smile was as much a part of his face as the arroyos that ran from his nose to the corners of his mouth.

He sat down crosslegged on the pine needles and waited for me to join him. The white, cylindrical object was a thick, tobacco cigar, wrapped in cornsilk. After I sat, he lit it, extended it to me, and I smoked. We passed it back and forth in silence. The smoke was potent; I began to get dizzy. When I motioned to him, Jim finished it by himself. Then he stared at me politely, waiting for me to speak.

I hesitated a moment, then said, "Is there anything you're supposed to tell me?"

"There something you want to ask me about?" he countered.

Might as well be blunt, I figured. "Are you a medicine man?" I asked.

"I'm a friend of yours," he confided, as if that explained everything.

"Oh." I wondered if I had committed some sort of blunder by asking. Probably.

"Everyone knows some medicine," he continued. "A friend will frequently give his medicine to another friend who needs it."

I relaxed. "What sort of medicine is good for confirming visions? For helping to pin them in the real?"

His round dark eyes probed mine gently for a while. There was something mild and inoffensive about him that I liked. Despite that strong presence, or maybe because of it, he had a spontaneous humility . . . an air of being just a man doing the best he could in whatever way seemed appropriate.

"Your spirit sees things, and your body wants to see them too, huh? And you want to work in this way, bringing the spirit through. Peyote is good for that."

"Uh-huh. Well, I've done hallucinogens . . . ."

Jimmie cut me off. "Peyote is medicine. It is not for being high and foolishness. It mostly is to help the singing. If you misuse it, you will also misuse your spirit and find out some bad business." His tone was grave, even though his smile was there as much as ever. "Spirit power is supposed to be used in a good way, and to help people."

"I realize my understandings have been different. I don't want to damage your understandings, so . . . ."

"You are not a bad man," Jimmie said. "So don't worry about being a bad man until you are. It's inefficient." He said the word "inefficient" with considerable relish. "You can't find out about peyote meeting by talking," he continued. "The only way to find out about peyote meeting is to go."

"Sounds true. But how do I get invited? I don't want to force myself in. . . ."

"Roadman will decide whether or not you are invited. You must come and meet Roadman. There will be two meetings soon. One July Fourth, for blessing the country. One tomorrow, for blessing a papoose. If you wish to go to that one, ride with Mesquite."

I was struck by a sudden thought. "Are you Roadman for these meetings, Jim?"

"You must come and meet Roadman," he asserted. His tone informed me our conversation was concluded—not cut off, but closed, because all necessary information had been transmitted. Further talk would only obscure the sound of the wind in the pines.

We went back to work.

Nasrudi, in her overwhelming drive to be of loving service to everyone, had constructed a sweatlodge.

It was a squat tipi not more than ten feet in height or diameter, on a high field overlooking the buildings of da Gama. On one side of the sweat, the coals of a wood fire glowed in and around a stack of smooth, flat river rocks. South of the tipi and downhill, a creek had been interrupted in its meander by a dam of logs, rocks, and packed earth, forming a deep, cold pool. This was a favored playspot of the da Gama children. No matter where else they showed up on the grounds of the Center, one could always find a smudge of mud on hand, face or clothes to show that they had been playing there.

Today the pool and sweat were to be used for purification, particularly by those attending the peyote meeting. Nasrudi squatted by the fire, poking at it, arranging the coals in glowing hieroglyphs.

"Hi guy!" she said. "You'd best strip and get in. I'm about to steam everybody's clam."

I shucked my clothes and stood for a moment by the fire, feeling its starchy warmth on my front and a cool breeze on my behind. "You comin in?" I asked.

"No sweat," Nasrudi said. She cocked one eye up at me as she squatted there, her thin brown body folded comfortably up on itself, her tumbleweed of hair nodding gently in the breeze.

"Huh?"

"I busted ass in the garden all day; I don't have any sweat left," she explained. "I'd be the only one in there with a dry skin. I'd get shriveled into a piece of jerky." She winked the cocked eye. "But you; show manhood. Go in."

I raised the flap, and crawled in on my hands and knees.

At least ten naked people were already in there. Most were women. I felt I had wandered into the monthly meeting of some ancient fertility cult. I wormed my way carefully across the knees and ankles and watching breasts to a space at the back of the lodge. I found myself across from Sarai. We appraised each other with a glance in the dim light, able to detect only the flash of the whites in each other's eyes. Still, I was sure it was her. I knew I would be going with her to the meeting.

171

The flap slid open. A shovelful of red-hot riverstones magically extended into the tipi, tilted, and fell onto the hearth.

Sarai, high priestess of the mist, sprinkled the stones with water and small twigs. Clouds of fragrant steam swirled out around her and began to fill the tipi. Sarai began to chant something in Arabic or Hindu that others in the lodge knew, and took up after her.

I closed my eyes and sat still. The chant, the steam, the smells of scorched willow and sage, filled the tipi with a thick, charged atmosphere. Bullets of sweat stood out on my face, collected, slid together, dripped off my chin. Then it seemed as if I fell *inward*, fell away from the scene in all directions at once. The sweatlodge and my body seemed something far, far away . . . .

I was standing on the ridge in Arkansas. Rich Mountain. My body was white, cool and translucent. I could see through it . . . could see, through my outstretched hand, wet footprints on the smooth grey rock of the path before me. I had been this way before. I looked up, out, and saw, or thought I saw in the distance, a glimmer of the *presence*, that storm star that had been the elusive, omnipresent goal of my voyage. It was different—in some subtle fashion—from the presence I had felt in Jimmie; I was sure of that now. And it drew me just as strongly and mysteriously as it ever had.

I was flying, a smooth, inertialess motion over the path, then up and over the mountain, launched from it into a realm of pure crystal radiation, where laser-like colors wove together in combinations I could almost grasp. Vast, vast, . . . then I was through it and into the virginal emptiness.

And the *presence*! The presence was not there, but somewhere beyond again.

Don't freak. Make do. Use this. I was not ready for all the absolute freedom that surrounded me. For that, I would need absolute integrity. But since I was returning to a place where my co-creators—both conscious and unconscious—had massive realities underway, to return with some of this freedom would be a good thing. Unsure of my ability to transport it, I swung on my center and swaddled myself with freedom and darkness, like a runner who has soared out beyond the stars to scoop up a dipperful of space, then dove back toward my native sphere . . . .

Like a carnival diver landing on his sponge, an infant squirting into the midwife's hands, or a mechanic shrugging on his work clothes, I came back into my body. Ahhggg! It was cloying, hot, and oppressive! It was as if solid walls of flesh had suddenly rushed in from all sides, and wrapped themselves around me with the embrace of a lovesick octopus. This flesh was not only solid and earthbound, but poisoned with fears and deranged patterns of behavior, subject to the politics of power, the price of wheat, and the pull of the moon. I was snared by the month of June, 1973, and the inevitability of my own death.

My eyes snapped open. Hot steam, smells so pungent they seared my nostrils, close walls of the tipi, weird grey-yellow light! Uttering a strangled cry, I crawled for the flap, slithered out under it, rose, and staggered into a run. The pool. I homed in on it, reached the edge and dove in. The icy shock was tremendous. The water came just to neck level, as some instinct brought me up to my feet. My heart gave one convulsive beat, and stopped. Although my eyes were open, my vision narrowed to one dull red spot and vanished. I was adrift in the darkness I'd brought with me in my brief excursion beyond existence. I floated back and forth without tether, through the fluttering, ruptured membrane between dimensions.

Then my heart beat again. And again. The dull red spot reappeared, dilated, and the scenery of da Gama, the mountainside and the plains of New Mexico, unfolded before me. Sensory input rushed into the vacuum of my brain, with a crisp, singing newness to it.

The breeze was freighted with the mingled scents of pine, the incense of the sweat lodge, and the smells of cooking rising from the round roof of the kitchen down below.

Nasrudi had come up to the pool edge and was watching solemnly as I emerged from the water.

"Hey, are you all right?"

"Yeah," I said, hearing strange and beautiful music in both voices.

"Whew! You turned all white while you were in the water."

"Yeah," I said. "For a minute there, I forgot what color I was."

She smiled her thin, flayed smile, all the muscles in her face standing out in relief. She handed me my clothes.

"Well, you better get down there pronto. Everyone else who was going to the meeting left the lodge before you."

She reached out and touched me on the chest. "Goodbye. Come see me when you get back."

"Bye Nasrudi. Thanks for being. I sure will."

Then I turned and ambled down the path. Uncreated space was all around me, interpenetrating everything. In the same way that particles of fog at night stand out against the black sea in which they float, so the thick mist of this earth, this time, and this flesh, was suspended in an immense realm of possibility. I breathed carefully, reverently. I admired the way my feet moved on the path I had chosen. Just for kicks, I held out one hand compounded of being and nothing, and flexed it. The fingers waggled hello. I smiled back.

"Hey-y-y, Getane!" Someone yelling for me at the main dome. It was Mesquite.

"Yowzah!"

"You comin to the meetin, or what?"

"I'se comin Massa Mesquite, jus ez fas ez Ah kin!"

I walked up to him and began to put on my clothes.

His bored, impatient attitude suggested that my very presence cast an annoying shadow on the glow of his enlightenment. Of course, I was in good company, since nearly everyone was Mesquite's acknowledged spiritual inferior. In the case of Winbhag Dass, he made an exception which I, lacking knowledge of esoteric Hindu chants, could not hope for. But I was content to remain an untouchable in his cosmology. I had no ambition.

"Would you mind hurrying?" he said.

"I grovel at your whim, effendi."

"That's a switch," he said, grinning broadly. His face began to change. He took a deep breath, and the body of Mesquite began to fill out with muscular weight. The face had become round and dark, the hair dark and short, and Mesquite's scrawny beard collected and rearranged itself into a pair of magnificent mustaches.

I was staggered to find myself looking into the face of Art Saruthaz. But where Art's eyes were grey, these were golden and dancing, faintly mocking, and fairly pleased with themselves.

"Push, baby!" I said, overjoyed. "I thought you were gone for good! Now, I see my fears are realized. You're not."

"Well-l-l, ya gotta take the bad with the worse, bud. I dropped by 'cos there's a little riddle in this whole astral junketing business that you're missing."

"Oh God. Still gleaning up after me?"

"Somebody's got to do it. Give a listen." He waggled an arrogant Aryan finger in my face. "You had an appointment with a disembodied entity you called Goodbye-To-Rains, whom you knew only by the taste of his energy and a string of complex aliases. Yet after a hazardous journey to the only possible source of his manifestation, you found nothing. Howcum?"

"Hum," I said. "Riddle, eh? Well, I found only nothingness. But *I* was there to find it . . . ! Therefore, I must be. . . ."

"Goodbye-To-Rains," Push finished for me. "Brilliant."

I repeated this statement to myself several times. It seemed at best only partially true. However, the part that seemed true felt real good.

"Check," Push agreed mildly. "You also are not him. To put it simply, from this perspective, Goodbye-To-Rains is your existence in the realm of the Uncreated. He is a disembodied presence who is constantly making himelf real through your body. He, she, it, or you, however you want to label it. His ceaseless challenge is that you continue to become him.''

A gust of wind came along. It blew about half the molecules out of the body of Art Saruthaz and scattered them across the meadow. I could see the outline of the main dome behind him coming through his body. By now, I could recognize a dematerialization when I saw it coming.

"Wait!" I said. "When will I see you again? How can I call you back?''

"What for?'' he asked lazily.

The outline of a man flipped over, becoming reflective, like a piece of glass you can see through, but which also gives you back your own image.

"I don't know yet!" I said. "Maybe just to beat you in a game of chess.''

"Just ring the chimes to the engineroom, chile,'' the reflection said. "You-all give the orders. I only work here!''

Then, at last, I knew I had a free hand.

X.
The
Magician

(The End)

This book was edited by Russell Fuller
and designed by Georgia Oliva. The mechanical
was prepared by Carolyn Cappai. The text
type is Garamond and Garamond Bold, set by
Ann Flanagan Typography, Berkeley. The
cover and title page type is Garamond Oldstyle
set by Omnicomp, San Francisco.

Also available from **Island Press**
Star Route 1, Box 38
Covelo, CA 95428

Headwaters: Tales of the Wilderness, by Ash, Russell, Doog, and
Del Rio; Preface by Edward Abbey. Photographs and illustrations.
$6.00.

Four bridge-playing buddies tackle the wilderness—they go in
separately, meet on top of a rock, and come out talking. These
four are as different as the suits in their deck of cards, as
ragged as a three-day beard, and as eager as sparks.

Wellspring: A Story from the Deep Country, by Barbara Dean.
Illustrations. $6.00.

A woman's life in tandem with nature—the honest, often beautiful
telling of one woman's life in a rugged setting, both
geographically and emotionally. This book is at once a
pioneer's journal and a record of our times.

The Christmas Coat, by Ron Jones.
Illustrations. $4.00.

A contemporary fable of a mysterious Christmas gift and a father's
search for the sender, which takes him to his wife, his son,
and his memories of big band and ballroom days.

A Citizen's Guide to Timber Harvest Plans.
Illustrations and charts. $1.50

A comprehensive handbook to timber harvest plans, including
up-to-date California law, the citizen's right to a hearing and
action if his livelihood or recreation will be affected by
timber harvesting, detailed instructions for full participation
in this process.

Please send $1.00 for postage and handling with all orders. A catalog
of current and forthcoming Island Press titles also is available.